STARDUST ANGEL

J. S. NATHANIEL

Publsihed in

DENVER, COLORADO

ALSO BY J. S. NATHANIEL

Dominion of the Divine

Juliet + Juliette = Love in Mafia Land

Everything Spontaneous in the Land of Doll Parts

Primitive Beauty: Author's Sketchbook

Narrator of Lies

CONTENTS

READER WARNING

The characters in this novel are crafted to reflect the complexities, motivations, and contradictions that make people seem real. Though, they are fictional creations, intended to immerse readers into a realistic yet imagined world of sometimes difficult themes, including coming-of-age, the impact of sexual assault and crime. Any resemblance to real persons, living or dead, is purely coincidental. Readers are advised that the narrative contains references to sexual assault and violence as part of some characters' experiences and development.

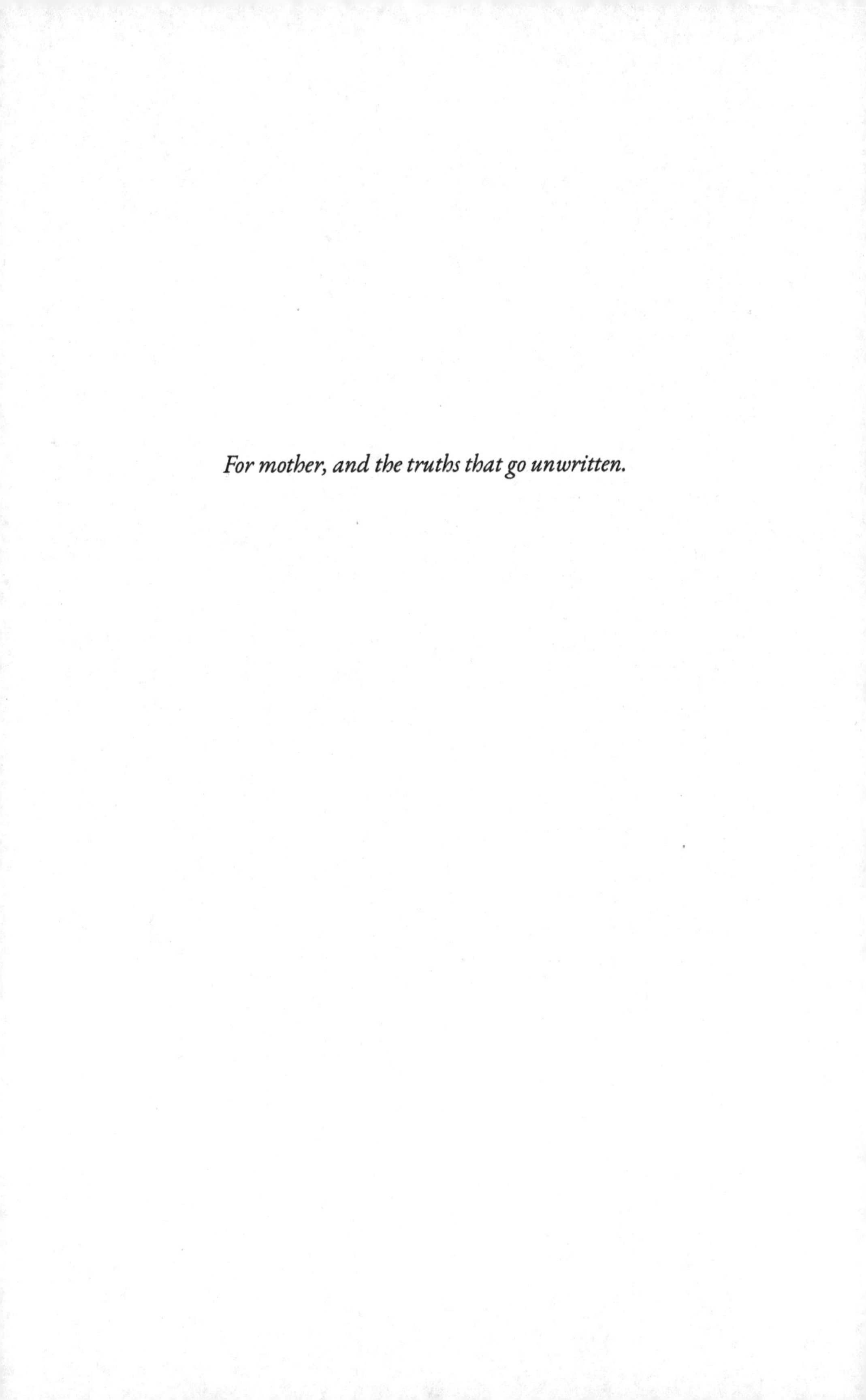

For mother, and the truths that go unwritten.

ONE
PSYCHO BUNNY

She had few options. That's what Dr. C later told a jury with tears in his eyes. Much later. Before I had a nervous breakdown and was transferred to a mental health facility. I couldn't blame juvenile hall for the breakdown. Still, it didn't help.

But before telling you why I murdered my parents, I had to first dispose of the bodies. That was step one. Step two came later: how to get away with murder. I had a sneaky suspicion, somewhere deep down, I'd do just that. Not because I was playing the angel. Sometimes you must play the devil to kill the devil.

Emma saved my life. She gave me the courage to leave this house. Even now, I wondered if she had sacrificed herself for me. I'd go to my grave wondering about that. *Our freedom belonged to us. It had always belonged to us.* I wished I could have told her that before she died.

I was a Mondragon. Though, if you'd asked Andrew about my Mondragon status, he'd have told you I wasn't. He'd further convince you I'd never had Mondragon blood pulsing through my veins. His last words before I stole his dying breath, were that I'd always be a coldhearted Gray. I figured it takes one to know one.

I supposed there was some truth to that. Abby Gray, my stepmother, had an exotic taste for cruelty. Evil lived in her heart, so screamed Emma, after getting caught climbing through the window at sunrise. Though, I wasn't a Gray. Not by blood, anyway.

He was mistaken about one thing: the Mondragons and Grays were the same. These bloodlines were a deadly concoction when mixed in equal parts. Sort of like a tsunami. The ocean is breathtaking at first sight. But don't go sightseeing just yet. A deadly tidal wave can hit any moment once the earth fractures beneath the sea. Thus, creating a holy shit moment.

I recalled Mr. Peters saying something to this effect in Earth and Science. Not the holy shit part but the former. That was the Mondragons and the Grays for you in a dysfunctional nutshell. They were the holy shit show nobody saw coming.

At twelve sharp, I popped in to see why death was dragging its feet. Waiting for death was a real buzzkill. You never knew if the cops were on the way because you did something dumb, like peeked out the blinds too many times. To be fair, it was just paranoia stealing my sanity. On this sleepy, little block, everyone turned a blind eye. Including Nurse Maggie. At least our neighbors never called the police when Emma and I screamed until the bats clustered around the streetlamp at night.

Once Andrew finished terrorizing the house, and everything fell still, I'd hear countless bats pelting their wings against the lamp's glass eye. But the mimicries haunted me more. As though they carried our silent agony toward heaven.

First stop was Abby's room. Her crystal figurines all lined up on the dresser glared at me once I entered. Soldier vibes with dust caked on top. No shame in their eyes. Even though they were dancing naked in years of gray snow. Staring up to the left. Expressionless. To where? Who knew? Maybe at Jesus tacked to the wall.

The steady hum of the oxygen machine was still going. Warm to the touch. Still pumping air into Abby's lungs that stopped doing their job. Damn that rigor mortis lag time. I couldn't wait for her face and hands to gnarl up, vampire like, once the sunlight struck.

I'd heard Andrew take his last breath but not Abby. I'd missed that one. I was too busy tending to Andrew's needs. His needs outweighed Abby, always. Right to the end. Andrew's needs smashed the entire house to smithereens.

Is that a psycho wish? To hear my parents gurgle their final breath. I didn't get all stabby. That's retro. Like those crystal figurines sitting on Abby's dresser. Retro gets you caught. And, also, I was the only one left to clean up the mess. I imagined a body was pretty fucking heavy for this slight frame to lug around. Then, times that by three. That would be the last to do, or my last to do, ever. And I wasn't a betting girl on which one would come first.

If I walked out the front door in handcuffs, covered in blood, like a psycho killer, then I elevated myself to a stale-sandwich serial killer.

Nobody knows a social media public execution like a teenager. Even toddlers pack phones and are itching to hit the record button, so saith Jesus—I meant, Andrew. Contrary to whatever you believe, this bitch had goals. I wasn't trying to go out OG. OG was sloppy. OG will get me one-way to the slammer.

At first, most who read my confession will think me a monster. And perhaps I was. I did not intend to have you believe I was an angel. How could I have been with parents like these?

Unlike Depeche Mode's "Playing the Angel," I wasn't playing at anything. Nor was I dying to wilt away in a cell. As I suspected I would have, once the authorities uncovered the truth. I still had plenty of time to tidy a homicide in progress.

There's a funny thing about the truth. One easily sees what floats to the surface. But people often ignore what sinks to the bottom. Forgotten. Lost at sea, so saith Jesus. You know who I meant. Yes, the actual evidence was lost at sea.

Well, it was now time to work up a sweat. Dispose of things. Maggie—Nurse Maggie, as Andrew loved to correct—would arrive at two. As always.

"Jesus, bless her soul," Abby slurred between bathtub martinis the moment Maggie walked through the front door.

Abby played a good game. She pretended to be happy to see Maggie. With her fake smile. That fake laugh. Sweet-as-candy voice. Sometimes she even fooled me. But I knew the truth. Abby was only eager to lock eyes on the prescription pills inside Maggie's bag.

It was hard to say if I'd regret killing my parents. Maybe in a couple years. But I'd regret killing Maggie. I hoped I wouldn't have to. To be fair, it might get slashy in the Mondragon house. Though I'd do my best to prevent casualties.

I saw her lift Andrew from the bed during diaper change one fine afternoon. She didn't even break a nail. She lifted him like he was a feather. There's no way Maggie would stand by and watch me kill my parents. She'd try to stop me. Or dial 911.

I worried I might have to kill her. Did you think I'd hand myself over to the police wrapped in a pink bow? Remember what I said before? I didn't plan on rotting in prison. Plus, that was a terrible place for a baby.

It's easy to dispose of a body. One, two, three times is a charm. Thanks to the internet. After the third one, you're elevated to a serial killer status. Don't worry, I had this covered. I never dared to look up "how to dispose of a body" on the internet at home. Googling sulfuric acid on a home computer would have given me the lethal injection. Premeditated murder would have been a bad look in front of a jury of my peers. Which made little sense. I'd never heard of a teenager serving jury duty.

Death by lethal injection was still on the table here. Besides, I could google nothing at home anyway. We didn't own a computer or a cell phone. Our childhood home used only landline service. People who don't know what a landline is, just watch a black-and-white.

I WENT to a gamer café to do all my research. I used a prepaid credit card to buy time on the computer. Which, the day before, I'd bought in cash at Walmart. I wore Emma's sunglasses that cloudy day and a ball cap. I thought I'd better cover all the bases. If the investigators tried to pull up security footage of my purchasing prepaid cards.

Don't worry. After Andrew and Abby were knocked out, I burned the evidence out back. Don't side-eye me, I didn't ice them yet.

Andrew told me I wasn't pretty countless times. So much so, I believed it. What I saw in the mirror only freighted me. Behind those innocent eyes was something indescribable. Whatever it was clawed its way to the surface sometimes as I tilted my head to the side. My neck muscles glistened when I caressed a pulsating vein. I was careful not to make direct eye contact with myself for long. Because those eyes were bottomless. Or maybe just soulless. It was hard to tell.

Sometimes I'd sit on the floor, leaning against Abby's bed. She'd stroke my hair while watching TV and say, "You're the classic ugly duckling. I don't see why he likes you." That was Abby, being nice. She only talked when the gin dried up. Abby didn't have dish hands. Her hands were pure cashmere. Mine were sandpaper. Digits and all. According to Abby.

Emma, on the other foot, was beautiful. Hollywood beauty. All the boys wanted to... Let's just say in a gazillion years from now, she'd never run out of boys. But she never chose. A boy, I mean. She never got to fall in love.

Abby could be charming. That strangely coincided with empty gin bottles spilling from the front door. All her drunken deeds seemed to evaporate. She lived a double life. Three lives, really. She spent her first life as a mean drunk. Then, when sober, almost maternal. Andrew was her third life. That one we don't speak of. But the drink stole her most days.

Still, I wasn't sure what she meant by calling me a "classic ugly duckling." Like, was I beautiful inside, rather than out? Or in reverse?

Andrew's message was crystal. In his eyes, I was a little dummy who couldn't think worth shit. A disgusting pig. Those were his words. "Oink, oink." He'd nuzzle my ear with his scratchy upper lip. Breathing through snot-caked nostrils like a pig. His pig-like grunts haunting. Andrew was brilliant at extinguishing souls like cigarettes. As I'd mentioned before, he smashed the entire house to smithereens.

Although Mario disagreed wholeheartedly with Andrews's assessment. I met him at Walmart while shopping for monthly supplies. You know, the usual. Adult diapers, baby wipes, ointments, and medications. Baby powder causes cancer, did you know? We went through cases of baby powder at the house. I bought it by the truckload. You've got to have goals, you know what I mean?

Mario thought I was beautiful. He gave me that look as I walked by. Girls know. Mario came looking for me while I was standing at the self-checkout. I wasn't even giving. I'd disguised myself by wearing oversized everything.

He said, "Damn, girl, you're clean as fuck," while staring at my ass and biting his lip. I was guessing "clean" meant "beautiful."

Mario's tattoos were grim. Especially the teardrop near his eye. I never liked tattoos. Andrew had tattoos. Army tattoos. Even though Andrew had never seen a day of action in his life. That's what Abby shouted one drunken night after he'd smashed her face into the floor. He'd enlisted as a draftsman. Who knew how deadly that was? But he loved to brag.

We hooked up on the first date. In the back seat of his Civic. We made it as far as the Walmart parking lot. It was over in a blink, and he lay on my chest panting the rest of the time. I finally told him I had to go. I wasn't trying to move in or anything.

His breath was minty against my cheek. That scent floated upward and made the strands of my hair quiver. His body spray made my eyes all watery. He smelled like a boy in my class. Mario's only saving grace was silky skin. It felt nice. It reminded me of Abby's hands.

My lasting impression was locking eyes on the headliner. We both stared up. Sprawled like starfish as customers rushed past the Civic. Some peeked in. Then went about their day. The headliner was dangling above my head like a soiled diaper. It brought me back to Andrew. It's funny how sharp turns in life bring you back to the place you try to escape.

Mario was rough. I didn't expect that. My neck creaked at an angle. Hair bird-nested against the door. His mitts crushed me. I kept begging for a moment to breathe inside my head. Maybe Andrew was right. I wasn't that smart. What kind of person hooks up with a stranger?

I broke it off with Mario the moment I exited the Civic. He kept calling the house with a stalker vibe. Waiting for me outside the Walmart every day. He screamed, "Every day, bitch!" I hated when boys called me a bitch. Just insert *girl*.

He tracked me down anyway. They always did. I showed up one day at Walmart, and there he was. I had the worst luck. He slammed me against the cinder wall outside. Pointing a dirty finger in my face, crying. Telling me he'd die for me. "I love you, fucking bitch, don't you see that!" He even got down on his hands and knees like he would propose with those goo-goo eyes. He surprised me. Those tattoos and the way he was crying made little sense.

To be fair, Mario wasn't right for me. Mainly, I didn't want to be loved that fucking bad. You get what I'm saying? Who aspires to be with a boy who calls you a bitch every other sentence? Learn your language. The only way you can get away with calling a girl a bitch is if you're *their* bitch. I thought, after Mario, I preferred girls.

In her last days, Abby watched *Criminal Minds* nonstop. Sulfuric acid was being investigated in one episode. I paid special attention to these gospel facts. Even though the episode blared and crackled as I perched at the edge of Abby's bed. I couldn't peel myself away.

I took notes. Word for word. I watched every detail unfold without blinking, while Abby snored away, the gin fumes making me gag. It's true what the Lord said—TV rots the soul, and so does the internet. According to Andrew's version of the Bible.

When the episode ended, the killer got caught. They always got caught for doing dumb things. You'd think this would change my mind. Forget about murdering my parents. But I took this as a sign from the baby Jesus above, so saith Abby. I saw this as my way out.

While shopping online at the internet café, I learned that lye, potassium hydroxide, dissolves human tissue and bone. The Mexican cartel labeled this process as "making pozole." How hard could it be? I could make pozole like those entrepreneurs down in Mexico.

But, I thought, *I better play this one a little smarter*. I just couldn't feed their remains to the pigs. I'd get caught. Although, I went back and forth about calling Mario. That teardrop tattoo got me thinking. But if he was crying over this, I hated to imagine how he'd react getting caught up in a triple homicide. It was best to exclude strangers from family matters.

I went from searching for chemical compounds to where to buy these delightful chemicals. I even googled "how to DIY a human corpse at home?" I was neck deep in my quest when an officer tapped me on the shoulder. Correction: two police officers hovered over me. Their faces read: *you're busted*.

"Ma'am," the younger officer said. "Remove yourself from the computer."

Inside my head, I screamed, "Stop giving me that goddamn look." I channeled Abby to calm myself. She loved that word. Goddamn this, goddamn that. That word she hung in dazzling lights whenever she got angry. That and Jesus. Especially the baby one.

I just sat there for a minute looking like a little dummy. Did he want me to stand up or something? I wasn't clear what to do next. Maybe I should hike my hands in the air. Then I ditched that plan. Guilty people don't raise their hands.

The younger officer waited for the other to give the go-ahead. "Come with us."

My throat pounded as though my heart was rammed inside. Remember what I said earlier: truth doesn't always float to the surface. I played the angel. Though, inside, I was doing the devil's work.

"Why, Officer?" My hand clutching my heart. My Little Bo-Peep voice even fooled me. "Did my credit card get declined?"

Don't call officers pigs. According to *Criminal Minds*. It's pigs when they slap the handcuffs. If you say *officer*, it's a sign of respect. It also throws them off the homicide trail. If you want to get caught, for anything or nothing, just call them a pig.

Everyone in the café was eyeballing me hard. Like I'd dissolved a body right in front of them.

"Ma'am," the older officer said. "On your feet."

I complied. I was calm. My twitchy hand, though. Darn that twitchy hand. "What did I do?"

Now I know how Mario felt that day when he professed his love. Though, I wasn't professing anything. I, too, wanted to bawl my eyes out. Get down on my hands and knees and beg for mercy.

"We'd like to discuss a few things with you," the younger officer said. He pointed at the main entrance. "Outside."

He seemed more sympathetic to my cause than the older one. He would play daddy. Sit me down and have a serious chat. Clear things up.

My cheeks were pure fire. They always get rosy when I was about to get in trouble. Stomach acid gave my mouth a terrible jingle. I thought, *Oh, Jesus, now what, I'm so close.* A sensation tickled my brain. I asked the older officer before he placed me in the back of the patrol car, "Am I under arrest?" and batted my eyes.

He said nothing before shielding my head. So I didn't knock it against the hood of the car on the way in. I'm like, no honey, you smack that little head all day long, so I don't wake up in the slammer.

"That depends, ma'am." The older officer was all magisterial in his lint-free, inky getup.

Once the car door slammed, they huddled outside my window. Almost whispering to each other. Side-eyeing me occasionally, as though I didn't get what was happening. Hello, my processor works just fine.

The younger officer opened the door and said, "Identification?"

"What?" I said, as though I didn't hear him.

"Do you have an ID?" the older officer chimed in over the younger one's shoulder.

"No." I made direct eye contact and didn't blink. I had my hands tucked in my hoodie. And guess what? I was holding my ID.

"Where's your ID?" the older officer scolded. "You must carry an ID." He caught his breath. "It's the law."

"Ok mister, it's the law." I mutter inside my head.

Two days before, Nurse Maggie had gotten pulled over for speeding. She'd told me all about it at the kitchen table. Unlike me, she really didn't have her ID. Someone had smashed her car window and stolen her purse at a Quick Mart. She was inside getting a cup of coffee when a smash-and-grab went down in the parking lot. She was too busy chitchatting with Lorenzo, the hot Latin cashier. That's how I painted him inside my head.

The police officer let her go with a warning after she explained the whole mess. Being a hospice nurse helped her case. The police officer who'd pulled her over was married to an emergency room nurse. Small world.

Officers may sympathize with teachers too, I imagined. They'd probably let you go with a slap on the wrist. I wondered how many teachers got away with murder. *Why can't I be a teacher right now?* Tears began to warm my eyeballs. *If it worked for that bitch, it's got to work for this bitch.* Girls, it matters little how you play it, as long as you play it.

"Someone smashed my car window and stole my purse," I said, lips pursed and quivering, about to cry.

The younger officer gave me a consoling look as though a puppy had died in his arms. "Why would you leave your purse in your car?"

The question was valid. In fact, I'd asked Nurse Maggie the same one. "I was in a hurry."

It didn't matter anyway. I didn't own a purse. Some feedback: Jeans still didn't have deep-enough pockets. Emma was the only person who could stuff those tiny pockets. Then again, she was extra. Don't give me that bra energy, ok. Not every girl has enough to work with.

The officers appeared to be in deep derail. What to do with this girl?

Luckily, I stopped myself midsentence. I almost finished with, "I'm on my way to see a dying patient." How would I have walked away from that one?

The older officer's steely eyes burned right through my little skull. "Late for what?"

"For... for school."

"What high school do you attend? GW?"

"No." My eyes darted. "DU."

You see how the lies raced from the package? It was freeing being a teenager sometimes. The rules didn't apply unless someone slapped them into you.

"How old are you?" the older officer asked. "You can't be older than sixteen."

Sixteen and a half, thank you very much. "I just turned twenty."

My eyes stayed the course, unflinching. The younger officer looked as though he bought my story. But the other one wasn't so convinced. "Oh yeah, what's your birthdate?"

That's when the oh shit moment hit me. Why didn't I say nineteen? Emma was nineteen and a half. I could have spilled her birthdate easy as milk.

"Why are you detaining me?" I'd heard this scripture from *Criminal Minds*.

"What were you searching on the internet in there?" the younger officer said. "Don't lie to me, young lady." That scolding tone rose once more. I'd have liked to slap his nervy mouth.

I batted the most innocent eyes. "How to dispose of a body? It's for research. I'm researching Mexican cartels."

It turned out I was a beautiful liar. I could lie on the fly, just like Nurse Maggie. When women lie like worms, men gobble it up like angry birds.

They looked horror-struck. "Why would a pretty thing like you want to research something horrible like that? This world is terrible, yah know?" He puckered his face as though he'd drank a cup full of pee.

I was willing to bet he'd never sleep a wink if he knew someone had already vandalized a pretty thing like me. Although, the pretty part, I relished. *Take the win, Lizzie.*

"I'm interested in forensic science." Another scripture from *Criminal Minds.*

Regardless of how depraved my internet search was, mentioning forensic science seemed to ease their minds a little. The light swam in their eyes again.

The older officer shrugged. "For future reference, gaming cafés monitor your internet searches. And they alert the staff when someone uses keywords. You seemed to hit every red flag there ever was."

I was so tired of the red flags already. The whole goddamn world is awash in red flags.

Thank you, Officer. I'll store that one for future reference. "It was purely for research. You must arrest boys all day long."

"What was that?"

"I'd hate to see their internet searches."

He shrugged again. This time with a stony glare. "Why aren't you using the computer at the DU library? They're free, aren't they?"

"Wouldn't I get in trouble over there too?"

"No," he said, as though it should be obvious. "DU is a law school, for Christ's sake. Those kinds of things, I think, are the norm there, not here."

Those kinds of things. Good Lord, Officer, as Nurse Maggie would say after changing Andrew's diaper. "Oh, okay."

The older officer played a game of don't blink. He waited for me to elaborate. Now they were both staring me down. "Well?"

"Yeah," I said. Pretending to be oblivious to his line of questioning.

"Why aren't you at the DU library?"

"Someone stole my ID, remember? They won't let me in without it. So I came here."

The lies just clicked into place. It dawns on them finally. I think they're buying it. Lies are nothing but Hollywood beauty.

They stepped aside and whispered among themselves a minute longer. Side-eyeing me midsentence here and there. The younger officer helped me out from the back seat. "Next time, use the DU library."

The older officer said, "Your research is finished for today. If I receive another call, I'll arrest you."

The younger officer shook his head, flailed his hand, and mouthed, "Just go."

TWO
LINCOLN

After my run in with the police, I took their advice and rode the bus down to the DU library. I had little choice. The officers had rudely interrupted my research. My plan was missing an important piece of the puzzle. I needed to know what kind of container safely dissolves a body.

The worst thing that could happen was for my victims to spill out onto the floor in a bloody, toxic slurry because I got sloppy. Remember this: lazy people get caught. Do the research, you won't regret it. Besides, there's always plan B. Burn every trail—in a literal sense.

Oil drum. Porcelain tub. Believe me, I googled every type of vessel. I'd even thought about dissolving their bodies in the cellar. Let them stew like pozole on the dirt floor. But then I changed my mind. Desperation is no excuse to willy-nilly things. I'd never desecrate consecrated ground. But, I must admit, I was palpitating like crazy over the entire mess.

Does a human body smell while being liquefied? The internet would arrest me on the spot for googling that.

I'd come to terms with some things. Mainly, dismemberment. I realized it would have to play out on the fly. How gruesome it would get was anyone's guess. All of us would take this mystery to the fiery gates.

It turned out, the DU library didn't track who came and went through those mirror-finish, mahogany double doors. I waltzed right in. No questions asked. In the late afternoon, I blended in with the other students.

My oversized jeans, hiked past my hips, reassured that I was comfortable. Even retro. My Cure hoodie harkened back to wistful days. The one I stole from Emma's closet. Screaming, "I'm naive and promising." And when you look naive and promising, you can literally get away with murder.

EMMA, my sister, my angel, was a burner. She was a suicide bomb. Andrew and Abby drove her to drink bleach. One soupy day in October, I rummaged through her room for something. I got stalky. Which happened sometimes. So, I ditched the reason I went into her room in the first place and yanked open a drawer in her nightstand, uncovering a lighter stash.

There must have been hundreds. Bic lighters—smalls and larges. A color wheel's worth. She had butane fire starters. The ones with superslender flames. As sharp as Damascus steel. Emma had stashed a baby machete on the side of her bed. I saw it glinting on the floor near the headboard. I nicked my thumb from holding it wrong.

Funny thing about the angels in your life, you don't know their lives. I thought Emma lived the dream, even though we both lived the same hell. Her room was right next to mine. I guess it's true—you don't know what you don't know.

My first and only stop, the computer room; however, the computer required a key card. I went to the front kiosk where a girl sat behind an official kiosk. She looked bored. Space-case energy. Chin in hand. Hand lifting the entire goddamn world, it seemed. Hell night hung on her face, as Abby liked to joke. Her copper wires cobwebbing out into the universe somewhere. Ink eyeliner and nails. The girl wore emo hell—and then some.

My five-foot frame barely let my eyes skim the kiosk counter. So I tilted my head upward to lock eyes. "I need your student ID for a key card."

Those lethargic eyes sort of rolled. I wanted to take a nap with her. To end the misery.

"Someone stole my purse," I said, wearing goo-goo eyes. Like Mario's. But my damsel-in-distress routine didn't budge her ass one bit.

Then she nodded to the left. "Down the hall, there's an elevator. Take it to the second floor. Suite two-ten, administration."

"I'll be late for class." I pointed at the scientific-looking wall clock behind her. "My class starts at three forty-five. It's three thirty." I made it sound so real, so urgent. "Help a bitch out."

"Excuse me?"

"Yeah, it's a small world. You never know when this bitch will help you out."

She turned to look at the clock.

"I need a computer."

She gave me a look of disrespect. With a sprinkle of "I don't care about your life." Same look Emma used to give. "It's a very small world, honey."

She spewed a sigh. Her eyelids fluttered. Then jammed a key card in my hand.

Whatever I resurrect inside her is why a bitch can't catch a break. Hear me out for a sec. The entire world conspires to erase a bitch, including other bitches. I'm thinking, where can a bitch go to get a drink around here?

I was more cautious about the landscape this time. I scouted a computer near the back of the room. A corner cubicle where I sank low and vanished. If I needed to give the police the slip. *Criminal Minds* energy all the way. Sunglasses. Hoodie. Ball cap. The works.

I scanned for the perfect vessel. A human-sized cubicle. The Mexican cartel cooked pozole in a fifty-five-gallon steel drum. What to do? The only places that sold these were online. Doesn't it twist your undies when you have to buy the stuff online? Meanwhile, you've got a triple homicide in full swing. If I were a little dummy who couldn't think worth shit, as Andrew often said, I'd order three steel drums online and have them shipped to the front door. But I couldn't do that. So, I bought another gift card from Walmart and shipped the drums to the neighbor's house, the Smiths. They were quintessential snowbirds spending six months wintering in Florida. What a life, right? I cherished two things in life: consistency and dedication.

I went back to DU the following day. Where a boy, older than me, handed me a key card. I think he liked me because he just handed it over without a fuss. Again, not giving. He gave me dreamboat eyes. Along with a side of creep vibe. As though he would lock me up in his basement and force me to have his babies. I wondered, though, would he best Mario? A basement would be a lot of steps below the back seat of a Civic. Still, he didn't look like a guy who would bawl his eyes out if I ghosted him.

Looks are deceiving, though. Mario didn't seem the type who'd bawl his eyes out either. And he did. And he was kind of grim. Who knew killers had hearts too? But, if you create a beast, be ready to feed it.

I went overboard and ordered a lifetime supply of drop cloths. Someone on Reddit wrote *cutting up a body is a messy and laborious task*. Oh, for sure. Whoever you may be in the world of Reddit. Especially for the inexperienced. That part killed me. I thought this person might be the real deal. I couldn't complain, though. *Thank you for the heads-up, serial killer from afar.*

When I returned the key card to the creepy boy at the front desk, he came for me like Mario had. Once again, I wasn't even giving. He got all touchy. He even grazed my boob with those clumsy, hot dog digits. The nerve. I said, "Is this a hookup? Because you got my attention."

Don't get judgy. I didn't want to ruin a good thing. I may need to access the DU internet again. Like I said before, this bitch had goals.

We met up later in the day. He bought me a Frappuccino with extra whipped cream. What a lady killer. But he had my digits all right. I loved whipped cream. Even the imitation stuff. He ordered a triple espresso for himself. I guess he wanted his wits about him. Stockpiling energy for what I hoped translated into a better endeavor than Mario.

Turns out, he outplayed Mario. Not in a good way. If I had a choice, I'd choose Mario. At least with Mario, it would be over in a blink.

His skin was pure boy. As if showering and using a loofah was against his religion. A tinge of BO lingered. His tongue tasted like weed and tobacco married and had Rosemary's baby. I saw that movie with Abby on a good day. Still, that cigarette afterburn turned my stomach.

His name was Lincoln. Like the sixteenth president. After he was done, we sprawled on his dorm bed with starfish energy. It was like Mario 2.0. We just stared up at the ceiling. Believe me, it dwarfed the comfort of a Civic; however, my surprise was palpable. He didn't imprison me in some basement.

He asked me if I wanted to smoke grass. I didn't know what that was, so I declined.

It wasn't until he pulled out a joint that I realized grass was weed. He tried handing it to me. But I refused.

Emma got me high at thirteen. All I could remember was being scared my heart would explode, racing faster than a Ferrari. I could hear my eardrums beat loud inside my head. Time lapses are a thing too. Sorry to say, I wasn't a grass girl. I was a pass girl.

Emma calmed me down after I started crying. It felt like time had stopped. I was stuck inside a dark universe. Slowly sinking into the mattress. My body lay marooned and starfish-like. Sinking in endless waves of nothing. Never again would I smoke grass.

Lincoln told me I had a soft pussy. He said it like a serial killer. This gave me the chills.

Then, he asked how old I was. I told him, "Sixteen."

What else was I going to say? I didn't want to get his hopes up. Bread crumbing, remember? I'm not trying to bake cupcakes with him for eternity. He went all silent at first, then he wailed. I mean, *wailed*. He cried way worse than Mario. I tried to calm him down by saying, "I'm sixteen and a half," but mentioning the *half* part made things worse.

"I'm going to fucking prison!" he screamed while bawling his little eyes out. "Your pussy isn't that fucking great!"

He kept shouting—*fucking* this and *fucking* that. I'm pretty sure everyone in the building could hear. The walls were paper-thin. I heard someone playing video games next door. At one point, his face turned primal red.

I told him I wouldn't press charges. He screamed, while still crying, "Your fucking parents will!"

Drool seeped from his nasty lip. Like, what was that all about? He wore the face of a rabid dog or something. I was like, "I don't like your tone."

He calmed down once I told him my parents were dead. They weren't. Not yet anyway. That seemed to soften the blow. Get this, he came for me again. I told him, "No way." I said, "I'm not in the market for a boy right now." Another scripture from *Criminal Minds*.

The situation was finally ok, but Skylar, Lincoln's roommate, barged into the room. Weed wisps were still dancing around. Skylar swiped a few from his face like cobwebs. The smell seemed to annoy him. The atmosphere was on the skunky side.

"I told you not to smoke that shit in here, bru. I have asthma."

Lincoln didn't reply. He quickly covered himself with a smelly blanket and didn't bother to share. Skylar saw everything. "You fucking babies now, bru?"

"What?" Lincoln's eyes burned brighter than the lunar launch.

"Yeah, look at those baby tits. Her body's tiny. I'm surprised you didn't break her."

Break her. Break her. I guess I was made of glass. I looked at Lincoln to see his reaction. His eyes watered again.

"I'm nineteen and a half." Emma was nineteen and a half when she died.

"That's what a baby would say." Skylar glared at me. He was quicker than most.

I blurted my sister's birthdate. Skylar narrowed his eyes. Still suspicious. Though he gave that same lustful look Mario did once when he thought I was legal.

After having sex with Lincoln, I gained unlimited computer privileges. Our relationship was a complex mix of shame and prison time. After that, every time I walked up to the desk, his eyes beamed lunar. Or it was the fear of prison nipping at his eyeballs. Perspiration leaking from his brow. Jittery hands. You see, it all worked out.

The one thing coursing through my mind was boys. They don't care about the details. The police officers thought I was underage. Mario and

Skylar suspected, which they knew I lied. Lincoln only bawled his eyes out thinking about going to the slammer. After that fear left him, he was down to hookup. Good.

Baby body, tiny tits, and glass girls. All my life, boys boiled me down to toy energy. Same with Emma. It seemed like twenty-first-century boys were all Paleolithic. Foreplay for them is choking you out so they can drag you to their basement.

THREE
GRASSY BAND ME

I REGRETTED ONE THING—NOT seeing Abby gulp her last breath. When I realized her chest wasn't all rattles and chains, my heart pounded like a million fists beating a door. The world swayed beneath this baby frame. My skin was sweaty suddenly.

I thought maybe I'd died and gone straight to hell. My body was so hot. I fought to keep my eyes open. I perched at the edge of the bed for a while, peering up at Jesus tacked to the plaster wall. "Am I pure evil? Tell me, please."

Jesus's eyes were in their usual place. Slumped to the left, or right, depending on your position in the room, as though he'd just ran a marathon. But I knew different. I knew the look of a beatdown. Mouth cracked. A halo of thorns. Driblets of blood painted on his temple.

Then I thought, *Maybe I looked like Jesus tacked to that wall right after Andrew got done with me.* Like I said before, Andrew was a genius at putting out souls.

Abby's face looked tired and horror-struck. Except her eyes told a different story. They were starry and glued upward. As though the ceiling didn't exist. Those eyes melted through plaster and wood and shingles and went someplace else.

The house was finally still. Emptier than ever. Funeral-parlor energy collapsing all around. Emma was gone. Baby Fay. They were never coming back. Now, Andrew and Abby would join the apparitions of the house.

I got scared of the silence playing tricks on me. Thinking Emma was still pacing the halls. Andrew's frightful laugh echoing from downstairs. That dead silence made it hard to breathe. Hard to process what was before me. I couldn't measure death. I wasn't capable of that. I hated to admit it, but Andrew was right. Cruel blood flowed in my veins.

Abby's room shrank half its size at its leisure. I felt high again. Everything inside me was paranoid and ultrabionic. I swore I could hear the mice get all chatty down in the cellar. A drumming heart that imprisoned my ears.

When my mind wandered at night. As far as it could go. Somewhere out there lay the good life. Someday we'd pack it up and leave. And the good life would welcome us. As though it were waiting for us the whole time.

I wished someone had told me the American Dream was stillborn. That maybe it never existed. And I thought my angel spared me from a broken heart by not telling me the dream never was. Or never could be. And I guessed when the light wouldn't shimmer across the face any longer, and the dreams morphed into chains, then what was the use?

The dead silence made me think too much. Dredging evil things from the past. I dared not grieve for Baby Fay or Emma while Andrew and Abby were alive. "Don't you dare shed a tear," Andrew had screamed before smashing my face with his boot.

The house playing chaos twenty-four made it easier to ignore everything on the inside. Noise muffles agony, if loud enough. Now that everything in the house has melted into ghosts, I could think about how they never got the chance to be. *Does anyone care about Baby Fay? Nurse Maggie, are you still playing the angel?*

The smell of gin and pee bathed the room. Abby always bitched about the rug smelling like cat pee. I didn't believe little Muffy was peeing everywhere until now.

Little Muffy's pee morphed into concentrated ammonia as the years snuck by on that shag. *She's a pourer, not a urinator*, I thought once. But now I realized she was both. You don't even know your critters' lives either.

Then, to my surprise, as I sat there in that gin-and-pee-infested room, a hot tear rolled down my cheek. I didn't know why. Emma, perhaps. Then another splashed onto the wood floor.

I felt myself about to wail as loud as Lincoln, when a rumble vibrated the bed. My eyes popped wide. My heart started burning nose candy like a broker's party. Abby came back to bite me with a smelly fart. I was terrified to place eyes on her. Part of me thought she wasn't dead. But I knew better. I pulled my shirt over my nose once the smell wafted by.

And before my mind could process, I started laughing. I laughed so hard I got a tingling sensation, as though high. After a while, my mouth got sore, and my eyes burned. I just kept laughing and sucking up Abby's stink of death. I didn't care that I was breathing whatever her corpse threw my way.

My skin crawled just thinking about laying eyes on Andrew again. But I had to know for sure he was dead. Within seconds of entering his room, the phone startled me by ringing that crazy, little tune. The ringer light flashing red on the nightstand.

I was terrified to pick up the phone. But, if I didn't answer, things would get extra pretty quick.

"Hello?" I said, all guilty pitched. I swallowed hard. My throat turned sticky.

I heard Nurse Maggie hacking up a tonsil on the other side, like little Muffy sometimes when she drank water too fast. I pulled the phone from my ear. Her raspy tone eventually said, "Lizzie?"

Of course it's Lizzie. Who else could it be?

"It's Lizzie." This time, I used my Little Bo-Peep tone, as though I was just hanging out.

"This is Nurse Maggie." She coughed again. Her voice bore a chain-smoker vibe. This time spitting through the phone louder than before. My ears rang. "I can't make it today."

I could hear Abby's voice scream inside my head, "Hallelujah! Jesus answered my prayers!"

"Okay." My tone sounded bubbly. Overly enthusiastic. It was hard to mask all the excitement brewing within. As if I'd killed Andrew and Abby twice over. Somewhere deep down, I reveled in their demise. My only regret: I couldn't rinse and repeat.

Still coughing away, she said, "I'll call the agency and find a replacement."

"No! I've got it!"

She paused. I could hear her nostrils rattling through the receiver. "Oh."

"Mom and Dad won't like someone new. You know how they get. They'll throw a fit."

Another pause. Her voice packed with phlegm. "That's a bad idea. I might not make it tomorrow either."

"That's okay." I twirled Andrew's plastic oxygen line around my finger, wishing I could wrap it around his neck for round two. His IV still channeling through the plastic-bullet thing. Still pumping into veins that don't circulate blood anymore. Eyes hung upside down. Hands elegantly folded on his stomach, as though he were in midthought. "I can do what's needed. It's better for me to look after them. They don't like strangers."

She sighed with another rattle. "Call me if anything happens."

I squeezed my mouth shut till I was blue. But my laughter was desperate for air too. I clenched my body as though I had to pee. I thought, *Well, Nurse Maggie, something has definitely gone wrong.* "Okay, will do."

"You have my number."

"Uh-huh, yep."

"Okay then." When she said *then*, the coughing spell got homicidal again.

"I've got to go. Dad's calling for me." I hung up and collapsed on the chair beside the bed with all my eighty pounds.

I stared at Andrew for a good while. Scrutinizing every detail of his corpse. A side profile revealed how big his belly was. Puffed out larger than a humpback. His arms and legs noodle frail. His fingernails, thick and jaundiced.

I couldn't tell which was yellower, his skin or nails. Everything else, shriveled and delicate as tissue paper. How could someone be so shriveled and fat in the same universe?

Regarding Andrew, a few examples from our childhood to mull. Andrew love bombed Emma. But he didn't love us. He never loved us. Why did he hate us so much? In his eyes, Emma's only worth came from her beauty. "A perfect Mondragon," he'd brag to just about anyone who would listen.

A week after Emma died, Andrew snorted, "At least she had the guts to see it through and finish the job, unlike some people," then thumbed in my direction. We both knew he meant me.

After the medical examiner removed Emma's body, I fell asleep in her bed. I didn't cry. I tried to muster tears. Some kind of emotion. But nothing bubbled to the surface. Was I a bad person for not crying over the death of an angel?

I felt empty and trapped inside a virtual world. Where someone had smashed the reset button to smithereens. Like someone had tipped me over and poured my entire universe all over that goddamn bed.

Andrew didn't shed a tear either. Abby locked herself away in the room and drank gin until she blacked out. Same old, same old. Once the house was soundless, I pulled the blankets over my head so I could smell her perfume. Emma's hair smelled like pears. Her scent was ground into the pillows.

I dreamed of her that night. She said I'd end up like her if I didn't escape. But the greatest thing my angel told me was that she was proud of me. It's crazy to hear the stuff you need to hear but don't think you need to hear it. There's no gift that can top that. Emma did all of that from the grave. Only an angel can deliver a message like that.

In the morning, I found a Polaroid camera hidden inside a shoebox in Emma's closet. Film, flashy cubes, and a stack of photos secured by a grass-colored rubber band.

She took pictures of birds and little Muffy. Too many of little Muffy. She even captured the decaying garden out back. She took selfies and nudes while standing in front of the vanity.

I didn't realize how miserable she was until I saw her selfies. The pain in her eyes went hell deep. They sparkled, stardust-like. But you could see all the misery bubbling to the top.

Her face weighed by all the agony the world could ever hurl. But a stranger wouldn't guess it just by looking. As I mentioned before, you don't know your angels like you think. Until they're gone. And when they're gone, they're gone. Take backs don't survive in this realm. Nothing can stop death in motion.

I never even saw her naked toes when she was alive. Emma mastered hiding venerable parts. But now I thought she was more beautiful than before. Andrew was right, she was flawless. She was born with a poet's eye. A master at capturing the soul of her subject. Instead of extinguishing it. While Andrew was busy stealing everything from us, she breathed life into things. I was unaware that a genius lived next door.

And, for whatever reason, something inspired me to snap a selfie in the vanity. Do it like Emma. And I did. I mean, I tried. But my selfie sickened me. The lighting was soupy and dreary. It presented like a scary movie.

Emma's were far better. Somehow, even though the evil had collapsed all around her, every day, my angel spewed stardust. My picture looked as though I wore hell, and then some. What terrified me the most were my bottomless eyes. Had Andrew extinguished my soul too?

I slept in Emma's bed every night until the pear perfume fell away. I was warming the bed for her return. I washed my hair with mint shampoo and bathed myself in pear perfume to keep her with me.

Though I learned something new. Pear and mint didn't smell the same on me as they did her. Emma did it better. Angels are just better. All the way to heaven. My skin, my hair seemed to exterminate her essence. Maybe I put out souls too. Some things you can't escape. No matter how hard you fight. Some things are purely genetic.

From then on, I started taking pictures of everything. Within a few weeks, I ran out of film. I went to Walmart to buy more, but they don't stock Polaroid film anymore. I went online to see if I could purchase more. It turns out Emma's camera was super old. A prototype or something. I found a place that sold her film. The online shop owner wanted a hundred dollars per box. Per box!

The online shop owner twisted my undies over the latest auction price. Emma's camera just sold on eBay for twelve thousand dollars. Plus tax and shipping. Those flashy cubes sold for two hundred dollars apiece. I had five sitting in the box. The shop owner knew how to screw me better than Mario or Lincoln.

The worst part was, I needed Andrew's money to buy the film. He'd never give it to me. Emma could squeeze anything out of him, but not me.

Andrew and Abby didn't attend Emma's funeral. Andrew made a stink about Emma being cremated. But I wouldn't let him do that to her. He was so obsessed with setting my angel on fire.

I forged all the documents to deny cremation. I was the only person at Emma's memorial. Who would know the truth except me? I did my part and carried her empty urn to the mausoleum for show. But I'll have you know, they laid her to rest beside mother. Our real mother died when I was eight. Twenty-five days after Emma's twelfth birthday.

My angel's headstone read: *Here Lies an Angel. Her last words, if she could speak: "Alone" by the Cure.*

No one else knew how she wanted to go, except me. The household moved on fast. It seemed like Andrew and Abby were eager to erase Emma from this place. As if Emma never existed. Whenever I'd mention Emma's name, they'd do my angel dirty and give me the cold shoulder.

Andrew came from wealth. He could shit gold if he wanted to. That's what he shouted every time the bank account got too low, and I couldn't pay for the monthly supplies. He reshuffled his affairs while muttering over bank statements. Which happened often. Him, moving money around. But what did I know? I was a little dummy.

I never met his side of the family, so I couldn't elaborate. Except, somewhere down the line, his parents had died in a car accident when he was six. I wouldn't waste my breath on Abby's side.

We lived in the ugliest house on the block. Best guess, Andrew catfished everyone in his life, excluding us. The thing about an old house is simple: broke down is broke down and eventually needs to be put to sleep.

Though I did stumble into another important fact. While scrubbing the kitchen floor with bleach and soap. I ran across Andrew's bank statement. It appeared Andrew *could* shit gold. I was speechless to read he had accumulated over eight million dollars.

He was so cheap that he refused to buy me five-dollar jeans from the thrift store when my pants turned into capri. The war over undies and bras was primal. Request for new socks may have sunk his puny brain. "One day you're going to open that fat mouth to the wrong individual, and that will be the end," so saith Andrew.

My wardrobe was Emma's things. She was much taller, though. I wore size-six shoes. She wore eight. Her top half was smaller. So her tees and blouses were skintight on me. Choices are very revealing when you're not interchangeable.

Once I hung up the phone with Nurse Maggie, I called Lincoln and Mario and left them each a voicemail asking them to come over. The situation was critical. I used the Little Bo-Peep-in-duress tone. Don't give me that look. It meant Nurse Maggie would live. I was a five-foot baby everything. I couldn't lug Andrew's potbelly and Abby's pickled body down two flights of stairs and into the cellar. I wasn't Supergirl. Besides, I couldn't budge either from where they lay. I'd already tried. I had three days to dispose of the bodies before Nurse Maggie popped on by. Then, I'd have no other choice but to ice the bitch.

I powdered my eyelids with glitter and then layered mascara. Moistened my lips with lip gloss. Slipped on Emma's white summer dress. I curled my hair. "Perfect as doll hair," my angel would say. Is this how black widows get their start?

Something Abby taught me: men are suckers for sandwiches and ice-cold beer. Especially if they're doing you a favor. No need to spill the tea here. Just know, Andrew wasn't too happy paying fourteen thousand dollars to remove a monster aspen growing in the backyard. Its roots ate all the pipes.

Have you ever seen grown men cut down a giant tree? It's a real show. Watching from the kitchen window, Emma, Abby, and I were mesmerized as we saw these Tarzans terrorize the neighborhood with their chainsaws. They were more trapeze artists than anything.

Abby waited on them hand and foot the entire time. She kept serving them endless supplies of sandwiches and ice-cold beer. Those men would have killed for that woman after all she had slaved over. They gave her real puppy eyes too. She even got them to shave the price by a few thousand. I guess that's why Mario didn't move me. You can't bullshit your way through puppy eyes.

I arranged geometric sandwiches on a platter just as Abby had taught and set them on the coffee table closest to the door. This would catch their eye first. The smell, their guiding light. I speedily substituted ice-cold beer for gin. Cold as ice is key. Liquor is liquor. There's no way I'd have pulled off getting beer.

I stood by the window for an hour. The mood—to die for. I peeled back the blinds every time I heard a car drive by blaring its radio. Two hours later, I lounged on the sofa and read a magazine. Then watched TV.

Daylight burned fast, and I was starving. I went to the kitchen and fixed a peanut butter and rye. Ten minutes later, I plopped on the couch and watched more television. Survivor was on, and all I could think of was the lengths people will go for money. And that got me spinny.

So, I called Mario and Lincoln and offered them ten thousand dollars each. All they had to do was get their asses down here and help me. I screamed, "Right now! I'm not joking! I'll tell."

Andrew had eight million dollars squirreled away, and I didn't care. The baby's freedom was priceless. I'd give anything to hug Emma one last time. Baby Fay too. To be fair, money won't love you back. It's not a shoulder to cry on. It doesn't care about your feelings. Money buys steel drums for pozole. Money buys a lot of junk but fails at immaterial. I'd give Mario and Lincoln every cent if they'd walk through the front door.

I lied there on the couch daydreaming about the way Emma used to hold me at night. The way her mint-scented hair tickled my nose at three a.m. Her spellbinding giggles. No one giggled like her. The things I missed most were the annoying things.

When the angel in your life dies, they elevate to God's status. But I was no dummy. Emma was a heartless bitch to me sometimes. Far from God's status. But she was my perfect bitch, see? She was the only bitch in the world who cared for me. Loved me. Even despite myself. Because I didn't make it easy for people to love me. And Emma did. Emma protected me. She even chose me before her own baby. Who can say that?

I woke to a dazzle of fuchsia cast on the walls. The TV somehow played cartoons now, and I wasn't sure who had turned the channel. I could hear a car alarm in the distance. Somewhere out in the starlight, a dog's ear-shattering bark approached.

I stole a quick glance at the clock, and it read two a.m. in laser red. Lincoln and Mario never showed their ugly faces. I called again and left more voicemails.

Gin bottles crowded Abby's personal cupboard. Except for a bottle of Glenlivet. I cracked it open and poured a glass. Lemon wedge chomping the rim. This stuff burns on the way down. It did warm my belly, which settled my stomach. A prickling sensation fluttered from the back of my neck. My first impression of Glenlivet made me think Abby's homicide was now a mercy killing. I gave her liver some time to breathe.

I kept thinking, while drinking more Glenlivet, how could Abby drink this stuff? But I soon discovered, it's easy after the first glass. I then chugged the bottle.

Morning light needled through the blinds. I woke this time to music. It howled through the kitchen on a rampage. For a sec, I thought Emma was still alive. That the last few months was only a nightmare. She was the only person who dared blare the kitchen radio like that. Emma was Andrew approved, no matter what.

I bolted upright. The earth melted beneath me. My head ballooned as though ready to pop. A sourness crawled its way to my tonsils. The sofa cushions toasted my body. A funny feeling slapped me silly. I thought Emma was alive.

"Emma?" My voice was hollow. Lost in the empty. I got to my feet and walked toward the kitchen. "Emma?"

Glenlivet sat empty on the kitchen counter with nothing left to give. Emma wasn't there. Not where she was supposed to be. Dust still caked her chair. The sight of it ripped a hole in my heart. The music droned and split my skull. My world kept swaying somewhere to the left. Morning breath drenched in liquor numbed my tongue. That scotch had supernatural powers. I could feel it oozing from my pores.

Within a few seconds, I got so dizzy. My knees hit the kitchen tile. I threw up all over myself. I tried to stand, but Glenlivet slammed me back down. Peeling myself from the floor proved futile. My body became heavy as lead. The world kept spinning at hyper speed. I squeezed my head, hoping to stop this morbid ride.

As I lay paralyzed, head cocked toward the refrigerator, that little shit Muffy was peeing two inches from my eyeballs. Then I thought, *Why did Emma keep this from me?* The blackness rushed in and stole everything else.

FOUR
RESERVATION FOR THREE

The kitchen Spanish tile cooled my cheek and soothed my achy head. My face throbbed in violent waves like a heartbeat. I thought I might have smacked my face on something on the way down.

My eyes heated at the sight of little Muffy's poo. Sudsy vomit sat beside me and smelled of scotch. Half-digested rye and chunky peanut butter brightened that dreary tile. This was Abby on a good day, if you substituted for gin. I could taste fermented lemon painted inside my mouth. My whole body quivered from the fumes that sought to end me. Those fermented lemon vapors dug deep and twisted my belly. I was doing my best not to throw up again. Like most things in my life, the scotch wanted more than I could give.

I was angry that I woke up here. *When will I be free of this place?* Because even after icing Andrew and Abby, the world still wanted more from me.

The day was almost spent. The sun had turned low and casted a ghostly shadow on the kitchen tile. I peeled myself from the floor to see if Mario and Lincoln were waiting for me outside. I hoped they were. I hoped they still wanted me enough to help get rid of the bodies.

Maybe they were outside right now. Chitchatting about me. How they might get caught for having sex with underage girls. They weren't the only ones with prison on the brain. I had a sneaky suspicion I'd get another tap on the shoulder from the police soon. Except this time, they'd slap the cuffs on me for life.

Maybe my Little Bo-Peep number—oh, forget it. *It won't do a bit of good this time. This time you really screwed up, Lizzie. And you know it.* I couldn't shake this feeling that I better get used to the idea of life behind bars. My gut was telling me I might die in prison. *Correction, you will die in prison.* After all was said and done.

My knees could give at any second as I walked to the front window. I struggled to peel the blinds, my digits tingling so badly. I must admit, a come-to-Jesus moment sobered me when Mario and Lincoln weren't pacing the porch. Waiting for me to answer the door.

The street was ghostly, and nightfall was almost here. Still, I waited to see Mario's white Civic race onto the driveway and screech to a halt as though running from the police. *I don't know what kind of car Lincoln drives, but the same applies.* Deep down, I knew they weren't coming.

In my neighborhood, it rained the industrial sectors. People who weren't afraid to roll up their sleeves, so boasted Andrew. Real Americans, working real-American jobs. But even he poked fun at the neighbors down the street. They cleaned houses for a living. Which wasn't glamorous enough for him. I was ready to puke just thinking about Andrew's bull.

It got me thinking how many hardworking Americans had eight million dollars squirreled away in the bank. Two things were wrecking my undies right then, even if memory is faulty. Besides Andrew's military stint, I didn't recall him ever holding down a job. Where did he get all that bank without a job?

I melted into the couch and eyeballed those sandwiches. The tuna was now waxy. The bread turned powdery. A nasty fly was buzzing around, annoying me. A terrible smell was creeping down the stairs. All I could think about was Andrew and Abby.

The telephone's ringer light pulsed beside those sickly sandwiches. Someone had left a voicemail. It had to be Nurse Maggie. Who else could it be? I already knew those boys were a lost cause since the day I'd met them.

The digital voice screamed, "You have eight new messages." My heart sailed to the pit of my gut. I closed my eyes and prayed to baby Jesus and listened to the messages.

First Message: "Lizzie, are you there? It's Maggie. Call me. I'm checking on things. You've got me worried."

My digits trembled faster than a Ferrari. Another sickly wave almost knocked me down again. Nurse Maggie's voice turned frantic pretty quick as the voicemails piled up. But her last message left me lightheaded.

"Lizzie!" Nurse Maggie's voice was still nasally. "It's been two days since I spoke to you. Where are you, young lady? Why haven't you picked up?" She stopped talking to let out a violent spell of coughs. She wouldn't shut up either. The message kept going. Still sounding hoarse and panicked, as though she'd been fired or something. All I could think about was two days. I was in la-la land for two whole days. "I contacted the agency. They don't have a replacement. If you don't call me by five, I'm coming down."

I set the phone down and glanced at the clock. It was 5:32 p.m. I did the only thing I could. I dialed her back in a trance. Her phone went straight to voicemail. I hung up and dialed again and still got a voicemail. I dialed three more times and decided, it's fate. I didn't want to go this route, but Nurse Maggie has to go.

I bolted up the stairs and stood in the hallway for a hot minute. My heart was revving like an engine. As I was standing there, thinking about what to do next, a strange, fruity scent wafted out of their rooms. That sour corpse smell had no place to run. I had stupidly left the bedroom doors wide open.

I plugged my nose. But that masked zilch. My timing was too late. The entire second floor was drowning in human rot. My knees sailed to the floor, and I started dry heaving.

There I was, doubled over in the hallway. Everything inside me bone dry. I braced against the wall, but nothing stopped the spinning. Pass out point was near. *Don't do it. Don't you dare.*

Out of the corner of my eye, I saw velvety flies jet from Andrew's room. It amazed me that, despite being so fed, they could still make the journey. Then it dawned on me. The fly downstairs must have started life up here, and it had worked its way through the house. I just got that feeling. I was lying on the floor, gagging, and these stupid velvety flies had the nerve to buzz around my head as if they owned something.

When I finally collected myself, it took me back to Abby. She'd say, "Collect yourself," after Andrew did what he did. Come to think, she always said that whenever Andrew did bad things to us.

I hiked my collar over my nose and entered Andrew's room. His tummy was fatter than a bull's. Most likely loaded with hot air and toxic gas. Thanks, *Criminal Minds*. Your insides, once putrefaction sets in, expands like a giant balloon. Everything under the tissue liquefies. Except bone. All the gases you've collected in a lifetime releases inward. Because there's no place left to run. Think about that for a second.

At first glance, I thought a plump worm was crawling around in his nose. But closer examination showed red foam. A combo of gas and blood was dribbling out faster than a Slurpee machine at Quick Mart. His eyes turned half-light with a mini-blind vibe to it. His tongue wasn't full-on raspberry but close enough. Dentures asymmetrical.

"Oh, Andrew, you're a complete disaster, my dear," Abby often said at the sight. The *complete* part always got me. As if you could half-ass a disaster. Well, Abby, I must confess, his face was a masterpiece of disaster.

"Oh, Andrew, you're bleeding all over the place. Do tidy that piggy face, my dear." Little Bo-Peep energy, whispering in his ear. I sat at the foot of his bed and grinned. Something devilish was filtering its way up from the pit of my gut. A sense of elation came over me. And the power of freedom provoked reckless behavior which, as you know, gets a bitch locked up.

I could run a mile right now. For eternity. And not barrel over from exhaustion. Here's the thing—I didn't care if Nurse Maggie walked through that door. It's true what I'd said before. If I had to ice her, well, that was just the burden I'd have to carry.

The longer I perched at the foot of the bed, something tugged my funny bone. It trickled out like Andrew's bloody Slurpee. First, a tinny squeal escaped. I slapped my mouth shut in shock. The shame made me question why I'd laugh at a time like this. But it desired the light. And I laughed until my chest burned.

I had to stop laughing once a dizzy spell hit. For a second, I swear,

Jesus appeared. *If he's real, I'll go straight to hell.* I broke all ten in less than a week. *Is that a record?*

Two days ago, was the first time I got drunk. The scotch was not done with me yet. I could feel it running through my veins like hot gasoline to a Ferrari. So, I went to the bathroom to brush my teeth. But even a gallon of toothpaste wouldn't scrub away the funk.

I had to pee. It snuck up on me while I was playing with my gums. And while I was sitting on the toilet, I got to thinking. Maybe I didn't have to ice Nurse Maggie. Maybe I could convince her that Andrew or Abby left town. I could lie on the fly. Everyone seemed to believe me. Even if they suspected something, they errored on the side of caution.

Abby had told me once, "Work with what God gave you."

I was a gifted liar. If God hated liars, then why did he build me so goddamn good? Aren't all stories just another form of lying?

I sprung from the toilet and raced to Andrew's room. I covered him in a mountain of blankets to mask the smell. I shut the door behind me. Then I rinsed and repeated with Abby.

After I was done, Andrew and Abby were almost invisible under the mountain of blankets. I did other things too. I unplugged the machines. Packed everything into the closets. Even the medical equipment upstairs. I covered my tracks. As far as Nurse Maggie went, Andrew and Abby had left town for an emergency.

I climbed into the attic and hauled down an industrial fan. Last year, the cellar flooded, and Andrew made me buy this contraption to air everything out. It was clearly a large metal fan. But Andrew insisted on calling it a contraption.

There's something magical about scotch. Because my head was full of ideas all the sudden. My mind lightning sharp. I had no plans of slowing down.

I set the fan in the hallway and turned it full blast. The fan created a vacuum, and one by one, all the doors slammed shut like falling dominos. Even the plaster walls shuddered in the wake. Though, none of this made me flinch. Not until I noticed Emma's bedroom door had slammed during the chaos. How can angels fly when there's no way out?

I changed clothes. Washed off my makeup. Teased my hair. I dressed in dirty clothes from two days ago. I didn't have time to slip on a bra. It didn't matter anyway. I wanted her to think I was bumming around the house.

I got rid of the empty scotch bottle and tidied the kitchen. Muffy's poo was rock hard and chalky. "Good Lord, what the heck is she eating now?" Then I think, please let it be the remains of Andrew or Abby. *Good girl, mama loves you.*

It took me some time to scrub whatever was glued to the frying pan. Whatever it was made me gag. The flames of the gas burner still spitting low. Why didn't the frying pan melt into smithereens after two days? And, further, why didn't the house burn to the ground? Saltines seasoned the counter. Cans of opened sardines set near Muffy's water bowl. Apparently, this bitch knew how to party.

The digital clock tacked above the stove read 6:08 p.m. in laser red. Nurse Maggie threatened to head down if I didn't call her by five. Nurse Maggie lived thirty minutes away. And for whatever reason, I grinned. I couldn't help thinking she'd died in a car accident on the way.

My stomach was bloated, like all those little pigs locked in the stalls. I wasn't hungry, or at least I didn't think so. But, for some odd reason, I shuddered. I was weak at the knees and thirsty as hell. Everything on the inside was super dry. My tongue a prickly cat.

So, I dumped a can of frozen orange juice into a pitcher and filled it in the kitchen sink. I snatched a coffee mug and mixed orange juice and gin. Don't judge, it got rid of Abby's tremors. Besides, it's best to be a little tipsy when getting booked for homicide.

I moved the party to the living room. Plopped my feet onto the coffee table and spread out. While resting my eyes, those tuna sandwiches emitted deadly fumes like Andrew and Abby. Enough for Muffy to steer clear.

I forced my eyes open when my body shuddered again. My jittery digits couldn't cling to the mug anymore. So, I grabbed a straw and got to sipping. My hands were so messed up I almost dropped the remote before turning on the TV.

A commercial blared. "News at six, News at eleven. News nonstop."

The world melted before my eyes. I felt shell-like, as though I was the third wheel in my own life. That same out-of-body experience when

Andrew touched me. I somehow turned invisible again. I sipped some more, just thinking about it.

The anchor woman was all bells and whistles. She had stardust angel hair. "This just in," she said with urgency, "Mario Tuffin, a twenty-two-year-old man from the Denver area, has just surrendered. Ending a ten-hour standoff between Mr. Tuffin and the SWAT team. Denver police have arrested Mr. Tuffin related to the death of Jennifer Combs."

Channel seven broadcasted a mugshot of my Mario. I inched up from the couch like a mindless zombie. I turned the TV louder. I saw them toss him into the police car like a wild beast. He shouted something at them. I bet he was calling them pigs as they slapped on the cuffs.

"Sources say Jennifer Combs was just twenty weeks pregnant. She posted a picture of an ultrasound on social media days prior to being abducted. Mario Tuffin could face multiple murder charges. Under the new statute, killing a twenty-week unborn child is now considered fetal homicide. More about this story later in our upcoming news coverage." The anchor woman turned to look at her cohost. She gave him a disgusted look. "Back to you, Charlie."

I couldn't agree more. I clicked off the TV and just sat in a dreadful daze. An evil spell. I could see my reflection on the black screen. It sort of buzzed to the left on its own. It wouldn't stop moving. *Am I moving?*

Muffy jumped on the couch and walked across my lap and startled the shit out of me. Her tail slapped my face while she purred on by. Emma always said Muffy had a sad detector installed inside. Muffy only visited when I was heartbroken. I stroked her velvety fur. She hummed Ferrari-like while sifting through my digits.

Tears fell on my lap. I couldn't help it. I didn't love Mario. I didn't think Jennifer Combs loved him either. *Does anyone love Mario?* Emma didn't escape. Baby Fay. Neither did Jennifer Combs or her baby. *Why do I get to live?*

Like I said before, Mario was a choker. He reeked of grim vibes. Without a passerby shouting, "Get your hands off that girl punk, or I'll call the police," Mario would have choked me against the Walmart cinder wall.

Mario had homicidal eyes. The same as Andrews. The more I

thought about things, the more I cried. Tears washed my face. Muffy sat on my lap, looking up at me with sad eyes. Her little detector must have broken to tiny bits.

"What's wrong with me?" I rubbed my eyes. I hated when I got like this. I wiped my nose on my sleeve and took Muffy to the kitchen to pour a bowl of milk. I just sat there watching Muffy drink gracefully from the bowl when a clamorous buzz, buzz, buzz startled the whole house.

I flinched as my heart took a nosedive. Muffy sailed to the floor and landed on her feet. She rubbed up against my leg and peered at me like I'd done something. I paused, hoping whoever was at the front door would leave.

Then, buzzzz, buzzzzzzz, morphed into bang, bang, bang. The front door rattled on its hinges. For whatever reason, Muffy went to investigate the noise. "Get over here."

"Lizzie?" I faintly heard Nurse Maggie's voice tunnel through the door.

I decided not to answer. But I wouldn't leave Muffy behind. *Who will take care of her when I'm gone?* While I was on the subject, I'd rather go kicking and screaming like Mario did. *They'll have to break down the door and drag me to the police car.* Dead or alive. You know which one I'd choose.

Buzzzz, Buzzzzz.

The ringer light sparkled and danced all the way to the kitchen. It was now playing that ridiculous tune. I tiptoed my way to the living room window and peeled back the blinds. Enough to get a glimpse of the front porch.

My eyes fluttered fast, and the fear evaporated once I laid eyes on Nurse Maggie. She was alone and appeared frazzled. She hammered the doorbell again.

"Nurse Maggie," I said innocently.

"Yes," she said, aggravated. "It's me. Open the door right now, young lady."

What's with this young lady shit? Jesus, Nurse Maggie, alert the entire goddamn neighborhood while you're at it.

"Hang on a second" I scouted the living room in a tizzy. What to grab? "I'm naked. I just got out of the shower."

The shower? My hair isn't even wet. Jesus, what a little dummy you are. I expected a response. It was so quiet now. You could hear a leaf cry its way to the dirt.

"Okay, young lady! You have exactly two minutes to open this door."

I saw her glance at her watch. My eyes went wild. My heart pumped blood like a speed freak. I sprinted up the stairs and hurled myself into the shower and turned on the water full blast. I gasped while a thousand icy needles pummeled my body. I couldn't even breathe, the water was so fucking cold.

I forced myself to endure. I thought I might pass out. I sprung from the shower so fast I smacked my head against the tile. I hit the floor hard enough to rattle pictures on the wall. Flashes of light and drizzle from the shower rained down on me.

My legs went numb, and I couldn't rise. I reached for the toilet and spewed orange juice and gin. My nose burned once I sat up. Eyes swirling in pain. I thought vomit might have poured through my nose. All I could taste was gin.

Somehow, I made it to the stairs. Wet clothes clung to my skin like a cast. I could barely bend my knees. My drippy hair blinded me. A burning sensation lit up my right side. My teeth chattered when I mounted the first step. I rested on the third step, and the wood planks groaned under my weight.

Buzzzz, buzzzz "Lizzie!" Nurse Maggie called. Bang, bang. "Lizzie!"

I was panting, and everything went fuzzy. Before I realized I had just opened the front door, Nurse Maggie's angry face glared at me. "You're soaked from head to toe."

Her voice was still hoarse. She touched my forehead.

I put on my pitiful eyes, this time genuine.

"You're bleeding."

Nurse Maggie tried to barge through the door and move past me, but I wouldn't let her. "We have the blues," I said.

Her face grew more concerned. She whipped out her phone. "You're soaking wet and bleeding. I better call the doctor for both your sake."

"No." I surrendered to the moment.

Nurse Maggie dabbed my eye with a tissue. "He needs his breathing treatment. Your father is missing half his lung. That's nothing to play around with. He could die from pneumonia. What did you do to yourself?"

Then my greatest fear dawned on me. I'd killed Andrew, retro style, when I should have poisoned him with pneumonia.

I gave Nurse Maggie the "I don't give a shit" face. Like the girl from the DU library. Like Emma.

"He could die, Lizzie, you don't want that on your conscience, do you?"

His death was certain. So, I gave him a few extra pills to speed things up. I did what nobody else would. This go around; I tried like hell to shine my innocent Bo-Peep eyes.

"How's your mother?"

I gave Nurse Maggie a blank stare.

"Well, is her oxygen level at 98 percent or better?"

I drew a blank. As though someone had tipped me over and dumped out my brains. So, I shrugged. My shoulder ached, and my head was super hot. Ice droplets kept sizzling down my neck. Or was it blood?

"Step aside, young lady, I need to assess the damage." She dug her feet into the threshold and used her meaty leg to spread my thighs. What a little bitch. "I need to check. It's my job."

Assess the damage? It's safe to say; the bastards are sunk. Think, Lizzie, think. "Aren't you contagious? That will make them sick to death."

I used Nurse Maggie's tactics against her. She'd told Emma the same thing once before. After Emma got Covid.

Nurse Maggie peered at me with angry eyes. Shocked I'd accuse her of doing something wrong. "I would never endanger your parents. Now let me through."

A violent wave hit me. My knees were shaking. Eyes all watery.

"Lizzie, you're white as a ghost. Sit over there, so I can look you over."

I couldn't seem to find the right words. Even though I wanted to.

"Lizzie?"

"Andrew and Abby are fucking dead." I laughed and mumbled something else.

"Excuse me?"

"Check for yourself."

"What?"

I gripped the doorknob, my body pure lead. I was too heavy to stand and winded. Then, I kissed the floor.

"Lizzie!"

I was hollowed out. The lights faded. The Cure played inside my head while my eyes rolled back.

"Lizzie!" Nurse Maggie screamed again, patting my forehead. "Can you hear me?"

I can hear you, Nurse Maggie. But I'm speechless at the moment. Leave your name and number. I'll get back to you soon.

"Lizzie!"

Little Muffy's sandpaper tongue licked my face. She knew when bad things ran about. *Is she licking my face? Or am I daydreaming? I can't tell. Nurse Maggie is moving my body. Turning me this way and that. Her lips are moving, but someone killed the goddamn volume. I see Nurse Maggie pick herself off the floor and run upstairs.*

I drew all the strength I had left, lifted my hand, and said, "Don't go upstairs."

Signing off for now, Nurse Maggie. Try not to scream after you open the bedroom door.

FIVE

JUST BURNS

DETECTIVE ROSE GAVE me that guilty-as-charged glare like the officers from the café did. I couldn't manipulate those law-abiding eyes. I tried my best. It seemed she could see something no one else could. She wasn't buying my story. Not one bit. Her line of questioning was really twisting my undies.

"Elizabeth." Her tone had a calm resonance. A voice you could trust. But I knew better. "You're not in trouble. We know what your father did to you and Emma. We know everything. You don't have to lie anymore." Detective Rose placed Emma's diary on the table.

I wanted to pee my pants when she scooted the diary forward.

"It's not my fault," I said with my Little Bo-Peep tone. "I really tried."

Detective Rose snatched my wrist with a tense vibe. I yanked my digits free. Her tone shifted. I didn't like it. "Listen, Elizabeth."

I casted evil eyes on her. "It's Lizzie! My name is Lizzie." Elizabeth belonged to Andrew and Abby. *And I've got news, Elizabeth is dead. And she isn't coming back.* Elizabeth died the moment those two fell into rigor mortis.

"Okay." Detective Rose adjusted and softened her posture. She side-eyed her partner, Detective Bones. "Lizzie, all we want is the truth.

42

You're not in trouble. We know something happened in that house. Bridget Sullivan."

"Bridget." My eyes said it all.

The detectives exchanged a glance, confused. "You don't know a Bridget Sullivan?"

I shook my head and lowered my eyes. Emma would know what to do in this instance. My angel could navigate these waters without breaking a nail. She did all the heavy lifting for me at home. She protected me from Andrew and Abby.

"The traveling nurse who visits your house every day. You don't know who that is?" Detective Bones clarified.

My eyes went starlight. "Are you talking about Nurse Maggie?"

The detectives looked relieved.

"Yes. She reported your mom, and dad had died of an accidental overdose. In her report, she stated you couldn't have known the correct dose to administer. The state wouldn't allow you to provide care, including narcotics, because of your age. She further stated it was her legal duty to contact the agency to find suitable coverage during a leave of absence and failed to follow policy." Detective Rose, still skimming the report and talking at the same goddamn time. "She stated she was sick for a few days. Is that correct? Was she sick?"

I nodded. My eyes burning a hole into the table. I wished I could burn a hole right through my little heart and end things right now. I could feel Detective Rose mentally noting all my reactions to her line of questioning. Detective Bones too. I could feel myself ready to ball worse than Mario and Lincoln. *Pull it together, bitch, you're two steps from the gold.*

She ruffled more documents. I picked at my cuticles under the table where the detectives wouldn't see my guiltiness grow fierce. I dug so hard I hit blood. Warm liquid oozed from my digits. My hands became a waxy mess.

That didn't scare me, though, because I was no quitter. Andrew could think whatever he wanted about me. Besides, he was eating dirt for all eternity now. And just to show him I didn't give a shit anymore, I dug even deeper. He adored perfect nails.

"The examiner's report ruled your parents' death accidental. The examiner agreed with Bridget Sullivan's report. Ms. Elizabeth Mondragon, who's only sixteen—I'm paraphrasing here. Doesn't have the medical expertise to administer non-lethal doses, like the ones given to Andrew Mondragon and Abby Mondragon that resulted in death. All three medications used in combination were a perfect storm. Only a well-trained doctor or pharmacologist would know this drug combination is deadly."

Detective Bones walked over to the table. "Lizzie, you did nothing wrong. It was an accident. That's not why we're here. We'd like to discuss your sister, Emma. We have evidence that suggests she didn't commit suicide. Did you witness anything out of the norm the night Emma died?"

"It's Angel!" I said, way too loud. My knees kept bouncing like an angry fish. Vibrating faster and faster. Enough for the table to rumble forever.

The detectives gave each other a strange look.

"Are you anxious about something, Lizzie? You keep fidgeting down there."

I ignored Detective Bones as Emma helped me get my knees under control.

Detective Rose shooed Detective Bones. "We examined Emma's body. Did you know she was a burner?"

Burner froze my mouth. My universe. But my brain twirled on, despite it all. *Emma, help a bitch out again, please. I'm begging you.* But my angel and I knew pleads only run a lifetime while stationary. The damage done to my angel was irreversible. To Fay. To me. The past was immutable for us.

When I didn't answer, Detective Rose rifled through more papers. "I'm going to assume your silence is a yes. How did Emma get all those bruises? The examiner noted numerous old bruises on her body."

"Stop!" I scream so loud my ears ring. "Please!"

Detective Rose ignored my major fuck up. She knew I was fucked in the head. She continued on with her dark language. Things we dared not speak. "The examiner reported evidence of a sexual assault."

Oh, my Jesus. Emma, please, if you're listening.

"He also notated genital-tissue damage and scarring. Which could support repeated assaults."

"Shut up!" I squeezed my eyes shut. "That's my sister!" I covered my ears to liquefy the noise. My heart was flying fast. And now, I was daydreaming about how to administer a deadly concoction to this bitch.

Then something stopped me from springing from the chair and slapping her. My body went limp. The world spun and everything was awesome again. Here, in the cold, dark silence. Where nothing could hurt me.

Detective Rose delicately pulled my hands free from my ears. "Lizzie, I know this is tough. I've interviewed many girls, just like you. Now is the time to tell us the truth. Your father can't hurt you anymore, sweetie."

I couldn't help it, but a tear spurt out like the beginning of a tsunami. Then two more. I was so furious I couldn't breathe. Now I got why Abby's blood boiled. Mine was piping hot. Why couldn't my body do what I needed it to do? Why must everyone own me? *Is that why you did it, my angel? To be free? Is that why you left me alone to die in this place?*

"Detective Rose is correct on this one, Lizzie. Now is the time. We've read Emma's diary. Did she mention the diary to you?"

"Nothing happened, I swear to Jesus," I snorted out of fear. "Nothing ever happened. It never goddamn happened!" I held my head from bobbing. Still, I was rocking myself like a baby.

"What didn't happen, Lizzie?" Her timbre changed gears. "Your father can't hurt you anymore. You can trust us. We want to help you, Lizzie." Detective Rose kept tapping the end of her pencil on the table. A steady tap. Tap, tap, tap. Like frail beats of a dying heart. A hollow snare.

I looked up and saw stars glinting everywhere. As though I'd swam the universe. Or a meteor shower. I couldn't tell which. Everything in the room liquefied before my eyes. Detective Rose's voice slipped away.

I could feel tears truck down my cheek. My face was full of lava that burned my digits to ash. I dug and dug some more. I wanted to strike beyond the bone. Until smithereens, I wanted to feel my bones disintegrate. I wanted to feel my soul evaporate. *Emma, my angel, I need you.*

The door swung inward with a bang. The entire room shuddered. "That's quite enough," a woman said. "Do you realize you're traumatizing this girl even more? Hasn't she gone through enough?"

I looked up, the detectives wearing shame.

Detective Rose said, "Lizzie must face reality if she's going to move on with her life."

"Move on," the woman said, annoyed. "Do you hear yourself?" Detective Rose stood and tried to rebut. The attorney palmed the detective. "I'm ending this interview. Ms. Mondragon, you don't have to answer any more questions."

"We haven't finished." Detective Bones rose.

"The court appointed me as legal counsel and temporary guardian. My job is to protect Ms. Mondragon. This line of questioning is causing irreparable harm."

"Now you're a therapist?"

"I may not be a licensed therapist, but I see that this line of questioning is emotionally damaging to my client. Not to mention the legal ramifications."

"Why did your father leave Emma eight million dollars? Why would he do that?"

Lizzie's lawyer threw Detective Rose a look of disgust. "You don't have to answer any more questions, Ms. Mondragon. This interview is over."

I looked up to lay eyes on her. But I couldn't see her. My world painted by all those twinkling stars. Still, my body mysteriously lifted from the chair. I was scared my head would float away. My legs stepping forward, one at a time. I couldn't think of anything anymore. I was no more.

"I want to go home," I said.

The room was deadly still. Like home. The only thing missing was the bats. And all those mimicries.

"Miss?" I said.

A voice swum out from the darkness. "Yes?"

"Can I go home now?"

"My name is Maxine." A warm hand touched me. "I'm taking you someplace safe."

"Maxine..." I said her name again because, in that moment, Maxine was elevated to angel status.

LESS IS MORE

Hana and Maxine sandwiched me while the detectives asked questions about Andrew and Abby's deaths. This was the first time I'd met Hana. They worked at the same law firm.

Detective Rose was there too. It appeared the entire police department wanted to know if I'd killed my parents. Or was it an accident? I think everyone at that station was betting on the former. Things were unraveling faster than I could catch up.

They moved the interrogation to the conference room. I didn't mind. The bigger room smelled shampooed. The small one had metal chairs and smelled of burnt coffee and stale pastries. The sugary kind you get from Walmart's bakery.

"Elizabeth."

Hana corrected Detective Bones. "Please refer to our client as Lizzie or Ms. Mondragon."

Detective Bones glared at me with incorruptible eyes, powerful enough to rummage through the soul for truth. "The examiner ruled your parents' death accidental. But there are a couple things we need to clear up before we close the case."

I forced a look of concern. I wanted to seem agreeable under the circumstances. When, in reality, I wanted to steer them off a big cliff.

Detective Bones was enormous. A real-life Goliath and scary. His shoulders propped baby heads on each side, his muscles trying to chew their way out of his suit.

"The toxicology report showed opioids, benzodiazepines, and muscle relaxants in your parents' blood streams. Non-lethal levels. Nothing crazy. Individually, these drugs aren't fatal in low doses. But together," Detective Bones set the toxicology report on the lacquered conference table, "they call it a triple-threat cocktail that causes respiratory failure. You ever hear of a triple-threat cocktail?"

I stayed very still. My eyes radiating angel energy. Concern sprinkled across my brow. There was a small hole in the cushion at the edge of my seat. My first digit tunneled the hole and spread it even bigger.

"The funny thing is their toxicology report is identical. Identical. You gave them the same medication. Same dosage. Abby Mondragon didn't receive prescriptions for opioids or benzodiazepines, and that's problematic. They both had lung disease."

"Detective." Maxine glared at him. "Ms. Mondragon has already provided a statement. Everything you need to know is in that statement."

Detective Bones skimmed through more pages. "I've read it." He stopped at a particular page and tapped his finger against the middle part. "Ms. Mondragon states, and I quote, 'I gave them whatever medication was already in their pill organizer, labeled Monday.'"

I SHRUGGED. *Whoops, Detective Bones, I doubt I'd make a competent nurse.* Everything just turned to shit in my hands. The only competent thing I'd ever done was kill Andrew and Abby. I wish I'd done it sooner, before my angel got pregnant and drank a gallon of bleach.

To be fair, you don't need a flamethrower to burn your insides to smithereens. My angel turned her insides pure. So much so that her tongue exploded, and her esophagus slammed shut.

The examiner had remarked that it was the most tragic suicide he had encountered in his twenty-year tenure. "Damn near impossible." She had burned from the inside out. I guess chlorine gases built up and had no place left to run. The examiner kept saying it was impossible to drink a gallon of bleach. If that's so, then why was the bottle empty? Where did the rest of it go? Maybe the mice living in the cellar drank the rest. IDK. I'm kidding. I doubt a bunch of mice would hunger for bleach. Although the mice lived under the same roof. It's hard to rule out.

But Emma and I knew the truth. I didn't think Emma did it. Every time I thought of Emma sitting in that cold, dark cellar, alone, drinking bleach like gin, my heart ached. Was that her chance to escape? It mattered little how badly it burned inside because we had grown to love the burn. They'd groomed us to delight in it. While the examiner couldn't conceive of it, I could. But here's the thing: nothing burns forever. Eventually, someone or something will put you out like a cigarette.

Nobody knew Emma like me. Nobody. I just never knew why she didn't invite me to tag along. I cried a lot. And got scared. Who knows, maybe she wanted some space. Maybe she'd have lost the nerve with me there, wailing and begging her not to do it.

Emma knew me best. I think the only reason she didn't invite me was because I wasn't strong enough. My angel on the other foot was very strong.

"Ms. Mondragon," Detective Bones scolded.

I snapped out of it and sharpened my focus. I hadn't realized Detective Bones was asking me a question. Sometimes I faded into my little universe. That's what my angel called it. I leaned over and whispered in Maxine's ear, "What did he say?"

"Detective, please repeat the question."

"Ms. Mondragon, when did you realize your parents had died?"

If you must know, down to the final second.

"Ms. Mondragon?"

"I gave them their pills, I think, at nine?" I peered at the ceiling.

"And?"

"I vacuumed. I did the dishes. I cleaned out the closet. Then I gave Muffy a bath."

Gave Muffy a Bath? They were so stupid, they didn't even know Muffy was a cat.

"Ms. Mondragon," Detective Bone's voice grew aggravated, "you're not answering my question. I'm not interested it what you did *after* you gave your parents medication. When did you notice your parents were dead?"

"I'm not sure." My eyes moved toward Maxine's briefcase. "I fell asleep on the couch."

Another gem stolen from Nurse Maggie's playbook. She, too, had fallen asleep on our couch many times.

"When did you wake up?"

"I think morning."

"You think morning?" Detective Bones wrote in his notebook. The pencil in his Goliath hand looked as slender as a dried spaghetti noodle.

"And then what did you do?"

"I watched TV, then I took a shower."

"When did you take a shower?" His voice exploded with excitement. He was eager because he thought he'd caught me in a lie.

"I'm not sure."

"Try me."

I could feel everyone watching me. Ears perked.

"Well, I was in the shower when Nurse Maggie knocked on the front door, so whatever time that was."

Best thing to do under these circumstances was to be vague. My advice for when you're being questioned for homicide. Never use specifics. Vague is the key. Vague is girl boss.

"Mmm." Detective Bones rubbed his chin. "I just want to get a good picture of the events. So, by your account, after you gave your parents pills at nine, you didn't check on them for...two days."

I shook my head and puckered my lips.

"Yes, Ms. Mondragon. Your parents were dead for two days. You didn't bother to check on them for two days. According to you," he rifled through more papers, "you gave them pills from their organizer marked Monday around nine. Bridget Sullivan's official statement claims she arrived at the Mondragon residence on Tuesday around six twenty that evening. The ER doctor notated your clothes were drenched, but Bridget Sullivan leaves this out of the report." He dead-eyed me. "Do you usually take showers with your clothes on?"

"I don't remember?"

"Which part?"

"Detective Bones, I'm uncomfortable with your line of questioning." Maxine adjusted her posture, as though she was ready to pounce. "Ms. Mondragon has already provided your department with a statement, as requested. She's been more than cooperative under these circumstances. The examiner has ruled their death as accidental. Its sounds to me like you're fishing. And if you are, this interview is over."

"I'm not fishing, Counselor." Detective Bones sifted through more papers. "There are inconsistencies in your client's statements. Recent evidence has surfaced."

"Well," Maxine locked eyes on Detective Bones, "Please elaborate."

"There are brand-new oil drums siting in the basement."

"Oil drums?" Maxine rolled her eyes. "What does that have to do with my client?"

Uh-oh. I guess real life isn't just like Criminal Minds *after all.* I'd totally forgotten about the drums. And the chemicals. Oh, dear Jesus! The chemicals. Please don't mention those.

"And there's considerable amount of chemicals sitting in the basement next to the oil drums. Enough to dissolve ten bodies. Tarps, gloves. We call it a cleanup kit."

Maxine raised her palm. "I'm going to stop you right there, Detective."

"Ms. Mondragon, who covered your dead parents with a mountain of blankets? You claimed you didn't return to their room after giving them pills."

Maxine gave me a look. "Don't answer that question, Lizzie." She glared at Detective Bones. "Are you charging my client with a crime?"

Detective Bones got quiet. He stopped playing with the paperwork on the table and peered at me with those judgy eyes, a touch of sadness skimming the surface. He'd lost someone close to him. He had the mark of grief scribbled all over. I saw that same scarring in my own eyes when I peeked in the mirror. He'd lost an angel too. When you lose someone you love, your eyes turn bottomless and empty, forever. And no matter what you do, the emptiness finds you, and a pinch of sorrow props those eyes. Heartbreak glistens like the morning dew.

"That depends, Counselor." He pointed at me. "Your client needs to cooperate with the investigation. This isn't a game."

SEVEN
JUVIE

WHEN THE JAIL guard points and tells you to line up against the cinder wall with all the other prisoners and wait to be processed—pay attention. Because if you don't, they'll strip you down and humiliate you in front of everyone. Then they'll throw you in the shoebox cell called "solitary" where you can touch all four walls with your hands and feet without getting out of bed.

Which happened to me. I was visiting my little universe when the jail guard screamed at me to stand against the wall. Several times, I guess. That's what a girl told me. But I was too busy daydreaming of a better life and didn't follow directions.

Solitary is like fool's gold. You think you've hit the jackpot. When, in reality, it's just a lump of shit. That's solitary. I know. I spent my first forty-eight hours there. A cell fit for a mouse. Even the mice at home get the whole cellar.

Brawls and screams played day and night. They kept the lights stoked white hot at all hours. I was in a puddle of sweat when the sun came up and only chattering teeth at night like an addict. A paper-thin, scratchy blanket to pad a metal bed.

I found out *Criminal Minds* wasn't so biblical. That show

glamorized jail. It portrayed prison life as squeaky-clean floors and punctual guards. The other day, I took a hot minute to realize one guard wasn't a prisoner. She blended a little too well.

It's a wonder how my cellie, once I got one, slept sound at night. Something I couldn't seem to do. The landscape of juvie was just this: someone always screaming. Or banging on their cell door. Which sounded like demons escaping the underworld. I won't even mention the beatdowns. It seems the universe is out for blood. Even the roaches that skate by now and then.

I heard a girl crying so long she melted into the background. I forgot she was crying until a new girl entered the pod and said, "That bitch better stop crying, or I'm finna give her reason."

Time had skipped this place. Each new day felt like yesterday, my life stuck on repeat.

I could hear a girl on the second floor throw a fit in her cell. She clobbered the walls and doors twenty-four. The guards kept her locked down the whole time. That's how they deal with "problem children" in this place.

She kept shouting, "Someone help me! Someone, please, help." Bam. Bam. Bam. Bam. She wouldn't stop. That girl made bricks shudder all the way to the ground level.

They serve primal food in solitary. Just enough to keep your little heart ticking. Bread and orange-colored water with a hint of rat poison. That's what it tasted like. Anytime Abby didn't care for the taste of something, this phrase would fall from her tongue: "That tastes like rat poison! Are you trying to kill me?" My response to her, underneath gritted teeth: "You just wait and see, bitch."

I didn't know what the orange-colored water was. Not until a girl told me they served Kool-Aid day and night, which has retro energy scribbled all over it. Some girls here will end you over red Kool-Aid. The guards serve it once a month. And guess what? It tastes just like orange Kool-Aid.

"Are you ready to cooperate, young lady?" Why does everyone call girls *young lady*? A guard with short, spiky hair with bleached tips stood before me. From afar, it looked like a porcupine slept on top her head.

"Yes." I sprung from the metal bed and raced to the door.

The guard pointed. "Take your blanket with you. You won't get another."

I didn't know why I was in a rush. Heaven didn't shine its light here. Never would. I'd soon discover, levels of hell are always identical.

I trailed behind Spiky. Zigzagging through a maze of corridors and loud buzzers that screamed whenever we entered another door. She took me back to processing where I had a problem listening to simple instructions.

She fingerprinted me and tried to strip search me. Spiky wanted me to get naked and squat and cough. She tried to poke me with her digits. I said, "Get your digits off me, bitch, I don't do that." I was tired of people forcing me to do things I didn't want to.

Back to solitary I went. Back into the shoebox where my bones froze like steel in winter. I shivered in the fetal position for a long time. I stopped eating whatever they tossed through the slot. In no time, food trays tiled cold concrete. I didn't have the energy to get up. I just lied on that metal bed and watched a tiny roach scurry back and forth under the door. It would visit the trays first, scout things out, get drunk on bread and whatever else. Then it would speed away with Ferrari energy.

As the days marched on, that tiny roach became my angel. My angel and I started having chats. To be fair, roaches are humble listeners and can morph into whomever you want them to.

The first shoebox they put me in didn't smell. But this one did. It smothered me like Abby's soaked Muffy-pee shag rug. Except, in this place, a hint of mold clung to every cranny.

A teeny window on the door gave me my only view. But to where? The glass had hellish scratches and shattered bull's-eyes as though a wild animal had tried to tunnel out. Had it not been for the shadows and food trays visiting, I'd have thought the world had melted into some starry apocalypse.

I drowned in a sea of angels until the fifth day. It could have been the fifth. Nothing was certain here. I added a few bull's-eyes of my own to say, "I was here. I am here."

Spiky finally let me out and processed me. I copped a squat, naked, like a lifer. I guess the smart ones just dropped and squatted like no biggie. And the dummies got hazed.

The guards had us line up single file when heading to the pods. That's what they called cells, *pods*. Spiky hollered while navigating the corridor. "Keep your head down and your nose clean, girlies. Do those two things, and you might survive."

A girl in line mocked Spiky and made faces as we marched single file. "Keep your head down and your nose clean. Keep your head down and your nose clean." Her witch-like voice changed pitch every time she said it.

The girl ahead of me had sleeve tattoos. Queen of hearts on her left elbow and ace of spades on the right. Mother Mary and thorny roses everywhere. I figured she had a thing for roses. Or thorns. I couldn't decide. She had a teardrop tattoo under her eye, as Mario did. "That bitch is dotted up!" Viking's exact words.

Everyone called her Kit. Short for Kit Kat. "Buy her zoom-zooms from commissary, and she'll protect your ass," my cellie whispered one night. "Cute little booties like you don't survive."

I didn't know what zoom-zooms were. Later, I overheard a girl tell a new bootie zoom-zooms were candy and cookies. "Anything with sugar —zoom-zooms. Get it, ho?"

I bought Kit Oreos, and she rejected me. I'll tell you something: commissary is no Walmart. So, I waited every day, like Mario did for me, for commissary to stock Kit Kats. And once they did, I bought her some.

Kit's face was Emma beautiful. Even though she had a bulky frame. Six-two everything. Detective Bones still had her beat, though. She was my age.

Viking was my cellie. But Spiky called her Mariposa. Viking and a few others hounded me for days. It seemed everyone wanted to know what I did to land here. "You too straight edge to be in juvie. Someone like you gets ate here." Viking laughed.

I thought back to when Detective Bones had arrested me, my mind leaping into a strange universe. He'd said a bunch of things when slapping cuffs. But someone had hit the mute button. I think he read me my rights. Once the detective locked the cuffs in place, I couldn't hear a thing.

Even Maxine had mouthed something to me. My universe had lost sound all of the sudden. Maxine locked eyes on me while Detective Bones did his thing. I still don't know what she tried to tell me. I wish I could travel back in time.

I might have been clueless in certain areas of life, but I wasn't dumb. Remember one thing: I was a killer. I was convinced Detective Bones had arrested me for double homicide.

The universe may fall from my lips whenever the mood strikes. But I wasn't about to run my mouth in the place. I saw how girls treated Kit. Even Spiky feared her. Every time Kit walked past, girls would whisper, "That bitch murdered her uncle."

Kit was on trial for murder, like me. She had stabbed her uncle twenty-three times with a butter knife. That's what Viking told me while we were eating choke sandwiches at chow time. Who serves peanut butter sandwiches with no jelly? Each bite was like swallowing a teaspoon of cinnamon.

Nobody dared mess with Kit. But girls still talked shit behind her back. I heard one girl joke in the shower, "Better stay in your lane, or I'll get Kit to shank you twenty-three times." The girls laughed so loud it rang in my ears.

They never did it to her face. Every girl in the pod knew better than to talk shit or misbehave when Kit was around. All I knew was that pod girls were mean to killers. And who knew what those girls would whisper behind my back if they knew.

I wasn't built mean-girl tough. Though, I will say, Spiky had screamed, "This girl's got giant balls for being scrawny," when wrestling me to the floor before taking me to solitary.

Not that Kit was a beastie or mean-girl vibe. Sometimes a knife is the only way toward freedom. Just because you're the one operating the goddamn thing doesn't mean you're evil.

But if you were to ask Monique, she'd rephrase: "Kit allegedly stabbed her uncle twenty-three times. *Allegedly*." Anytime a girl in the pod confessed their crimes, Monique would correct them, and say, "*Allegedly*. Remember that word when the judge aks, bitch."

Monique had allegedly strolled up to an old lady while she was pumping gas at Quick Mart and pointed a gun at the old lady's head and said, "Give me all your shit." The old lady screamed and dropped everything in her hands. Her keys and purse crashed into the pavement. Monique snatched the old lady's shit, including the keys to a hundred-thousand-dollar SUV. She forced the elegant old lady to lie on the oily pavement, and Monique peeled out of the gas station in that SUV. She tried to outrun the cops and ended up sideswiping another car and crashing into a ditch. This was the first time she had ever driven in her life...allegedly. The ditch entombed the SUV and boxed her in. Monique couldn't roll down the windows, so she tried breaking them for a quick escape, but they were bulletproof or something. Monique got stuck inside until a tow truck winched the SUV out.

When I woke to buzzers sounding somewhere in the distance, I thought I was home. It took me a minute to realize my angel was gone. I had a dream we were swinging on the playground. I should have known it was only a dream. My angel never smiled like that in real life. Despite the white light illuminating her, her face remained overshadowed by darkness. I told her I was sorry. I never got to say sorry for the things I'd done. The night before my angel died, I screamed, "You're a bad sister! You never protect me from him!" Those last words still haunted me. Sometimes, life offers no second chances.

She got quiet and went to her room after that. I heard her rummaging around late at night like an apparition. Part of me wanted to apologize, but my angry side hungered for blood. I tossed and turned all night, ignoring a strange persistence living inside my heart.

I made excuses. Emma could get like that sometimes. Then the next day, she'd emerge cheery. That was her ritual. Things just fixed themselves in our house. I fixed myself too.

I realize now that I hungered for Andrew and Abby's blood. Not my angel's. Eleven years of hunger makes you desperate. Homicidal. Hate had melted my love for her in the moment. The worst part: I didn't get a chance to say, "I love you." I wonder if my angel knew I loved her. *Still* love her.

Something had eluded my heart until it reached a rolling boil. I can't explain it. Well, I can try. We had a nurse visit the house prior to Maggie.

I think her name was Jennifer. Anyway, she only came to the house twice. On the second day, she hardly said a word to Emma and me. And before she left, she said, "I'll see you girls tomorrow." Her delivery unsettled me. It felt like a last farewell. She stood at the front door for a hot second, staring at us. Like she didn't want to leave. But had no other choice. Emma wore those same eyes that night when she walked past me in the hallway. Cold and empty, like she'd made up her mind and wasn't coming back.

Signs exist for a reason. I bet only a handful of people intervene when they notice them. The problem was, I ignored the signs until it was too fucking late. I wanted to scream. I wanted to bawl my eyes out forever for what I'd done to my angel. But I was scared to feel this way all at once. I might just lose my mind to hurt this bad. If I wasn't careful, I could end up like Emma. That was my biggest fear. I wasn't strong like her. I was afraid to die.

Once I sat up in bed and realized where I was, I walked out to the common room and sat next to Viking. Viking and Monique were sitting at the circular tables eating breakfast. They wouldn't even look at me and pretended like I wasn't sitting there next to them.

They gave each other a weird look and stood with their trays and moved to another table. My heart sunk when they did that.

Emma was the only friend I ever had. I never had friends before this. How could I? Mean girls flooded the high school so bad they spilled out every door. And I thought these girls might be friends. But it's true what Abby said, "Guardian angels don't fall from trees."

I stood and looked around. Whispers filled every crevice as glares attacked me. The vibe turned darker than homicidal thoughts. One girl snapped a dirty look my way while chewing, mouth wide. The table behind was a tower of murmurs. The murderous vibe in that room caused my hands to shake.

I sat back down and slid my tray to the side. I wasn't hungry anymore. I stared at my food. "Act like you don't give a shit, or they'll fuck your world," Viking had told me.

The eyes in the room began to smother me and burn a hole through my soul. Scrambled eggs jittered on the plastic spork as I tried to swallow a bite. *I can't believe I'm eating eggs.*

I scooped another bite when something wet hit the back of my head.

"Skank," someone yelled in the distance.

I checked to see what had hit me and ran my fingers through my hair —chocolate pudding. I peered down to see a half-empty pudding cup at my feet.

I was close to bawling my eyes out. And I wanted to grab my tray and go to my cell. But you get solitary for sneaking trays into cells. I didn't want to go back to solitary. So, I scraped the contents of my tray into the trash and stacked it on the return cart and laid on my bunk.

After a few minutes, Viking came into our cell. She made no eye contact, as though I were being shunned. She collected all her belongings and moved out. Monique crowded the doorway, staring me down with whatever fire she had. Monique was Viking's new beastie now.

I didn't eat or leave my room for three days. Girls kept walking past, whispering. They'd scream loud in my room and clobber the door at random times. It startled the shit out of me at first. But after a while, it faded into the background, like that girl crying on the second floor.

On the third day, Kit came into my cell and sat on the top bunk. Her feet almost touched the floor from where she sat. "You better eat, or they're gonna drag your ass up to psych. Trust me, you don't want psych. It's worse than solitary."

"I'm not hungry." My throat was raspy as hell.

"I heard the guards talking. You better force yourself."

Kit lowered her hand to my eye level and gave me a Kit Kat. I pushed her digits from me. "I can't eat."

"You're shaking like a leaf. You've got no choice."

"They're going to throw things at me again. They hate me."

"They don't hate you. They're just scared of you. There's a difference."

"What did I do?" I peered up and tried to find Kit's face.

"Manslaughter. Two counts. Everyone knows you murdered your parents."

"Oh, dear Jesus." My heart exploded into tingles. I was dizzy all the sudden.

Kit snickered. "This is juvie, there's no secrets here. Someone's bound to spill some tea up in this bitch. My guess is a trustee ran her mouth. Trustees can get their hands on anything for the right price. It doesn't take much around here. You'll see how it is."

"I can't." Tears blurred my vision.

Kit hopped off the bunk and landed with a boom. She reached out her catcher-glove-sized hand and said, "Come on, don't let them change you. Trust me, no one's going to fuck with you while I'm here."

I sat with Kit in the common room and ate loaf. Or tried. Kit said loaf is a bunch of mixed ingredients formed into bread pans to make prison meatloaf. I swallowed my canned peaches and vanilla pudding and gave Kit my loaf and red Kool-Aid. I just couldn't eat loaf. I almost puked twice until Kit took over.

I still felt the eyes on me. Whispers and murmurs swim behind us like a girl-eating shark. I heard someone say my name and laugh. Still, no one messed with me while Kit was there. I didn't get covered in chocolate pudding, and that was a win.

Kit and I played cards until lights out. A game called hand and foot. She moved into my room. I took the top bunk. The first few nights, we talked little. Kit was polite and reserved. She wasn't like the others. Most girls in juvie spilled their stories in seconds. My first night in juvie, Viking had talked my ear off until chow time. Viking was too busy spilling her guts that she never asked about my life. Come to think, she probably didn't care.

Kit's life resembled mine. We just didn't share with strangers. Kit and I learned to hide truths. If she stabbed her uncle twenty-three times, allegedly or not, I envied her. I wish I'd had giant balls to stab Andrew twenty-three times. A million had a nice ring.

"They sent my little brother to foster care," Kit said, pushed to tears.

"Where are your parents?" I knew better than to ask a dumb question.

"They're little bitches too."

Conversations with Kit mirrored those with Emma. I guess angels do fall from the tree.

"They're serving time." She cleared her throat. "My uncle took us in after they got sentenced. Everything was cool for a while. Then he started messin' with my little brother. And he wouldn't stop. And then..." Kit grit her teeth and pursed her lips.

When she told me her uncle wouldn't stop messin' with her little brother, I went quiet too. I kept thinking about Andrew. Andrew didn't understand the word *stop* either.

"Don't be like all these bitches up in here." Kit's voice grew the color of fire. "You can't trust none of them. You're in for murder. And these bitches will trade you for Oreos. They'll snitch just to save their own asses. Trust me."

I shook my head.

"You can't even trust me." Kit got out of bed and locked eyes with me in the dreary light. "Trust no one. If you killed someone, you keep it to your damn self. Mona confessed to the wrong girl. Now Mona's serving a dime in El Paso, and the girl who snitched is free as a bird. That's how bitches are in this place."

I don't think I want to kiss a girl anymore. From what Kit said, I can't even trust them. Girls might be worse than boys. *Yeah, from here on out, it's just you and me, my angel.* "That's how bitches are." Did you hear that, my angel? That's how bitches are. Was I that kind of bitch to you? Was I a good sister? You were trying to tell me something with those eyes that night. Was that what you were trying to say?

Kit and I talked all night. Until the morning light crawled across the worn concrete floor. I had talked a little since my angel was alive. I think my angel intervened. Saved me from this place by giving me Kit. My angel must have made our paths intersect.

Our cell had slender, rectangular windows. Almost the width of a ruler and six times taller. You couldn't see anything out of them. Some girls spent days craning their necks in windows just to see trees and people. You might steal a peek at those things. But it was impossible to see the sky. Still, somehow, the sun filtered through all that muck.

After lunch one day, I did what those girls did on the second story and craned my neck to peek at the sky. Thinking the higher you go, the better chances you have. I wanted to see clouds and the sun. It felt like a lifetime since I'd seen them.

They let you out one hour a day for "yard time." It's nothing but a monumental brick box topped with a barbwire lid. There's nothing to see. Yard time is psychological warfare. I thought they were experimenting on us. How many days does it take to turn into a homicidal maniac?

I got myself dizzy and nauseous, smashing my face up against the window like that. Even if I could turn my head into a Rubik's Cube, I'd never see cotton balls surf a blue universe. And no matter how sore my neck got, I refused to give up.

EIGHT
SHATTER HALL

Kɪᴛ and I ate a strange breakfast. The trustee handed us a tray of slimy French toast and canned green beans and watery mashed potatoes and Kool-Aid. Kit loves mashed potatoes, so I gave her mine. I was about to tell Kit a funny joke when Spiky entered the pod. "Elizabeth Mondragon!" She screamed my name like a cringy witch.

I was scared to stand because I thought I'd done something wrong.

"Mondragon!" she shrieked again.

Kit warned me to get up, or they'd throw me in solitary again.

I rose and raised my hand.

"You have a visitor!"

Kit looked at me. "A visitor?"

My eyes raced across the room, fast as my heart. Guilt clouded my excitement. Kit looked jealous for a second. We both knew Kit would never have a visitor. Her brother was the only family she had. And he was in foster care. Kit got a letter from him the other day. He said the foster parents thought it was a bad idea for Kit to see him. Then he wrote, *I'll visit you when I'm eighteen. Then no one can tell me what to do.* They told him it would be too traumatic for him, since he'd saw Kit murder their uncle.

For Kit's sake, I did my best not to rush toward the door. But deep down, I wanted to sprint. "Don't worry. I'll be back."

Kit smiled with puppy eyes. But I knew that, inside, she wasn't smiling.

I scraped my tray and stacked it on the cart.

"This way, young lady," Spiky said while flicking her digits at me.

I trailed behind Spiky. A few times, I almost clipped her heel with the point of my shoe. I wanted to shove her along and make her go faster. I couldn't wait to see Hana. I mean, who else could it be? I doubted Nurse Maggie would visit. And I wouldn't count on Lincoln.

By the time we reached the visitation center, everything inside me was about to burst. My hands began to tremble.

Spiky smashed me into the seat by my shoulders. "You've got fifteen." She flashed five digits three times.

I sat there picking at my cuticles, expecting Hana. The minutes were tolling fast and still no sign. I got nervous. I thought maybe she changed her mind and left.

There are many things to despise here. But I'll stick to the point. For whatever reason, wall clocks are enemy number one. The moment you enter juvie, time ceases to exist.

The visitation center was empty. My mind was dead set on seeing Hana. But Maxine walked through the double doors. No matter how hard I tried, my face went the wrong way once I landed eyes on her. Not that Maxine was a horrible person. Maxine had teddy-bear energy. But she wasn't Hana. Hana knew what to say to make me feel better about things.

Maxine sat at the table and unloaded a finely stitched binder from a leather attaché case. Her perfume was luxurious. Something you'd buy at the mall. She layered herself in silks and fine wool. I almost forgot what the real world smelled like. Her entire being highlighting my dilemma. What I didn't realize until now. The smell of juvie becomes you. Right down to the hair follicle.

She folded her hands and sighed, as though out of breath. "How are you holding up?"

That was a loaded question. How was I holding up? *Well, I'm in juvie for homicide. All things considered, not well, Maxine. Not well at all. I'm this close to losing my shit. And if I lose my shit, I ain't never coming back.* "Where's Hana? Is she coming to see me?"

"No, she isn't coming." She peered at me. I think she saw the disappointment on my face. She grabbed my wrist. "They won't allow two people to visit at once. They only allow fifteen minutes per request. No exceptions for attorneys. It's unfair, I know. We all agreed."

"We?"

"Hana and Etten. We agreed I should be the one to visit since I'm your attorney. I bet you have plenty of questions, but we don't have a lot of time. So, I'll get to the point. I know you're scared." Maxine scans the visitation center as disgust infects her face. "I would be too. Just know we're doing everything we can to get you back home."

"When?"

"As quickly as possible. A grand jury has indicted as charged. The prosecutor is pursuing a case against you. You have an arraignment hearing next week." She grabbed my other wrist. Now she's clinging to both. Her face sparkles dead serious. "I don't know how to word this, so I'm just going to say it. The prosecutor is requesting a million-dollar bond. The prosecutor believes you're a flight risk. It's absurd. You don't even have a passport. I think their motion is shaky and the judge will rule in our favor and release you without bail."

When Maxine mentioned the million-dollar bond, my heart ditched my body. It palpitated the same way after opening Andrew's mail. I had to snoop. I stole cash from his checking account on the regular. How else was I going to buy prepaid Visa cards? He had no idea what was coming or going. How he kept eight million dollars in the bank for that long was a mystery. I read that somewhere, I think Japan, if someone does you dirty, they make them pay you "restitution." Technically, I wasn't stealing. I was collecting what was already mine.

Warm tears trickled down my cheeks. My lips quivered.

"Listen to me. We're fighting. I'm petitioning the court to release you on your own recognizance. I'm requesting the court to waive the bond. You have no priors, and age plays a part too. You're only sixteen."

"I don't have a million dollars." My voice quivered. "I'll never leave." I squeeze Maxine's hands with desperation.

"Actually, you stand to inherit a great deal of money from your father."

"Andrew!" I somehow rose above the tears and corrected her.

"I'm sorry. *Andrew* had millions in the bank. He also had sizable investments. All purchased through the Mondragon estate and placed in your sister's name. Complicated stuff. We had to hire a forensic accountant to make sense of it all. Did he ever mention this money?"

Tears filled my blank face.

"By the look on your face," she leaned back in her chair, "I don't imagine he did. Well, you stand to inherit over eight million dollars. It's plenty of motive to commit murder. The prosecutor's going to twist those facts. That's their job."

I opened my mouth to say something when Maxine raised her hand and shook her head. "No, don't tell me anything. Say nothing. I don't want to know the details. Keep your lips locked until we can discuss this privately, where attorney-client privilege can protect you."

I nodded and lowered my head. I was locked up for being a homicidal maniac, and I couldn't tell a soul why I'd done it. What Andrew had done to Emma and me. And now, Andrew's millionaire energy is mad disrespecting my chances of ever escaping.

I started picking my cuticles as my wild knees bucked.

"Lizzie," Maxine's tone shifted to concern, "there's something very crucial to discuss. What I'm about to ask will impact your case."

My head ascended from the dreary within. My eyes red from crying.

"The investigators found a newborn baby buried in the cellar."

"Oh, dear Jesus." I'd forgotten about little Fay. *What's wrong with you, Lizzie? How could a fucking baby slip your mind?*

"Lizzie," Maxine's voice broke through the darkness swimming inside my head. "As your counsel, I need to know if the baby is yours." Her voice dissolved into the nothingness.

I felt like I would throw up. The sourness was collecting on my tongue. The ground seemed to sway.

"Lizzie." Maxine furrowed. "They took DNA samples from everyone involved to determine who the baby is."

I stood. I couldn't feel my heart beating. I even clutched my chest, just to see if I was still alive. I couldn't feel the vibrations. All I could do was glare at Maxine. Her mouth was moving, but I couldn't hear a word.

"What?" I think I said. "What about Emma?"

I glossed over Maxine as though she wasn't sitting before me. I waited for her lips to say something. And when they moved, nothing came out. Without warning, the interior lights dimmed, getting darker by the sec.

Maxine faded into the background. Somehow, my heart fired up again, beating so fast and so loud in my ear. Each strike morphed into a paralyzing boom. I couldn't catch my breath. And the table disappeared. Then, everything slipped away.

NINE
MUSTARD

For the first time, I woke to darkness. I was drenched in sweat. The vinyl mattress had glued itself to my skin during the night. For a second, I thought I was free.

Until my eyes focused and I spotted the familiar water stain on the ceiling. The dark had turned that mustard patch on the ceiling to an inky mold, as though some demonic creature was watching over me. Waiting for me with those razor eyes.

"Are you awake?" I whispered.

I focused all my energy on that demon patch in case I had to bolt. The bunk seemed to move on its own. My head throbbed. And Kit didn't answer.

The room was still, like a vacant house. Too quiet. I didn't hear the girl on the second story banging on her cell. Or screams in the distance.

"Kit?" My voice louder this time.

But the room ushered silence again. I rolled to the edge of the bed and peeked at the bunk below: Kit was gone. Her belongings too. Her bed made perfectly with a military vibe.

When they shipped a girl to another unit, they stripped the bed clean. The metal frame symbolized an inmate's tombstone. Where did Kit go? Did she abandon me too?

I laid all night, staring at the demon patch. Until light crept through the window. My mind was stuck on Baby Fay and Emma and Kit and Hana and Andrew's millions. I worried Hana might ditch me too after Maxine told her all about that money. Maxine was right. Fifty-million reasons are plenty of motive to kill. I kept thinking Maxine had lied about the visitation restrictions. She didn't have the heart to tell me the truth. Hana probably didn't want to see me.

The moment I heard the buzzer scream, I sprung from the bed. When you hear the buzzer, that means they unlocked the cell doors for chow time. All done remotely.

I was the last girl to leave my cell. I hung back for a while. Too scared to walk out to the common room without Kit. Someone might hit me with something again. Or worse.

Everyone was sitting at the tables, eating breakfast. I did my best to mask my nerves. Though it mattered little. All eyes watched my every step. I went to the cart and collected my tray and sat alone.

Kit wasn't in the common room. An eerie silence filled the air. No one mouthed a whisper. There's something haunting when girls go quiet.

I sat at the table in the back, where I had a panoramic view. There, I waited for Kit's beautiful face to appear. I skipped eating powdered eggs and something wrapped in foil labeled NOT FOR HUMAN CONSUMPTION. The only item on my tray I wanted to eat was corn. Who knew canned corn got moldy? I suddenly had no appetite. I didn't care what Kit had told me earlier. I wasn't eating. The guards could throw me in psych. I didn't give a shit anymore.

From the corner of my eye, I saw Viking glaring at me. I scraped my tray clean and set it on the cart. *My ass gets beat daily, so bring it.* That's what one girl had told me the other day.

I needed to know what had happened to Kit. So I walked over to Viking's table. Monique and a new girl, Lexus, were sitting there too.

"Where's Kit?" I said too quickly, like I was terrified.

All three girls peered at my trembling hands.

Viking gave a devilish smile. Her eyes had a touch of sneer to them. "Bitch got shanked."

Lexus giggled and covered her mouth.

"Where is she?" A violent tone exited my voice box. Whatever had bolted from my mouth didn't belong. It belonged to someone else.

"She got shanked." Viking laughed. "You deaf, bitch?"

Lexus giggled. This time, though, she didn't cover her mouth.

"You better kick rocks, Killer Girl, before you get your ass shanked too." Monique fluttered her digits to shoo me away.

"That's good," Lexus said. "Killer Girl."

"What happened?"

Viking wouldn't answer, and Lexus giggled louder.

"Tell me!"

Viking looked at Monique, then Lexus, and rose from the table. She had the same chocolate pudding cup sitting on her tray that had hit me a while back. She grabbed the pudding cup and scooped a heaping portion with a spork. Cocked it back like a catapult and flicked the pudding at me. It splattered everywhere. And some of it landed in my eyes. "Skank."

Monique's eyes ballooned. "Ooohh shit," she said, covering her mouth.

Viking stood there, staring me down with those hateful eyes. Waiting to see my next move. I felt the tears climb their way to the tippy top. My lips twitched. My digits only angry rattles. My skin was so hot I swore I heard the pudding sizzle off.

The devil had me as I leaped over the table. My eighty pounds knocked Viking to the floor in seconds, clawing her face. Viking belted a horrifying shriek. I dug my nails into her eyeballs, trying to rip them from her boney head. Viking kneed me in the crotch and tried to throw me off her. A sharp sting hit me, but the rage wanted blood and fueled my anger. I could feel my nails sink into the jelly part of the eye. Viking popped with a curdling scream. Powerful enough to make my ears ring. I went from clawing her eyes out to punching her face to smithereens. Over and over, I landed wild punches. Her face cracked my digits.

She bucked and tried to wiggle free. Kicking and flailing. She ripped a chunk of my hair from the roots. No amount of pain she could deliver would make me stop. I kept hitting her wherever my fist landed, tenderizing her, pinning her to the floor. All Viking could do was scream and flail beneath my demonic possession.

The longer I hit her, the more Viking evaporated until I didn't see Viking anymore. I saw Andrew and Abby and Baby Fay lying in the dirt. My whole goddamn world blown to pieces.

If the guards hadn't yanked me off, I might have killed Viking. She was screaming and crying. Blood drenched her face. I looked at my hands, and they were bloody too. And I screamed. And kept screaming. And kicked. And swung at anyone who got in my space.

Everyone peered at me like I was a lunatic. A killer who had escaped some ward in hell. One girl cried and covered her mouth in horror. I wore hell and then some. I had finally morphed into that girl on the second floor, screaming and crying and banging every single day.

The guards slammed my face into the concrete and hog-tied me. I still had the energy to fight back, and I did. I screamed more. I flailed my legs wilder than Viking had. I kicked one guard in the face. I heard someone holler, "Grab the taser, quick!" Panic illuminating their faces. I spit a mouthful of blood in their faces and laughed.

Whatever evil was stored inside me had finally been unleashed, and I couldn't stop it. I didn't want to. I was no longer scared. I didn't see the taser touch my body, but electricity surged through me like a vampire to holy water. Then another high-powered jolt knocked me silly. My eyes burned, and I couldn't think straight. Then another surge caused my entire body to convulse, plunging me into nothingness.

TEN
MY ANGEL

"Wake up, sleepy head," my angel whispered. "The birds are chirping, the sun's out."

I heard Emma's voice echoing inside my head, but it throbbed something terrible. My ears rang a low hum. I tried to sit up but couldn't; my wrists and ankles were strapped to the bed.

The room was inching its way from me. Nothing would stay put, as though I were high. Like the time Emma got me high on flower. Same thing happened, where everything slithered in one direction all at once. Away from my grip. Stretching farther and farther out.

Uh-oh, you're in trouble, Emma whispered inside my head. *Here comes the doctor.*

"Shut up," I muttered. "You don't know that."

He's wearing a white coat and a stethoscope, hello.

Emma and her hello. Every time I disagreed, she finished everything with *hello*, as though it should be obvious. *Hello, Lizzie, you're an idiot*, mistaken once again.

The doctor peeked behind the door after he entered the room. I think he was checking to see if anyone was hiding behind it. "Who are you talking to?" he said with concern.

I was panicking but tried to stay calm. "I thought Emma…"

"Who's Emma?"

I grinned. I knew it was a strange smile because I always smiled strange when I was uncomfortable. "What?"

Lizzie, Emma said, *stop lying. Just tell him you hear your dead sister talking to you.*

"Shut up," I murmured through my teeth.

"Are you hearing voices, Elizabeth?" The doctor peeled my eyelids wide and shined a light in them. The light stung and blinded my pupils. His clean breath warmed my nose.

Go on. Tell him the truth. He's a doctor, he can fix you.

I shook my head to convince him I was sane. I could hear his feet traipsing around the tile floor, but I couldn't see where he was going. I still saw spots everywhere.

Something bit my arm bad. "Ow. That hurt!"

"It's just a pinch. It'll dissipate in a second. This will help with the hallucinations. Sometimes certain medications don't play well together."

"Why did you do that?" Anger surged inside. "I'm not hallucinating."

"I beg to differ. I know when a patient is hallucinating." He forced my mouth open so he could jam a tiny flashlight down my throat.

See, told you so, but you never listen to me.

"Shut up!"

"Hmmm." He rested a cold stethoscope above my heart. "I'll dial down the olanzapine."

"What's olanzerrrrpin?" I sounded like a blabbering drunk. The same way Abby sounded when she'd had too much gin.

Oh, I know this one, Emma said. *Olanzapine is an antipsychotic. It either takes away the voices inside your brain or makes you hear them. Isn't it amazing one little pill can do all that?*

"Please," I gritted my teeth, "shut up."

The doctor smiled. "This will help you feel better, Elizabeth." He ignored my crazy outburst. "Trust me, I've been doing this a long time, kiddo. Besides, this place is cleaner than a detention center, don't you think?" He dared wink at me with those woodsy eyes. "We serve better food. Well, that's the word on the street anyway."

Word on the street? Oh, dear Jesus, Doctor.

"Are you hungry?" the doctor said, cheery. "I can have the nurse bring you something."

I lifted my arms a smidge. The restraints clinked against the railing. "Eat?"

"Ah, yes." The doctor inspected my restraints as if I were a puzzle to solve. "I'll make you a deal. I'll remove the restraints, but you," he pointed at my chest, "must promise you won't get out of hand. These are for your protection and ours. It's a two-way street, kiddo."

"Okay," I said with Little Bo-Peep energy.

The doctor unlatched the cuffs on my wrists, then ankles. He hesitated once he came to the restraints crushing my waist. "I believe everyone deserves a second chance." He peered at me with Andrew eyes. "Don't make me regret my decision."

My eyes slumped low out of hunger. I was so hungry I could eat every digit.

"Okay." He removed the restraint. "I'll have the nurse order a burger." He glanced at his digital wristwatch. "I think they're still serving lunch."

Oh, no. Emma giggled. *Are you going to tell him you're a vegetarian, or will I have to?*

"Wait." I stopped the doctor before he left the room. "What happened to Kit?"

He walked toward me, brows scrunched. "Kit? Is that a patient here?"

"She's my cellie," I said, voice quivering. "She got shanked."

He rested a hand on his hip. "Privacy laws prevent me from discussing medical care with nonfamily members. You need to concentrate on yourself, kiddo. I'm sure Kit will pull through."

"Please."

Tell him you don't eat meat or else they're going to feed you a moo patty.

He sighed, standing in the doorway. His attention focused on whatever was happening in the hallway. "I can't make any promises, but I'll see what I can do."

When the doctor departed, my eyes scoured the room. What I was hunting for was a mystery. A medicine-and-disinfectant odor stung my nose. The heart monitor murmured tranquil beeps. My heart raced at fifty-two and holding. A significant pause between beats. I was afraid my heart would quit at any moment.

Lizzie, Emma scolded. *I'm no doctor, but I think fifty-two is low.*

"How do you know?"

Fine. I imagined Emma crossing her arms. I could hear it in her voice. She always crossed her arms when using that tone. *If your heart stops, don't come crying.*

The mere thought of my heart seizing elevated my status to sixty-five beats. I guess my heart had more to give. And if my heart had more to give, maybe I did too. Shit, I had to pee.

"See," I said, crossing my legs, trying to hold it. "You don't know everything." I couldn't finish my conversation with Emma. I shut my mouth fast when the nurse entered the room.

The nurse gave me that same look the doctor had. She aggressively cleared the whiteboard and scribbled her name on it. I hoped she wasn't upset with me.

Maybe she knows your dirty little secret, Emma said.

"Shhh." My legs stopped shaking. The pee went back into my bladder.

I hadn't realized until then that the whiteboard was divided into four parts:

Patient name: Elizabeth Mondragon/Gilliam Youth Center

Doctor: Dr. Clark

RN: Molly

MEDS: Olanzapine, fluoxetine, valium

Nurse Molly turned to me, still holding that same look. Inspecting me under her microscope like I was an insect. "Who are you talking to, sweetie?"

Sweetie, Emma protests. *Who is she calling sweetie? She's practically my age. She is on the pretty side, though. I don't know, what do you think, Lizzie?*

"Nobody," I blurted. Frustration made my voice all raspy.

She gave me a nasty eye. "It's best to be honest in this situation. It helps the doctor adjust your meds. Some medications can cause hallucinations." She tapped her temple with a finger.

See, I told you.

Nurse Molly yanked the blanket from my body. My feet and hands were freezing. "I'm going to unhook your leads from the heart monitor."

"Why?"

"Well, for starters, I need your weight. And a few other things."

"I hate shots!"

Oh, Lizzie. Emma sounded annoyed. *Let sweetie do her job. Stop being a baby.*

"Leave me alone!"

"Okay…" The nurse overrode my outburst and gripped my arm as though she were ripping it from the socket. She tore the sticky leads from my chest. "Let's get you out of bed and walking around. It'll do you some good, sweetie."

My backside was visible to the whole goddamn world once my naked toes landed on the tile. A cool breeze caused my flesh to pucker. I played hell with the hospital-gown straps in the back as they danced around like a kite.

"Here." Nurse Molly grabbed the straps and tied each one. "These are tricky little devils."

Now that I was standing, I felt lightheaded. My knees wobbled. Little prickles bit my tongue. All the juices in my stomach, Rage Against the Machine, like Emma's favorite band.

Lizzie, Emma whispered. *See if they have a wheelchair. I always wanted to ride in one.*

Nurse Molly had the same idea. "Stay here a second. I'll go hunt down a wheelchair."

"No."

The nurse paused.

"I don't want a wheelchair."

"Here." She extended her arm. "You can lean on me like a crutch."

I latched on to Nurse Molly, and we slowly went down the hall.

On our way to the scale, we passed a room with the door wide open, and a woman inside was weeping. I could only see her shadow beyond the privacy curtain drawn around the bed.

Nurse Molly unlatched my arm. "Okay." She motioned for me to the stand on the scale.

I mounted the scale all wobbly, as though I might tip over.

"What's your height, sweetie?"

I blankly stared at Nurse Molly.

Nurse Molly, we've never seen a doctor in our lives.

"Here. Stand with your back against the wall, like this."

She shows me how to stand. I stand against the wall, hunched.

"Stand perfectly straight, no slouching. Otherwise, I won't get a true measurement. Okay, sixty-seven inches." She scribbled on a pad. "When did you have your last period?"

I refused to answer the question. "How tall is that?"

Her eyes landed on the ceiling. Then she peered down at me. "Five feet six inches."

Lizzie, Emma's voice was bubbly, *you're taller than I thought.*

The digital screen on the scale flashed: 83.7

"Oh." Disappointment rose from Nurse Molly.

"What?"

"You're cutting it close, sweetie." Nurse Molly scribbled more notes on the lined pad. "Your BMI is low for your height. And you're a teenage girl. You should weigh more. At least a hundred." She peeled back my gown, inspecting my ribs.

I ripped my gown from her hand. "I'm vegetarian."

See. That's all you had to say. She'll get it.

"I don't care if you're Mary Shelley," Nurse Molly said. "Anything less than thirteen BMI, and we'd be having a different conversation."

Oh, dear Jesus. Mary Shelley was a vegetarian. I loved Frankenstein!

I smiled a fake smile. "Do you know what they serve in juvie?"

Nurse Molly wore heartbreak eyes. She extended her elbow like a chicken. "Let's get you back to the room. Order some food before the cafeteria closes."

On our way back, I heard the hospital come alive. Those same tranquil beeps swept from every direction like a gentle wind. Machines purred and bleeped as we navigated the hall. Everything fell under mechanical automation. A sharp smell of antiseptic dancing through the air.

We wandered past the weeping room again. The door remained open, but this time, someone had peeled back the curtain, and the bed lay empty. Not even a pillow in sight. The crying woman seemed to have evaporated and left no trace. Or perhaps she was a phantom of my imagination, like Emma.

After I mentioned juvie cuisine, Nurse Molly hardly said a word. When we entered my room, she fished a plastic cup from her coat pocket and handed it to me. "I need you to pee in this." She pointed to a metered line engraved on the cup. "Don't fill it all the way, just to the line." She tapped her forefinger on that color wheel meter, as though I was a baby.

I was relieved. I had to pee so badly my hands started to shake. I snatched the cup and rushed to the ladies. I tried to close the bathroom door behind me, but Nurse Molly stopped the door from shutting all the way with that ugly little clog.

Uh-oh. Emma's voice got serious. *She's going to watch you pee on a stick like Andrew did.*

"I can't pee while someone's watching."

Nurse Molly kept the door open for the whole world to see and stood at the threshold. She glared at me with meanie eyes. "I have to make sure it's your pee."

My heart sailed to the floor. "I don't know how."

"Do you need some help?"

"No!"

I lined the cup as best as I could. I couldn't see what I was doing. Nurse Molly watched my every move. The air around me was boiling all the sudden. I began to sweat. I was so nervous, I couldn't get any pee to come out.

Oh, Jesus. Nurse Robocop takes her job to the extra.

I think Nurse Molly read the embarrassment on my face. She started tapping her foot as though I should speed things along. After a minute, Nurse Molly peeked at her digital watch and said, "I'll turn around, see if that helps."

The moment Nurse Molly turned her back, I sprayed everywhere. Whatever was left trickled all the way to the back. Oh, dear Jesus. It was a miracle any pee entered the cup.

"I guess you really had to go."

I passed the cup to Nurse Molly, dripping with pee and all. My hands still shook. Nurse Molly didn't look happy about the condition of the cup. And she stepped back and hesitated to grab it as though a deadly virus was in there. She pointed to the bathroom sink. "Set the cup on the sink. I'll collect it when I have gloves."

My legs were trembling and weak. My bones had turned to jelly. Nurse Molly helped me to the bed and hooked me up to the heart monitor again. My heart rate spiked.

Nurse Molly quickly looped the blood pressure wrap around my arm. "Relax your arm and lay back. Don't cross your legs, and try not to move."

The blood pressure wrap expanded, then choked my arm, cutting off circulation. She placed two digits on my wrist and glared at her watch. I could see her eyeballs jittering as though they were counting. "One twenty over ninety," she said, ripping the Velcro cuff from my arm.

"Is that good?"

"No. It's high, considering your age. The medication in your system is supposed to lower your blood pressure and heart rate. Even during physical activity. You weren't very active. You're not jogging the block, are you?" She scribbled something on a pad. "I think you're dehydrated. I'll see if the doctor wants to start a round of fluids."

Dehydrated? Emma laughs. *I think Lizzie's too hydrated. Did you not hear Niagara Falls in there, Nurse Molly?*

"Shut up, Emma!"

Nurse Molly scribbled more on the pad and gave me a weird look. "The cafeteria isn't vegetarian friendly, but they have salads, fruits, vegetables, umm," I can see her thinking inside her head, "soups—no— maybe not soups."

"I like fruit."

While you're at it, tell her about your weirdo obsession with peanut butter and rye.

I roll my eyes and ignore Emma.

Nurse Molly looks a little relieved that I'd mentioned fruit. "Okay then. That certainly narrows it down."

Nurse Molly put on latex gloves and retrieved the pee cup from the bathroom.

"Why do I have to pee in a cup?"

I can tell I interrupted Nurse Molly's train of thought. I always messed up Nurse Maggie's train of thought too. Bombarding her with questions when she was elbow deep in a task. "Your health, for one. You can learn a lot from urine. And we need to know if you're pregnant. It's hospital policy."

Oh, dear Jesus! Why did you pee in that fucking cup?

ELEVEN
FIDGET

"Good morning," Etten said brightly. Smiles for days in her luscious voice. She gestured for me to have a seat. "How are things?"

I sat on a grass-colored velour sofa. The texture was butter sifting through my digits. Etten drew a chair closer. "The last time we met, you seemed a little apprehensive about going to New York?"

I said nothing.

"We haven't seen each other in two weeks. I'm eager to hear about the show. I bet that was exciting."

My eyes crawled up to the ceiling.

Etten perched at the edge of her seat and locked eyes. "I would like to prepare for our next session." She edged closer. "We're going to discuss some deeply painful topics. I don't feel that we've reached that point yet. But your trial is in three weeks."

"Etten?"

"Yes?" Etten leaned back and crossed her legs.

"Maxine told me not to talk about things that could harm my case."

"That's sound advice." averted her eyes. "Even though I must report your progress to the court, whatever we discuss in this room is confidential. This is a safe space. We can talk about anything you choose."

I stared off.

"I want to make the best of our time today. It's vital we discuss what you may encounter while taking the witness stand. The prosecutor will ask you to testify about the abuse you underwent. You'll have no other choice but to comply. The judge will require you to answer the prosecutor's questions. Once you're in the courtroom, you may feel attacked with no place to land. I want to help ease those anxieties."

Etten made everything sound pleasant. But she would drill me on the ugly details. She never talked about pleasant stuff. Never. My knee started to bounce. I dug at my cuticles.

Etten peered at my blood-stained fingers and stood. "That reminds me, I bought you a gift." She walked over to the desk. "I was shopping at the Sixteenth Street Mall the other day, and I popped into a novelty shop. It caught my eye because it had all these interesting gadgets displayed in the window." She held a fluorescent triangle thing in the air.

"What is it?"

She spun the triangle between her fingers. "It's a fidget spinner. When I saw it, I thought of you. Would you like to try it?"

Etten placed the fidget spinner in my palm. I spun it a few times. The thing spun and spun between my digits. Faster and faster. Making a zzz sound. *Zzz. Zzz.*

"It's pocket-size, so you can take it wherever you go." She edged closer again. "Every time you feel anxious or sad or are just having a crummy day, I want you to use the fidget spinner. When we discuss uncomfortable topics, I want you to spin the fidget really fast. I mean really, really fast, if the topic is incredibly tough. That way I can gauge our conversation. Would that be all right with you?"

"Yes." I spin it between my digits. *Zzz. Zzz.*

"I have one more suggestion."

I was still spinning the fidget, not so nervous now.

"If a topic is unbearable, just—"

"Like when I can't breathe?"

"Right." She crossed her legs. "Exactly. When you feel you can't breathe. Stop spinning the fidget, and I'll change the subject, okay?"

"Okay."

"In our last session, we briefly discussed the abuse Emma endured."

I stopped the fidget.

"Hold just a sec."

I liked when she said *sec*. It sounded cool.

"We've discussed Andrew at length over our sessions. I'd like to delve a little deeper into Emma and Abby."

I spun the fidget again.

"Was Abby aware of Andrew's abuse toward Emma?"

I gave a look.

"Did she ever witness the abuse?"

"Yes."

"Was she aware Andrew was abusing you as well?"

When I didn't respond, Etten knew what that meant.

"Did she witness the abuse, particularly the sexual abuse?"

I froze as though I'd seen the ghost of Andrew rise.

"Did she ever try to intervene in any way?"

"No." I spun the fidget faster. "She blared the TV to drown out the screams."

Etten gulped hard, as though she had a rock stuck in her throat. "I read the report, and it stated Abby had Paget's disease."

"They only told us what we needed to know." I leaned back onto the cushion. "Abby told me her bones broke easily."

"Abby wasn't your biological mother, correct?"

I nodded while playing with the fidget.

"Did you know Emma was harming herself?"

I just looked at her for a sec.

"The investigators noted several burns on her arms and legs. Did you ever notice them?"

"Emma wore baggy stuff. One time, I barged in on her undressing. She had scars on her back. She yelled at me to get out of her room. I only remember seeing scars on her back." The spinner stopped. I stared at Etten. But I wasn't staring at her. I was staring through her.

"Let's change the subject."

"I found her lighter stash. She had a machete on the side of her bed. She was my angel." Tears spit from my eyes. "I don't know if I was her angel because I didn't stop Andrew. It's my fault. I could have stopped him."

"Remember the golden rule we established during our last session." Etten sat taller. "We don't blame ourselves for what others do. We cannot control the actions of others." She twirled both hands, around and around, to remind me of the fidget spinner.

"It's not my fault, and it's not Emma's fault. Andrew and Abby are to blame." I spun the fidget again.

"That's exactly right. There's nothing you could have done to save Emma. Emma couldn't save you. You're not responsible for the pain inflicted upon you or Emma. Both of you had zero control over what happened in that house. Andrew and Abby are to blame."

"What if I—"

"You couldn't control happened in that house."

"When I heard Emma scream the first time, I should have done something. I shouldn't have obeyed Abby."

"Okay." Etten perched on the edge of the chair. "We can discuss this a little further. But then we need to switch gears. Tell me what Abby told you do to in that moment."

"I heard Emma screaming. I was in Abby's room, feeding her pills. Her and her pills." I smashed my fist into my palm.

"I would like to know more."

I was panting now. It was hard to breathe. "I picked up Abby's cane from the side of the bed and was going to run in there and smash his face in." I was spinning the fidget superfast. *Zzzzzzzzzz.*

"What stopped you in that moment?"

"She said if I went in there, Andrew would, you know, hurt me." I gave Etten that look. "She looked at me and said, 'Do you want him to hurt you too?' But she used the other word instead of *hurt*." The fidget stopped. I couldn't keep the tears from falling. My hands were shaky. My body shuddered.

"Lizzie." Etten put her hand on my wrist. "That would fill me with fear and make me avoid that room if someone told me that. You did nothing wrong. I'm going to sound like a broken record here. What Andrew did was not your fault." Etten stared at me, but my eyes were on the floor. "It's not your fault. It's not Emma's fault. Andrew and Abby were to blame. I think it's best we move on to another topic and circle back later."

Etten walked over to her desk and poured some water in a glass, placing it on the coffee table in front of me. The outside of the glass was crying, like me. "Sometimes taking small sips can ease anxiety."

I drank a sip. Now, I had soaked fingers. I looked at Etten. "I can still hear my angel scream at night when I'm in bed. I just wanted the screaming to stop. I just wanted the screaming to stop. I hate Andrew! I hate Abby. I wish I killed them sooner!"

I squeezed my head as tight as I could. I couldn't breathe anymore. Etten kneeled in front of me. She looked worried. I could see her lips moving, but no words came out.

<h1 style="text-align:center">TWELVE
NEXT DAY</h1>

Etten opened the door to her office with a smile. She had a warm smile. Her bright eyes comforted me. "How are things?"

I tried my best to put on a smile. But the sadness, the emptiness, shone through, no matter what. My face could tell a thousand tales in one sec. "I'm okay."

"Where would you like to sit?"

I plopped down on the chair facing her desk. I wasn't angry at Etten, just tired. Etten gave me a look as though I was hiding something.

"The desk it is."

Etten had a lot of degrees hanging on the wall behind her desk. "Hana told me you're friends. Are you besties or just friends?

"Oh." Etten smiled. "We're very close."

"How long have you known her?"

"Well," Etten took a seat at the desk, "we grew up together. And went to the same college."

I pointed at the mustard diploma on the wall. "Did Hana go to Harvard too?"

"Yep." Etten swiveled her head to look at the diploma. "And so did Maxine. We were sorority sisters." She made finger quotes.

"Is that why you're my therapist? Because of Maxine and Hana."

88

Etten gave me a queer expression. "Lizzie, I believe trust is the key to establishing a safe, therapeutic environment." She crossed her legs. "To answer your question, yes, I accepted you as a patient because Hana asked me to. I rarely accept patients as young as you. This isn't my particular field. Although, my residency included a year of child therapy and development. But we're not here to talk about me. We're here to talk about you. So let's do that."

"Do you feel sad for me? Is that why you agreed to be my therapist?"

"No." Etten averted her eyes. I could see her trying to think of the right words to say. "I think you're incredibly brave. You survived a hellish upbringing. I'm sorry to use powerful language, but I feel this best fits." She rolled her chair closer to the desk. "There are adults who walk through those doors," she pointed to the office door, "who aren't nearly as courageous as you. It's never a question if someone is or isn't strong enough to endure trauma. Or process trauma the right way. That's not what I mean. Every session you make progress. You do the hard work. Even when topics become unbearable. You never shy away. You face them head-on. That takes a lot of guts. And believe me, you've got a lot of guts. I accepted you as a patient because I believe I can help you learn to live a healthier life with these traumas. Not because I felt sorry for you. I feel quite the opposite."

She made me smile. I didn't hate myself as much now.

"I want to apologize for yesterday. I rarely end sessions like that. I felt it was in your best interest to stop. In light of that, I'd like to discuss other topics that don't include Andrew or Abby."

"What about my angel?"

"Yes, we can discuss Emma. I will caution you, though. It's best we steer clear of any discussion surrounding assault. We're moving too quickly. Therapy can improve our daily lives. But therapy can also do a lot of harm. You can take on too much too fast, and that can have disastrous results. Let's take things a little slower."

"What about the trial?"

"We're going to take a different approach today. I want to focus on coping mechanisms. There are ways to counterbalance anxiety and past traumas, making it easier for you to process these events when they come up in court."

I stuffed the fidget spinner in my pocket. I wouldn't need it today. I stood and walked over to the grass-colored velour sofa.

"Before we begin, I wanted to know how things went in New York?" Etten's eyes filled with anticipation. "Only if you feel comfortable talking about it. No pressure."

"The food was delicious."

"Oh." Etten sat taller in the chair. "What's your favorite restaurant?"

"I don't remember the name."

"I always scan the dessert menu first." Etten snickers. "That's my favorite part."

"I forgot the name, but it was homemade Italian donuts. They had preserves and chocolate and lavender dipping sauces." My face lit up just talking about it. My tongue tingled and watered.

"Wow." Etten giggled. "That sounds like a fancy place. I think they call Italian donuts *bombolone*."

Etten said *bombolone* with an elegant accent. Fancier than our waiter did at the Italian restaurant. "Yeah." My eyes grew eager. Heart racing and everything. I could almost taste warm, sugary *bombolone* melting on my tongue. "Have you ever tried one?"

Etten smiled. Even her eyes did. Her face warmed me. Her presence eased everything on the inside.

"Yes, they're very delicious." Etten put on a serious face. "I know we got sidetracked yesterday, but I was curious to know how things went in New York. The art show, in particular." Etten's eyes lit up. "Your show."

I wasn't energetic enough to talk about the art show. So, I stayed silent.

"Did things not go well?"

No, things didn't go well, Etten. Not at all. I never want to go back. Well, maybe eat at that restaurant again. Their bombolone *was perfection. My angel said a mouth full when she fell in love with delicious food too.* "It's fine."

"I'd like to know more." She showed concern on her face. "If you feel comfortable."

"Everyone kept staring at me. Whispering things about me. It was weird."

"Weird?" Her eyes sharpened.

"Everybody thinks I'm a serial killer." I threw up my hands.

"Did you overhear someone say that?"

I said nothing.

"What supports this thought, Lizzie?"

"Because." I squeezed my eyes shut. "Every time I walked past someone they'd whisper stuff like, 'That's the girl who did it.'"

"I can see how that would make you feel uncomfortable." Etten sighed. "I wasn't present, but I think maybe they're referencing your Polaroids."

"A couple people stopped me and asked questions."

"About Andrew and Abby?"

"No." I pulled out the fidget and spun it. Etten stared at the fidget. "One person asked me where I got my inspiration. Another asked if I'd consider my work rep...something rep..."

"Representational."

"Yes, that. They said other things too. I can't remember what they called it."

"Did you have time to meet Keith Mayer?"

"He was at the exhibit."

"Keith is a close friend of ours. He started his career just like you. Well, not quite like you. He was much older when his career took off. He was in his forties, you're sixteen."

"Seventeen now."

"Yes, you're right. Pretty soon you'll be an adult. My gosh. I recall Keith saying similar things during his first exhibition. There's an art lingo, he told me once. He didn't know the art lingo." She threw her hands in the air. "And he was self-conscious about it. He didn't think anyone would take him seriously because he had a difficult time articulating the motivation behind his work. There are even college courses on art lingo, if you can believe that. The art world, from my understanding, is difficult to navigate. Even for adults."

"Why were they talking about me?"

"My best guess is because you're only seventeen and a prodigy."

"It makes me feel weird when people talk about me." I looked at the carpet.

"I'm going out on a limb here, but I think their intentions were very positive. I won't say it never happens. Let's just say it rarely happens. That a seventeen-year-old presents their first art exhibition at one of the most prestigious art galleries in the world."

"Not in the world."

Etten locked eyes with me. She never dead-eyed me before. "Famous artists like Sandoval and Liu have exhibited their work there." I must have looked confused because Etten straightened her posture, as if ready to dig in. "Their work sells for millions. Only the best artists exhibit work at Ezra Gallery."

"I just take pictures like my angel did."

"Do you like taking pictures? Or do you take pictures because Emma did?"

"I take pictures because I feel closer to her. When I want to see her, I take pictures. That's the only way I can see her now."

"You see Emma? Lizzie, this is significant. Do you physically see Emma, or is this a figure of speech?"

Something in Etten's face told me I should lie. I stopped spinning the fidget. Etten looked at my hand. I tried not to look scared. I wouldn't tell her I saw my angel in the camera. *I won't tell our little secret, my angel. I won't tell. I'll keep our secret until I die.*

Etten inspected me. Suspicion in her eyes. My mind would horrify her if she could read it. But I play the angel card with my face. It worked because she moved on.

"Well, I think you just found your inspiration. When you have your next show, if you feel comfortable sharing with potential buyers, you can just say, 'My sister is the inspiration behind my photos.'"

"What if they ask about my angel?"

"Share what makes you feel comfortable. If a question makes you feel uncomfortable, just pretend you didn't hear it and move to the next."

"What if it makes me sad?"

"You don't have to share anything that makes you sad, Lizzie. I want you to share only when you're ready. When you feel comfortable to share. You're in charge."

"Is it okay to share something sad with a stranger? Sometimes I want to share. I want to tell the truth. But I'm scared people will think I'm a bad person. Or stupid. Or a lunatic."

"When you share traumatic topics, no matter what it is, you won't be able to control what someone says or thinks. I think the key here is to prepare for anything. When you share, some people may provide encouragement or empathize. But also prepare for criticism too."

Etten peered at her watch, then looked up. "We have twenty minutes left. Are there any topics you'd like to discuss that we haven't already touched on?"

I glanced at her.

"How are things going at Hana's? I know a new environment can bring unexpected challenges. Living in the same house as strangers isn't always a simple transition."

"Hana's kind."

"How is Graham?"

I stopped fidgeting.

"Does Graham make you uncomfortable?"

I shrugged.

"I'd like it if you could tell me more."

"He hates me."

"How did you come to this conclusion, Lizzie?"

"He's not nice." I resituated myself. But I still couldn't seem to get comfortable. "He thinks there's something wrong with me. He gives me salty looks all the time. He wants me to move out."

"Have you discussed these concerns with Hana?"

I just glared.

"Lizzie, it's important to communicate your feelings to Hana. Do you feel comfortable enough to discuss important matters with her?"

I shrugged.

"Is it a safe space?"

"Yeah."

"Help me understand why you don't feel comfortable discussing your concerns about Graham."

"They fight at night in their bedroom. I can hear them arguing about me."

"How do you know they're arguing about you?"

"He says my name a lot when they argue. I spied on them one night. He doesn't like me. He wants me to move out of his house."

Etten sneered.

"He told Hana that foster care would be a better place for me or a mental institution. He said *mental institution* three times."

"Lizzie, I'd be happy to discuss your concerns with Hana. Would you like me to do that on your behalf?" Etten's eyes were piping hot. But her voice was still as elegant as ever.

"I don't want Hana to get in trouble."

"Hana isn't in trouble. It's important for her to know you're aware of these arguments. May I speak on your behalf?"

I shook my head. I shouldn't have said anything. I should have kept my mouth shut. I gave her a look to move on to another subject.

"We still have a little more time. Is there anything you'd like to discuss before our next session?"

I wanted to ask Etten something, but I was too scared, afraid she'd say no. But it was hard to disguise my expressions.

"Lizzie, are you sure you have nothing further to discuss?" Etten perched at the edge of her seat. She always did this when she wanted me to dig deeper. "You can tell me anything. I won't judge. I'll never judge you." She waved her hands in a circular motion. "I'll never share what we talk about unless you give me permission. Not even to the police, okay?"

"Do you think my Polaroids are good? Because I don't think they are. My angel was better."

Etten leaned back and crossed her legs. "Well, I'm not an authority on art. I don't have an artistic bone in my body. Medical school was my strong suit. But I will say this. When Hana shared your Polaroids with me, the images moved me. I don't know the difference between good art and bad art. But your Polaroids are deeply powerful. One Polaroid hit me right here." She patted her heart. "I believe you're a gifted artist. Your Polaroids have certainly left an impression on me."

"DETECTIVE ROSE." Maxine peered down at her notes. "Please tell the court how long you've worked for the Denver PD."

"Twenty-two years this August," Detective Rose said, as though she was exhausted.

"Have you been a detective in the sexual assault unit for all twenty-two?"

"No." Detective Rose pushed her witchy hair behind her ears. Her gray strands spidered out and disguised the dark color underneath. She also had dark circles under her eyes. She looked grounded down like a cigarette butt.

"First five was beat. Mostly traffic. Five homicide. Two years special unit. Last ten sexual assault."

"Ten years." Maxine's voice perked. She tucked those papers in an armpit and slid her eyeglasses over the bridge of her nose. "How many sexual assault cases have you investigated?"

"It's hard to say."

"Would you say a hundred?"

The detective rolled her eyes

"Best guess, Detective Rose?"

"Maybe five hundred."

"Five hundred, that's a lot of cases," Maxine nodded, still reading her notes. "Is it fair to say, Detective Rose, in those ten years you've developed a sixth sense?"

"You mean, do I know when a victim is lying about a sexual assault?"

"Yes." Maxine winced when the detective called the survivor a victim.

"Objection, Your Honor, defense is asking the witness to testify if a person is lying or telling the truth. It's all speculative. It's the detective's opinion. Not based on fact. The detective isn't a clairvoyant, is she?"

Maxine snarled at the prosecution. "Your Honor, Detective Rose must investigate sexual assaults with every resource afforded. For instance, their perception. Interpreting a survivor's behavior is also key. Her expertise, or as the prosecutor put it, her opinion, is a major factor when charging a suspect with a crime."

The judge raised a stop palm. "Overruled. I'll allow it. I caution the defense to limit the questioning to relevant professional opinion."

"Detective Rose, on April fifth, you interviewed Lizzie Mondragon. Is that correct?"

"Yes."

"Please tell the court why you interviewed Ms. Mondragon."

"Well," Detective Rose sat a little taller and smoothed the wrinkles from her jacket, "Detective Bones and I were investigating the sexual assaults of Emma Mondragon."

"Assaults? As in multiple?" Maxine reiterated.

Detective Rose nodded.

"Please inform the court of Emma Mondragon's connections."

Detective Rose pointed at me. "Emma Mondragon is Elizabeth Mondragon's sister or wa—" Her response evaporated.

"Can you also tell the court why you investigated sexual assaults involving Emma Mondragon after she had already passed?"

"Emma Mondragon mailed a diary to the sexual assault unit."

"Were you aware of any crime committed against Emma Mondragon prior to receiving her diary in the mail?"

"Before that day," the detective kept smoothing the wrinkles from her jacket, "no."

"Detective Rose, is it unusual for your department to receive diaries or written confessions?"

"Diaries, yes. Confessions, no." Detective Rose snickered. "Actually, we get more mail from unstable types. But the diary stood out to me."

"Why the diary?"

"Well," Detective Rose squirmed in her seat, "it was very credible."

"Objection, Your Honor!"

"Overruled." The judge looked intrigued. "The witness will answer the question."

"I've interviewed hundreds of victims."

"Please, go on."

"There are markers I look for."

"Such as?"

"Well, Emma Mondragon's diary proved Andrew Mondragon repeatedly assaulted his daughters."

"Objection!"

"Overruled."

"I'd like to clarify this a little more, Detective Rose, so that the jury can gain a better perspective." Maxine didn't pace like the prosecutor. She claimed her spot near the witness stand. "After reading Emma Mondragon's diary, it was your professional opinion—"

"Objection."

"Overruled, Counselor," the judge snapped.

"You concluded Andrew Mondragon committed crimes against his daughters, Emma Mondragon and my client, Ms. Mondragon."

"Yes."

"After many years on the force, Detective," Maxine peered at the jury, "is it your professional opinion that the Mondragon girls were sexually assaulted by their father?"

"Objection!"

"Overruled."

"Yes. Emma Mondragon wrote a detailed account about her life in that house. There's no doubt in my mind. It was one of the most haunting things I've read in my career."

I'd forgotten my fidget spinner. I had no choice but to pick at my thumb. My knees started to bounce too. I knew what was coming next.

"For the sake of time, can you sum up the diary?"

"Emma Mondragon accused Andrew Mondragon of raping her several times. She also claimed she was pregnant with his child."

Some of the juror's gasped. More gasps sounded off in the courtroom. A steady barrage of murmurs ensued.

"Order!" the judge said.

"Objection, Your Honor. This is hearsay. Emma Mondragon cannot testify to these facts. And Andrew Mondragon cannot refute these allegations."

Maxine raised a hand. "Your Honor, I submitted the diary into evidence weeks ago. The prosecutor's office had plenty of time to object to the admittance of the evidence and chose not to."

The judge peered at the prosecutor, then at Maxine. He seemed deep in thought. Then he glanced my way. "Overruled. The defense can continue."

The prosecutor plopped into his seat, seething.

"Detective Rose, did your office formally investigate Emma Mondragon's claims?"

"Yes." Detective Rose edged closer to the witness ledge. "By law, we investigate every claim, no matter how outlandish."

"Was Andrew Mondragon the father of Emma Mondragon's unborn baby?"

The courtroom was soundless. Tingles ran down my arms and legs. I drew blood again. And rubbed the slimy liquid between my digits.

"Yes," Detective Rose said in a somber tone.

Gasps filled the air. Loud whispers crowded the courtroom.

"DNA evidence identified Andrew Mondragon as the father."

"Did you formally charge Andrew Mondragon?"

"No, he died before we could formally charge him."

"Did you collect a formal witness statement from Emma Mondragon?"

The detective lowered her head. "No. Emma Mondragon committed suicide before we could interview her."

"Did you inspect Emma Mondragon's body after her suicide?"

"Yes, my partner, Detective Bones, and I exhumed the body."

"Did Homicide get involved during the investigation?"

"Yes."

"Why would Homicide investigate a suicide?"

"Emma Mondragon showed signs of sexual assault. Her body exhibited bruises and burn marks. We then suspected foul play."

"Was there evidence of foul play?"

"It was inconclusive."

"Was Emma Mondragon sexually assaulted prior to her suicide?"

"Yes."

"Did your department collect DNA evidence from the sexual assault?"

"Yes, semen."

"Objection."

"Overruled.

"Was there a DNA match?"

"Yes, it belonged to Andrew Mondragon."

More whispers and murmurs rose.

"Quiet in the courtroom."

I covered my face. *My angel, did Andrew kill you? Did he kill you? Tell me.*

"Detective Rose, did you interview my client, Elizabeth Mondragon, during the investigation?"

"Yes, twice. Technically, once."

"I don't follow."

"I interviewed Ms. Mondragon about the sexual assault of Emma Mondragon. Homicide interviewed Ms. Mondragon the second time. They asked me to sit in. I asked Ms. Mondragon a few more questions during that time."

"I see." Maxine walked over to the defense table. "Why did you feel it necessary to sit in on an interview with Homicide?"

"My first interview with Ms. Mondragon was incomplete."

"When you say *incomplete*, Detective, what exactly do you mean?"

"I felt Ms. Mondragon was holding back crucial evidence."

"Like what?"

The judge looks more intrigued than the jury.

"I thought she was trying to protect Andrew Mondragon, her father."

"Objection, Your Honor. Detective Rose has no evidence to support these claims. The testimony is purely speculative."

"Sustained." The judge peered down at Detective Rose. "Is this your professional opinion?"

"Yes, Judge."

"Proceed."

"Your Honor—"

"The prosecution will take their seat."

Detective Rose glanced up at the judge. "I believed Ms. Mondragon was hiding a lot."

"What do you think she was hiding?"

"The way she was acting fidgety and nervous, I thought she knew full well about the sexual abuse. I think Andrew Mondragon sexually abused her too. She exhibited behavior consistent with sexual assault. Emma Mondragon's diary claimed Lizzie—I mean, Ms. Mondragon— would never tell."

"Objection!" The prosecutor headed to the judge's bench in a fury. "Elizabeth Mondragon didn't admit her father assaulted them during questioning. There isn't even a victim-impact statement. None whatsoever." The prosecutor swung his hands around.

The judge peered down at Detective Rose. "Detective, did Ms. Mondragon admit witnessing these crimes?"

"No, Judge."

"Sustained."

"In your professional opinion, did Ms. Mondragon display signs of sexual abuse?"

"Objection, Your Honor. The witness was investigating Emma Mondragon's sexual assault, not Elizabeth Mondragon."

"Sustained. The jury will disregard the defense's last question."

"I'll rephrase." Maxine approached the jury box. "Detective Rose, did you ask Elizabeth Mondragon if Andrew Mondragon ever sexually assaulted her during the interview?"

"Yes."

I squeezed Hana's hand so tight the blood scattered from my hand. I peered at Hana's hand, and it turned white as light. We were now light.

She stroked my hair. I loved it when she did that. My angel used to stroke my hair at night. Or after taking a hot bath. Sometimes I lay in bed at night crying. Sometimes I could hear my angel crying on the other side of the wall too. I was crying now, for the both of us. *Everybody knows the truth now, my angel. Everybody.*

"And what was her response?"

"She almost had a mental breakdown when I mentioned her father possibly sexually assaulting her. But she still wouldn't answer the question."

"Do you think Andrew Mondragon sexually assaulted my client, Elizabeth Mondragon?"

"Yes. Several times, I suspect."

Juror 13—I envision a grandmother from Kentucky, who moved to Colorado, and settled into her son's guest bedroom to watch the children while both parents work stressful, high-paying jobs—Gasped, dramatically. Then slapped her own mouth shut. Thinking, I didn't sign up for this shit.

"Objection!" The prosecutor rose with fire in his eyes.

"Sustained!"

FOURTEEN
DAY 3

"Your Honor, the state calls Elizabeth Mondragon to the witness stand."

The judge motioned toward me. It was almost like an authentic version of *The Price Is Right*. Come on down, Elizabeth Mondragon. Unless I won, I would spend the rest of my life behind bars. Freedom beat a shiny, new car or a washer and dryer. Still, I didn't want to go up there. I didn't have the strength to talk about these things.

I slid my chair out from under the table. Maxine smiled at me with confidence. How could she be so sure things would work out for the best? I looked to my left and saw Hana smile with encouragement too. The jurors peered at me with sympathetic eyes. Everywhere I look, it seemed the universe is smiling at me. I don't understand why everyone is so happy.

As I walk toward the witness stand, I feel the weight of a thousand eyes storm me. And I think to myself, this is just a live performance. I collected all those eyes, one by one, and placed them in my pocket. Maxine had drilled me day and night not to make eye contact with the jury as I walked past the podium. I didn't. So far, a win.

Don't make eye contact. Don't smile. Don't give dirty looks. Pretend you're a robot. A smile could show I had no remorse or that I had privilege. *Don't get angry.* Anger signified I had a motive. Of course I had a motive. In that moment, I felt like telling Maxine, *You be the goddamn robot. Try it on, see how it feels.*

I didn't understand why I shivered so bad, despite sweat bubbling to the surface. Even my lungs were as tight as skinny jeans. I could feel nothing below the neck. But I saw my patent shoes glide across the grass-colored carpet. I was outside my body, but I still closed in on the witness stand. My body was no longer mine. A strange episode of the *Invasion of the Body Snatchers* hijacked everything else.

I took my seat at the witness stand and locked eyes on Maxine and Hana. Just as we'd rehearsed last night. Their smiles said they were confident I'd win. But what if I didn't? What would happen to them if the jury found me guilty? I could live with a lifetime of guilt. That's how I was. Or maybe I was manufactured to absorb guilt.

The bailiff mouthed something to me, but I couldn't hear his words. He raised his right hand. "Do you swear to tell..." Then his voice got muted again.

I heard someone cough. The ruffling of papers. I got nervous and could feel laughter rising to the surface. *Don't you dare, Lizzie.* The bailiff was staring at me so hard, and I shied away from his gaze, then I mistakenly locked eyes with a woman sitting in the jury box. I turned my eyes away, although, in that moment, she gave me puppy eyes. Not the eyes of disgust, as I suspected. I saw sadness. I knew what sad eyes looked like. I saw those eyes every time I looked in the mirror.

The judge cleared his throat and motioned toward me. "Ms. Mondragon."

I swiveled my head and peered up at the judge. Disappointment etched on his brow. "Yes?" I said with a nervous-as-hell vibe.

The judge smiled. His voice was soothing as rain. "Do you swear to tell the truth?"

"Yes."

"Prosecutor," the judge said, "you may proceed with the witness."

"Yes, Your Honor."

The prosecutor was eager to destroy me on the stand. His voice was a trail of ugliness. The anger within himself, lit his face bright red, as though I'd run over his puppy. I'd seen this sort of thing before. Andrew wore it best, though. I knew one thing: evil finds a way. So much so that evil chisels the face like one of those marble statues. Those angry wrinkles didn't lie. He charged the witness stand. For a sec, I thought he was going to smack me a good one.

"Ms. Mondragon..."

"Yes?" My throat buckled under pressure.

"I'm not finished with my question. You say *yes* when I ask you a question. Do you understand?"

I looked up at the judge. He motioned at me. "Ms. Mondragon, you only need to say yes when asked a question."

"Thank you, Your Honor."

The judge got all salty when the prosecutor chimed in. "Don't speak over me. You'll carry yourself with a professional conduct while in my courtroom, do you understand?"

"Yes, Your Honor."

"Proceed with the witness."

I saw Maxine and Hana whisper to each other. I wondered what they were chatting about.

"Ms. Mondragon, do you attend high school?"

"Yes."

"What's the name of your high school?"

"Arapahoe."

"What's your GPA at Arapahoe?"

"Um, I..."

"Um, is not an answer, Ms. Mondragon. Let's freshen that memory of yours."

The prosecutor walked over to the prosecutor's table and retrieved a piece of paper and held it in the air. He walked back to the witness stand as though he had a smoking gun. "Your Honor, I'd like to submit into evidence Ms. Mondragon's Arapahoe High School transcripts as exhibit A."

The judge peered at Maxine. "Does the defense have any objection to the prosecution's submission of exhibit A, Arapahoe High School transcripts?"

Maxine stood and straightened her silky pants. "No, Your Honor."

"The court will allow it."

"Ms. Mondragon, are you aware that you're failing every single class? Every assignment this year was incomplete. You're the first high school student that went the other way. While most students strive for all A's, you accomplish all F's."

I shook my head. "I...I—"

"Are you also aware that you missed one hundred and fifty days of school out of one hundred and eighty? Why is that, Ms. Mondragon?"

"Objection. The prosecution didn't allow Ms. Mondragon to answer the question."

"Sustained." The judge side-eyed the prosecutor, then peered down at me. "Please answer the question, Ms. Mondragon."

"I took care of Andrew and Abby." When I blurted their names, I worried I'd blown it. "I mean, Dad and Mom."

"Andrew and Abby Mondragon," the prosecutor rephrased sarcastically, "do you always call your parents by their first names?"

"No. He'd smash me to the floor with his boot if I ever called him Andrew."

Murmurs and whispers rose in the courtroom.

"Oh, that's right." The prosecutor snapped his fingers. He walked over to the table and picked up another piece of paper. "Your Honor, prosecution introduces exhibit B."

"Does the defense have any objections?"

"Not at this time, Your Honor."

When Maxine took her seat, the judge motioned to the prosecutor.

"You told the investigators your father—I'm sorry, Andrew— physically assaulted you on multiple occasions. Is that right?"

"He did," I say with conviction.

"You also state he mentally and emotional abused you as well as," he was paraphrasing from the piece of paper in his hand and counting his digits, "sexual assault." When he said *sexual assault*, my heart skipped. My gut cramped.

"Your statement shows multiple instances of sexual abuse also happened to Emma Mondragon. You say, and I quote, 'I heard Andrew rape Emma in the other room.' Then the investigator asked you, 'How do you know Emma was being raped by Andrew in the other room?'" He stopped reading from the piece of paper and pointed at me. "Your statement also shows, 'I heard Emma screaming. And I could hear Andrew grunting.' Is that right, Ms. Mondragon? Is that what you told investigators?"

I peered at Maxine and Hana. Their faces were stern. Maxine gave me the nod of confidence. I tried my best, but tears ran down my face. My lips quivered. My throat was packed with shards of glass. "Yes."

"Your father was in poor health, wasn't he, Ms. Mondragon?"

"Yes." I couldn't stop the tears; my heart was breaking. I heard my angel scream inside my head.

"That's why you missed most of the school year, isn't that right?"

I nodded. I couldn't speak.

"Isn't that right, Ms. Mondragon?"

"Yes." My voice cracked.

The judge handed me a box of tissues. The prosecutor raced to the table again and retrieved a stack of papers this time, brandishing the papers at me. "Bridget Sullivan, your father's nurse—I'm sorry," he placed his hand over his forehead, "I forgot. You like to call him Andrew. Bridget Sullivan reported that *Andrew* had 80 percent diminished mobility and mechanics. Eighty percent." He aimed his eyes at the jury, as though they hadn't heard him the first time. "Isn't that right, Ms. Mondragon?"

"No."

"No?" he said in shock. "Ms. Mondragon, are you a trained medical professional? Do you have a medical degree?"

"No." I fidget behind the podium where no one can see me. I pick at my thumb cuticle. I dig until the blood makes my digits slick, and I use it like grease.

"What am I saying?" He smacked his forehead. "You don't even attend high school. Heck, you're failing the tenth grade. While most kids your age are home studying and going to homecoming, you're too busy murdering your parents."

Maxine sprung to her feet. Her voice was all fire. "Objection, Your Honor, the prosecutor is testifying, my client—"

The judge slammed the gavel on the podium. "Sustained." He raised his voice and pointed the gavel at the prosecutor, his face the color of a tomato. "I'm holding you in contempt, Prosecutor. I run a strict courtroom, and I will not tolerate misconduct of any sort. This young lady has the right to a fair trial, and your actions are undermining those rights. Do I make myself clear?"

The prosecutor looked scared. "Yes, Your Honor. It won't happen again."

The judge addressed the jury. "The jury will disregard the prosecution's last statement." He then peered at the prosecutor. "Proceed with a new line of questioning."

The prosecutor collected himself. He cleared his throat. His voice was softer this time. "Ms. Mondragon, Bridget Sullivan, a veteran nurse of twenty-five years, reported that your father couldn't take a shower on his own or even dress himself." He placed a digit to his lip. "In fact, most days, as Bridget Sullivan documents in the medical record, Andrew couldn't even get out of bed on his own. Is that right, Ms. Mondragon?"

"He lied." I accidentally glanced at the jury box again. This time I stumbled onto a man. He was handsome and looked at me as though I might be guilty. "He lied to everyone."

"That's awfully convenient for you, Ms. Mondragon." The prosecutor walked over to the jury box. "Why would Andrew lie about being disabled and then create an elaborate charade that fooled a veteran nurse of over twenty-five years?"

"To get Social Security."

"Social Security," the prosecutor said in disbelief. "Didn't your father have eight million dollars sitting in the bank before his death?"

Murmurs hit the courtroom like an undulation.

I nodded.

"The jury can't read minds, Ms. Mondragon. Is that a yes?"

"Yes, but I didn't know—" My knee bounced up and down, jackrabbit energy.

"Let me get this straight, Ms. Mondragon. Your testimony today is that Andrew was in tiptop shape. And, I might add, according to you, he was scamming Social Security. Scamming Bridget Sullivan. All of which is a serious crime. That's a very elaborate con. Why would a millionaire risk going to jail over that?"

"He got lung cancer."

"You mean a doctor diagnosed him with lung cancer?"

"Yes."

"What does that have to do with him conning all these people?"

"He said we couldn't afford to pay for cancer treatments."

"But Andrew could, in fact, afford cancer treatments, isn't that right?"

"I believed him."

"Isn't that right!?"

"I don't know."

"Ms. Mondragon, you just testified you knew your father—I'm sorry, Andrew—had eight million dollars sitting in the bank." He kept pacing the courtroom, making me dizzy. He walked over to the prosecutor's desk, then to the jury box, then to the witness stand like a windup toy.

Maxine rose. "Is there a question here, Your Honor?"

"Prosecutor, either ask the witness a question or move on to the next line of questioning."

The prosecutor nodded. "Ms. Mondragon, I'm having a tough time comprehending your testimony today. Help me help the jury make sense of what you're testifying to here."

"I didn't know we had money, so I believed him. I didn't find out until Em—"

"Ms. Mondragon, please tell the jury—"

"Objection, Your Honor."

"On what grounds?"

"Prosecution continues interrupting Ms. Mondragon during questioning. The jury must hear clear testimony to decide the case."

The prosecutor held up his hands.

"Sustained. If you don't like Ms. Mondragon's answers, Prosecutor, then don't ask the question. The witness will answer the question." The judge motioned to me.

"I didn't find out Dad had money until Emma died. He told us we couldn't afford treatments. He said if we didn't lie for him, he'd die of lung cancer."

"Thank you, Ms. Mondragon. Thank you for painting that pretty little picture." He smiled with nasty grinch energy. "You just testified that you willingly conned the government with Emma Mondragon. Just like you're conning us right now."

"Objection!"

"It's Angel," I roared. "Her name is Angel."

He held up his hands like he was surrendering. "Oh, I see. You seem to have pet names for everybody in your life, isn't that right?"

"Your Honor."

"I'll allow it."

Maxine fumed in her seat. She whispered something to Hana and scribbled something down on a legal pad.

"Dad..." I thought for a second. "Andrew used to say Emma's name weird."

"Weird," the prosecutor seems intrigued, "like how?"

"He said her name like he was going to do something to her."

"Explain, Ms. Mondragon."

"I don't know." The tears began to fall. "Something bad."

"Is that why you call Emma, 'Angel?'"

"Yes."

"I think this is the first time today you're actually telling the truth, Ms. Mondragon. So you do, in fact, refer to your father as Andrew. That's very disrespectful. The jury needs to see the *real* you, Ms. Mondragon. Just in case you've forgotten, you're on trial for manslaughter."

The prosecutor was right. Maxine knew the truth. Hana knew the truth. The whole goddamn world knew the truth now.

"Emma Mondragon is your sister's legal name, isn't that right, Ms. Mondragon?"

"Andrew gave her that name." Now I was picking at my left thumb, opening old wounds.

He walked over to the jury stand and placed his hands on the railing. "What's so wrong about that, Ms. Mondragon? Isn't it a parent's job to name their children?"

"My angel didn't like it." My voice was shaky again. Tears were screwing up my vision.

The prosecutor sprung over to the witness stand with a kangaroo vibe. "Ms. Mondragon, why did your sister not like being called Emma? Tell us. Tell the jury why."

"Because," I whimpered.

"Because why, Ms. Mondragon?"

I peeked at the judge. He seemed eager to know the answer too.

"Because."

"Because isn't an answer, Ms. Mondragon. Because *why*?" His voice was louder. He carried the voice of Andrew.

"Because Andrew liked to call her Emma."

"Yes, we've heard this already. Andrew called her Emma. Why's that bad, Ms. Mondragon?"

"Because Andrew whispered Emma. He whispered Em—"

He threw his hands in the air. "My God, Ms. Mondragon. Andrew whispered Emma." His eyes spun like a lunatic. "That's not a crime."

"He whispered it in her ear. He always whispered in her ear." When I said this, I saw meteor showers everywhere. Electricity pulsing through my body, killing every sense inside me.

"In her ear?" The prosecutor peered at the jurors. "In her ear... Well, Ms. Mondragon, I really..."

My eyes burned, and everything disappeared. I was swimming in the dark universe. I angrily pressed my digits into my eye sockets, as though I wanted to pluck them out. "He whispered Emma's name when he fucked her! He whispered Emma's name!"

The jury gasped. It sifted through the courtroom like a deadly wave. Once the gasps softened, the whispers rose. I couldn't take this anymore. I started slapping my head again and again. I compressed into myself and rocked to soothe.

"Ms. Mondragon, why didn't you report Andrew's abuse to the authorities?"

I plugged my ears. I didn't care anymore if I went to the slammer for life. I forgot to bring the spinny thing that made the pain go away.

The prosecutor walked up to me, saying something, but it was muffled. He kept talking, and I kept plugging. He couldn't make me talk.

The judge stepped down from the bench.

Then Maxine and Hana approached. It was quieter here in my

world. I thought I'd stay for a while. With my angel. I watched them argue about me.

Hey, why's the jury leaving? They all walked single file out of the courtroom. The women I saw earlier is rubbing her nose with a tissue. It looks like she had been crying.

The judge was coming this way. He towered over me. His eyes look sad. He twirled his digit. I think he wanted me to unplug my ears.

I cautiously removed my digits. Tears were in my ears. My heart fluttered in agony.

"Ms. Mondragon," the judge said. "Can you continue?"

I stared into his eyes like a wounded animal. I was sorry for spilling Emma's secret to the world. *Please forgive me, my angel.*

The judge waved Hana over to the witness stand.

"Lizzie, sweetie." Hana walked around to the side and knelt to my eye level. "The judge will grant us a quick recess. I think we should take a break."

I shook my head.

Hana looked at the judge.

The judge placed his hands on the witness stand ledge. "The trial won't proceed if you don't answer my questions, Ms. Mondragon." He gave me gentle eyes. "This is horrific stuff. Even for an adult. I need to know you can continue. Are you able to continue?"

I nodded.

He inspected me with those ocean-colored eyes. He probably wanted to read my mind. "Are you certain you can continue, Ms. Mondragon? What you've gone through," he shook his head, "there's no shame in taking a break."

I scrubbed my eyes with my fist. "I want to."

"If it gets too difficult for you to testify, give me a wink. I'll be watching closely, so don't worry about that. Then I'll know we need to take a break. Agreed?"

I nodded.

The judge seemed as if he didn't want to leave my side. Then he waved his hand. "Bailiff, escort the jury back into the courtroom."

It's a real show, I thought. The whole goddamn thing. One big, giant show. Everyone, take your places so the judge can scream, "Action!"

Even the prosecutor looked a little deflated. Unsure of himself. Unsure of his duties. Unsure of his justice. What is Justice? My angel once told me justice is in the eyes of the beholder, like Hollywood beauty. And sometimes, just lies are just.

"Ms. Mondragon," the prosecutor paused, "did Andrew ever whisper into your ear?"

I could feel the weight of the courtroom crush me. My chest was icy tight. All eyes were on me. "He whispered Emma's name."

"Yes, Ms. Mondragon, you testified to that already. Did Andrew whisper your name?"

I cast a quick look at the jury with shame in my eyes. I then glanced at Maxine and Hana. I could feel tears bubbling to the surface. It felt like my body was being burned alive.

"Ms. Mondragon, did Andrew whisper your name?" He beat his palms on the ledge of the witness stand.

I was speechless. Woozy.

"Your Honor, the witness will not answer the question."

The judge raised his hand at the prosecutor and leaned closer to the witness stand. "Ms. Mondragon, please answer the question."

I nodded. That's all I can give. I told Emma's secret. Now it's my turn. It's what they came for. It's what they all came for

Then I lowered my head in shame. "Yes."

"So, he did, in fact, whisper you name?" The prosecutor seemed more energetic this time. As though the truth had revived him like spring water. "How many times did Andrew whisper your name, Ms. Mondragon?"

Maxine sprung. "Your Honor, I object."

"On what grounds?"

"Relevance?"

The judge peered at me. Then the prosecutor. "Overruled."

"How many times did Andrew whisper your name, Ms. Mondragon?"

"I'm not sure?"

"You're not sure."

"I don't know."

"Well, which is it, Ms. Mondragon? You're not sure or you don't know?"

"I don't know."

"You don't know," he said, perplexed. "Is it perhaps because you're lying to everyone in this courtroom?" He jutted his hand toward the jury.

"I said, I don't know." I felt hot tears trucking down my face.

"You don't know because it's untrue, Ms. Mondragon, isn't that right?"

"I don't know."

"You don't know because it's untrue, Ms. Mondragon."

"I don't know." My voice cracked into a thousand pieces.

"Tell us why you don't know. Tell us, Ms. Mondragon. Tell us the truth for once in your life."

"Your Honor!"

"I lost count!"

The courtroom ruptured into a unanimous gasp.

The judge slammed the gavel on the desk. "Order!"

The prosecutor walked over to his desk and retrieved another paper and held it in the air. "Ms. Mondragon. The juvenile-detention center has a legal obligation to notify the court of the health and safety of its inmates."

"Your Honor, the prosecutor is testifying. He's not asking the witness a question."

"Make your point quickly."

"Were you pregnant, Ms. Mondragon?"

"I don't know."

The prosecutor headed to the jury box again. "Tell the court who's the baby's daddy."

"I object!" Maxine bounced to her feet. "Request to approach the bench."

"Overruled!" The judge flailed his hand. "I'll allow it."

I almost forgot about the baby swimming in my stomach. I caressed my belly. I didn't know if it was a girl or a boy, but I hoped it was a girl. If it was, I'd name her Stardust Angel.

"Ms. Mondragon, the court is waiting." The prosecutor walked toward the witness stand. "Who's the father of your baby?"

I thought I was done. If I said the truth, then I'd drink the bleach, like Emma did. And I wanted to see my angel again. I believed she lived inside my stomach now. That she came back for me.

I turned to face the judge. There was heartbreak in his eyes. Everybody was wearing sad clown faces today. I bet my eyes were sad too. I was sure of it. Then, I did the only thing I could do. I winked.

FIFTEEN
DAY 4

"Denver notified the examiner's office about the Mondragons' untimely death. Is that correct, sir?"

The examiner cleared his throat and adjusted the microphone. "That's correct."

"Sir, can you walk us through the specific steps you took during your initial findings?"

The examiner gave the judge a puzzled look. He then peered at the jury. "Well, processing a body is extensive work. It's not like the movies. I can walk you through my process, but, well, do you have a few days to spare?"

Maxine cracked a smile. Some jurors giggled.

"I'll rephrase." The prosecutor walked over to the witness stand. "You were the first examiner to arrive at the Mondragon residence, were you not?"

"Yes."

"Did you conduct a formal investigation?"

"Yes." The examiner straightened his posture. "This wasn't an unusual case, and that's standard practice for every—"

"Thank you, sir." The prosecutor sneered, went to his desk, and retrieved documents.

"Objection, Your Honor." Maxine stood. "The prosecutor asked the examiner to paint the jury a picture of the medical examiner's daily tasks when investigating a death, now he—"

"Overruled. The examiner already answered the prosecution's question."

"Did you interview the defendant, Ms. Mondragon, during your investigation?" The prosecutor pointed in my direction.

"No," the examiner said, now focusing his attention on me.

"Please tell the jury what stopped you from interviewing Ms. Mondragon."

The examiner kept looking at me. "Bridget Sullivan notified me that an ambulance had rushed Ms. Mondragon to the hospital."

"Bridget Sullivan is Andrew Mondragon's hospice nurse. Is that correct?"

"Uh, yes, I believe so." The examiner fiddled in his seat.

"Did Bridget Sullivan explain why they rushed Ms. Mondragon to the hospital?"

"She thought Ms. Mondragon had suffered a concussion."

"Did she elaborate on how Ms. Mondragon might have sustained a concussion?"

"No. Ms. Mondragon had fainted and was unconscious when the ambulance rushed her to the hospital."

"Is it possible," the prosecutor went to the jury box and grabbed the handrail, peering at the jurors, one by one, "Ms. Mondragon sustained a concussion by blunt-force trauma, say fighting off her attacker?"

I felt the electricity buzzing my brain again.

"Objection." Maxine sprung to her feet. "The prosecutor is purely speculating. There is no evidence—"

"Sustained. The jury will disregard the prosecution's last statement." He pointed his gavel at the prosecutor. "Prosecutor, you're on a slippery slope."

The prosecutor nodded. "Sir, can you describe the state of the bodies of Andrew and Abby Mondragon? Were there signs of a struggle? Was the crime scene in disarray?"

"Objection. Prosecution is linking the examiner's investigation to a crime scene." Maxine sat angrily. "It's not a crime scene."

"Sustained." The judge peered down at the examiner. "The witness will answer the prosecutor's question but will make no reference to a crime scene." The judge inspected the jury. "I want to make clear to the jury that the Mondragon residence was never investigated as a crime scene. The jury will disregard the prosecution's reference to a crime scene." The judge gave the prosecutor an ugly look.

The examiner almost looked confused, as though he didn't know how to move forward.

"The jury is waiting, sir," the prosecutor said.

The examiner eyed the jury again, particularly juror seven. I envision juror seven looked a lot like his daughter, who pasted from a fentanyl overdose.

"Uh... Andrew Mondragon and Abby Mondragon died at the scene. They were lying in separate rooms. The bedrooms were tidy. Spotless. The home was plain, what you'd expect. There were no signs of a struggle."

"Do you find that odd, sir? Spotless bedrooms? Maybe someone covered their tracks."

"Objection!"

"Sustained."

The examiner continued. "When I say *tidy*, I mean the deceased appeared well cared for. Clean clothes. Fresh linens. Fingernails trimmed. That sort of thing. There was a balanced meal, for instance, untouched, sitting on a side table near Andrew Mondragon."

"Okay, sir." The prosecutor held out his hand. "We get the picture. So, nothing out of the ordinary." The prosecutor walked over to the prosecution's table.

"Yes, definitely out of the ordinary." The examiner's eyebrows rose.

The excitement in the prosecutor's tone electrified the air. "Please, tell the jury how so! How was the scene out of the ordinary, sir?"

"Well, I've been an examiner for many years. Too many, really." He laughed a little. "It's not unusual to see terminal folks pass at home. It's quite common these days. Most people can't afford to die in a hospital setting."

"And..." The prosecutor rotated his hands, trying to speed things up.

"Andrew and Abby Mondragon were fortunate to have had the care they received. As I said before, someone took good care of them. No signs of trauma whatsoever. It's unusual for the sickly to be cared for in this manner. I could tell that the young lady loved her parents. I see every day how people in this country forget and neglect those who are terminally ill. Usually, they're unrecognizable once they reach death. Soiled beds—"

"Since it's so unusual, sir, could someone have staged the scene to make it look like Andrew and Abby Mondragon were well cared for?"

"Objection."

"Overruled. The witness will answer the question."

"No, I don't agree with that statement." The examiner shook his head.

"How do you know for sure that the scene wasn't an elaborate hoax?"

I envisioned the examiner was still distracted by juror seven. Every time he looked at her, his daughter's image flashed in his brain. But juror seven seems uncomfortable by the way he keeps staring at her. I bet she's thinking, "As if, I'm you're daughters age sir"

"Well, for one, Ms. Mondragon would have had a heck of a time staging a scene to appear accidental. You might get away with staging one body, but two? You're bound to miss something. Both bodies had clean fingernails. To get all the details right. That's a hard one to swallow, sir. I have difficulty just removing one body from a home." The examiner pointed at me. "Look how small she is. I've investigated countless scenes where foul play was involved. This wasn't one of those scenes. There was no evidence of foul play whatsoever. This was an unfortunate accident."

The prosecutor whacked the document in his hand. "Right here. On page eight. You say Elizabeth Mondragon doesn't know enough about medicine to understand the risks of those three drugs combined." The prosecutor gripped the juror rail. "You think only doctors and pharmacists know these meds could be deadly for people with respiratory problems? Is that correct, sir?"

"Yes." The examiner's tone rose. "I stand by my original findings.

There were no signs of foul play whatsoever. I will not change my findings. I did my due diligence, sir."

"You consider it an accidental death," the prosecutor paraphrased from the document, "even after the defendant served her parents a deadly cocktail. How can you not rule it foul play?"

"It wasn't foul play." The examiner beamed a confident tone of voice. "Not in this case."

"So, there are cases with similar circumstances where you suspected foul play?"

"No."

"No?"

"Andrew and Abby Mondragon had very low levels of medication in their system. If there was foul play afoot, they would have had high levels of narcotics in their system."

"How can you be so certain that Ms. Mondragon didn't have prior knowledge of this so-called triple-threat cocktail? I mean, the internet is full of useful information." The prosecutor pointed at me. "You told the jury earlier you didn't interview Ms. Mondragon. Yet, you wrote a report stating Ms. Mondragon had no expertise in this matter."

"I interviewed Bridget Sullivan."

"And?"

"Bridget Sullivan is a licensed medical professional. Many years as a hospice nurse. She provided information about Ms. Mondragon. She believed Ms. Mondragon was sixteen." He adjusted his position as though the chair was uncomfortable. He cleared his throat. "Even If Ms. Mondragon could get this information, she'd have to execute the plan perfectly. Not with just one body but two. Plus, she would have to possess the medical expertise to pull it off." The examiner raised two digits in the air. "As I said before, you might get away with the first one, but the second one gets them every time."

I saw Hana peering at me from the corner of her eye. The examiner was a perfect specimen. *Look, my angel, I told you everyone always underestimates teenagers. Do I deserve to get away with murder? I believe I'll get away with it. In every sense. Don't forget, I did it for the baby.* I peered down at my belly and caressed it for a sec. *Andrew hurt you too.*

The prosecutor was ready to have a go at the examiner again, but the judge slammed the gavel on the desk. "I'm calling a short recess. Bailiff, please escort the jury from the courtroom." The judge was scowling. "Counselors, meet me in judge's chambers."

"Your Honor." The prosecutor furrowed his brow.

"Prosecutor, we'll discuss any grievances you may have in my chambers."

Maxine wore a look of shock. She glanced at Hana, then at me. Hana squeezed my hand and gave me an encouraging smile. "Maybe you guys should get something to eat or a cup of coffee. This might take a while."

Hana looked scared. "Should we?" She side-eyed me. "Be concerned?"

Maxine squeezed Hana's arm. Then peered at me. "The trial is leaning in our favor. The prosecution is struggling to present a case. We're halfway through, and he has yet to provide a smoking gun, so to speak. The way things are going, I highly doubt a jury would convict. I'll tell you one thing, the jury despises, and I mean *really* despises Andrew and Abby. And they most definitely despise the prosecution for protecting—," she glanced at the prosecutor, "I just don't see a jury convicting Lizzie."

SIXTEEN
DAY 4, JUDGE'S CHAMBER

WHEN THE JUDGE dismissed everyone from the courtroom, Hana took me to a coffee shop—Arts and Crafts style with varying rooflines, so saith Abby. It looked like the Smith's house. They served us curly cue foamed lattes but then asked if we'd like to sit in the mediation room. Hana thought that was a good idea. So we sat on yoga matts and closed our eyes. A nature soundtrack was stuck on a loop. Birds gabbed endlessly while a drizzle ran amuck.

I wasn't allowed in Judge's chamber, but as I sat there meditating, I envisioned this is what took place.

"Counselors," the judge motioned them to sit.

The prosecutor yielded to Maxine, letting her sit first.

"Thank you," she told the prosecutor.

Then the prosecutor settled in his seat.

"I called a recess to give both sides an opportunity to come to an agreement."

The prosecutor was bewildered. "An agreement, Your Honor?"

The judge locked eyes on the prosecutor. "How do you think things are going out there? Are you confident about the case you've presented so far?"

The prosecutor peered at Maxine, then the judge. "I think it's going as expected."

"So," the judge dug underneath his nails with a pick, "you weren't planning on winning the case."

Maxine leaned back and watched the prosecutor squirm.

"I'm unsure what your question is, Your Honor."

"Frankly, Counselor, I'm surprised the grand jury returned with an indictment. And I'm even more surprised that the district-attorney's office pursued this case." The judge pointed at the prosecutor. "Your boss."

"We believe we have a strong case against Ms. Mondragon."

"Strong... The prosecution's case is like," the judge tilted his head toward the ceiling, "going to Mars in a paddleboat when the journey requires a spaceship."

Maxine giggled. "Your Honor, I drew a motion to dismiss because of insufficient evidence, but—"

"I'll raise you one better, Counselor." The judge stopped picking his nails. "I'm of sound mind to rule in your client's favor for a lack of evidence, with prejudice, of course."

"Your Honor." The prosecutor bounced to his feet. "The prosecutor's office still has incriminating evidence that implicates Ms. Mondragon did, in fact, murder her parents."

"Sit down, Counselor. Now, I know you're new to the prosecution game, but I have to say, your courtroom manners aren't sitting well with the jury. Not with me either." The judge pointed toward the courtroom. "You tore that little girl apart on the stand."

"That's my job."

"No, no. All you're doing is making yourself look soulless. Let's face it," he peered at Maxine, "he's a soulless bully, isn't he?"

Maxine gave an uncomfortable nod, averting her eyes.

"You see, Counselor, the trial is almost at the finish line. There are only two witnesses left to take the stand. And one of those witnesses is in favor of the defendant. I have sat on the bench for four days waiting for the prosecution to present firm evidence against Ms. Mondragon. And all you've done is beat that little girl down in front of the entire courtroom. Day after day, you've dragged that little girl through the mud. And you know what, your strategy, if you want to call it that, has backfired. What you've done is make the jury fall in love with that little girl. You can't see it because you're so blind. That jury's heart is breaking for her. You won't get a conviction. I'm confident of that."

"Your Honor," the prosecutor sat taller. "I have faith the jury will see the evidence. I've presented valuable and reliable evidence. They'll rule accordingly, in my favor."

Maxine shook her head and rolled her eyes.

Sweat poured from the prosecutor's brow as he faced Maxine. "In good faith, I'm prepared to offer Ms. Mondragon a lesser charge—involuntary manslaughter. The maximum penalty is six years. But," he motioned to the judge, "he'll probably give her the minimum of two. She'll be out in no time with good behavior."

The judge didn't mask his emotions. He looked horrified by the plea bargain.

"I will strongly advise her to reject this offer. Your Honor, if the court convicts my client of a crime involving her father's death in Colorado, she gives up her inheritance." She then aimed her eyes at the prosecutor. "My client will require therapy for the rest of her life. That kind of therapy is expensive. She's already accumulated thousands in debt from therapy. She'll never know what it's like to live a normal life. Never. What Andrew Mondragon has done to his daughters is pure evil. It makes me sick to my core. He and Abby Mondragon are vile as it gets. I'll see that my client gets her inheritance. She's entitled to it."

"I guess I chose the wrong profession." The prosecutor scoffs. "I should've been a therapist."

"Do you have daughters, Prosecutor?" Maxine produced a sparkly glare.

The prosecutor's face turned red. He hesitated.

"I hope, for your sake...no, for your daughter's sake, that she will never know the realities and the pains Ms. Mondragon lived through in that house. I hope to God she never endures that kind of abuse."

"My daughters would have stood by their faith and not gotten an abortion. Make no mistake, Ms. Mondragon is a murderer."

"So, that's what this is all about. You can't convict my client for having an abortion, so you use this weak case instead. You realize that the father repeatedly raped my client, resulting in her pregnancy. DNA doesn't lie." Maxine aimed her finger at the ground. "And the newborn buried in the cellar was Emma's baby. Andrew Mondragon was the father."

The prosecutor shrugged. "Ms. Mondragon took it upon herself to take an innocent life."

The judge sat back and stared at the two for a minute. "You're a man of faith. Is that right, Counselor?"

"Yes, I am." The prosecutor puffed up. "That's why I became a prosecutor. I believe in dedicating my life to the Lord's work."

"Me too, Counselor, me too." The judge started rocking in his chair, thinking. "Raised in the church since I was this tall." The judge measured his hand in the air. "You believe Ms. Mondragon needs to atone for her sins, I gather?"

"Without question," the prosecutor said.

"Do you read the Bible, Counselor?"

"Every day."

Maxine had a worried look on her face, unsure where the conversation was going.

"Which version?" The judge snapped his fingers. "King James, I'm guessing."

"That's right." The prosecutor smiled and nodded, as though it were a parlor trick.

"How about you, Counselor, do you read the Bible?" The judge addressed Maxine.

"My parents raised me in the church, but I don't attend anymore, not for a long time."

"That's the same with our daughter." The judge pointed to a picture on a shelf. "We raised her in the church too. But she despises religion." The judge chuckled.

The prosecutor rejected the statement with a shake of his head.

"So far, you've provided no evidence Ms. Mondragon is guilty beyond a reasonable doubt. In fact, you've helped the defense's case more than your own. You heard the examiner. He testified Ms. Mondragon doesn't possess the knowledge to commit such a crime. He's not backing down from his initial findings. It's time to move on,

Counselor. I cannot in good faith proceed with this trial. You're a million miles away from winning the case."

"I'll appeal."

"It's within your right to do so. But let me ask you this, Counselor, just for the sake of argument. If Ms. Mondragon is guilty of murder, as you suggest, don't you think she's already paid a hefty price? I suspect Ms. Mondragon will keep paying for the rest of her life. With or without bars. Ms. Mondragon isn't lucky enough to sail off in the wind. Andrew and Abby Mondragon aren't innocent victims." The judge glanced at Maxine. "They're the definition of pure evil. I'll tell you what you've got. You have plenty of evidence proving Andrew Mondragon repeatedly assaulted his daughters and forced them to have his children. He should stand before my bench, not Ms. Mondragon. I'm the longest-standing judge in Denver County, and I've presided over some of the most heinous cases. But this one will haunt me. It should haunt you too." The judge raised his voice, scooted his chair closer, and etched a serious glare on his face.

The judge stood, tucked his chair under the desk, and hammered his finger on the mahogany. "Today, I'm going to intervene on that little girl's behalf because I believe God put me here for a purpose too, Counselor. God put me here for this moment. For this little girl. Someone has got to put an end to this nightmare. This is your moment to do the Lord's work, Counselor. Move to dismiss or I will."

SEVENTEEN
ELECTRICITY AND MISSING TIME

WHEN I WAS THIRTEEN, Emma convinced me to lick a nine-volt battery. I was too scared to do it, so she licked the battery first to show me it wouldn't sting. Her demonstration convinced me. As all her demonstrations did. So, I licked the battery. "You're a moth to the flame," she said and smiled, proud of herself after I'd licked the battery and got burned by the electricity surging through my mouth. I made a horror-struck face. Not from getting burned but from experiencing heartbreak and betrayal.

At first, it was scary realizing my angel could betray me. After being betrayed, I didn't know how to cope with all those feelings. Looking back, I was more stunned than anything else. *Why would you fool me like that and take advantage of my trust? Maybe you tried to build me wiser. Or less trusting. Maybe this was your way of insulating me from the horror all around.*

She was brilliant. But even brilliant people don't account for everything. She didn't consider the toll betrayal would take on me. The pain of betrayal burned worse than a nine-volt. But somehow, like everything in life, you learn to absorb the pain. Add enough betrayal in your day, and you'll develop immunity. And then, pretty soon, you hunger for betrayal, day and night. Betrayal is like a drug. The first time it enters your bloodstream, it's a once-in-a-lifetime euphoria. And you spend the rest of your life chasing it.

My angel was right about most things. But she was mistaken in saying I was a moth to the flame. Because I wasn't. I was a moth to electricity. A moth drawn to hurt. Is what I think she meant to say. That part is true.

I pretended to despise the sting of the nine-volt battery. My acting was so good, I convinced myself that I hated self-inflicted pain. Yet I loved electricity surging through my tongue at first taste.

When Emma wasn't looking, I slipped the nine-volt battery into my pocket. And after dinner, I snuck off to my room and tasted the zap again. I did this night after night. It became a ritual until, one night, the battery had no more venom left to feed.

Emma noticed circular scars on the tip of my tongue and told me to stop. Somehow, she knew what I was doing, but I didn't listen. I wanted what I wanted.

The weird part was, I thought I had plain worn out the little battery. Thinking my appetite was too great. I descended two flights of stairs to reach the cellar during the night. Where more nine-volt batteries sat on a utility shelf. I hungered for electricity so bad, I didn't retreat to my bedroom. Instead, I sat in that dank cellar and smashed metal prongs on my tongue.

Nothing happened with the first one. I threw the battery to the ground and reached for another and sucked on its metal prongs. Nothing. I picked up another. Nothing. Pretty soon, five nine-volt batteries laid in the dirt, and not one of them zapped my flesh.

My addiction was so potent, I sought help from Andrew. I made it a point to avoid him, regarding his presence as a black hole that would devour my soul if I stayed too long in its path.

Though his obsession to keep the carbon monoxide detectors and smoke alarms working was my way in. He agreed with me. We must purchase fresh nine-volt batteries from Walmart. Before the house burned to smithereens. Or we died in our sleep from carbon monoxide poisoning. If only. These were the things he listed off on his ugly, pudgy, jaundiced digits.

I liked the sound of dying in my sleep from carbon monoxide. "Put me out of my misery." Nurse Maggie often said. I obsessed over it. Wouldn't it be great to never wake in this house again? Wouldn't it be great to never see Andrew's ugly face ever again? Although it wouldn't be great to never see Emma again.

I bought three jumbo-sized packs of nine-volt batteries. I didn't even make it to the Camry before I planted one on my tongue. And I felt nothing. I tossed it to the ground and grabbed another one. And another. And another.

My little science theory had failed. I soon realized the batteries weren't the problem. I was. My tongue was the problem. My nerves. But how does one replace their tongue? Their dying nerves. Their brain. You can't rewire an entire brain, can you? Turns out, you can.

I later discovered the problem really was me. Those little batteries couldn't deliver the power my body required. Or should I say *my mind*?

This reminded me of the moment after I received my first application. Which the doctors called "my sessions" of ECT. Electroconvulsive therapy. I called it "dosing."

ECT. Where would I be without you?

They don't hook your brain up to a nine-volt battery. More like a futuristic car battery. That's what it looks like anyway. A car battery hooked up with a radio tuner and had a baby. The ECT machine had dials and gauges. The needles bouncing around, measuring electricity, right?.

I'm kidding. I have no idea what the needles do. I can't be that far off. I'm sure they measure something. I hope so anyway. I hope the doctors aren't just letting it rip like a chainsaw through my brain.

Anyway, they use tiny dumbbells. Metal pads are at the end of the dumbbells. Sort of like nine-volt battery prongs. But instead of placing them on your tongue, they press them against your temples and turn up the juice. And when they turned up the juice, I heard music. Wondrous things. I smelled popcorn. The flavor of metal flooded my mouth.

The doctors weren't little devils. They gave you a cocktail before putting the electrodes on your temples. Not the kind I served to Andrew and Abby. Muscle relaxers and anesthetics. That part wasn't so bad. Then they jammed a mouth guard between my teeth. Hooked me up with wires and stuff. And resurrected my little dead brain like the creature from Frankenstein.

Dr. C advised me, before my first application, not to be scared if my body trembled all over. I guess that's common. But I never felt the trembles. Though my face muscles kept twitching like crazy. When it ended, they rolled me back to my room, and it felt like I was riding on a cloud. I was calmer than before. Clearer. Like a factory reset.

Electricity surging through my body takes me back. I have ten more applications to go. And then, who could say? Dr. C said ECT would significantly reduce my symptoms. He had no clue he was feeding an addict.

I am unaware of the severity of my symptoms. But apparently, they're not so great. "Concerning, very concerning," said Dr. C during our private session. All I knew was, for whatever reason, I was missing time. I didn't recall these concerning symptoms when they happened. And sometimes, especially when I talked about Andrew, I'd see stars or meteor showers. Then I'd wake up someplace new. Not the place I'd started from. I was used to it. Waking up someplace new wasn't new to me. I think it all started when I was thirteen.

Dr. C said it was my mind's way of coping with traumatic-emotional something. I couldn't remember the medical term. My mind went on auto, and I checked out. But ECT was supposed to fix all that. I knew I was on to something with those nine-volt batteries.

Let's go back. Little did I know, Emma was perusing the camping section. Buying all the lighters her hands could carry. Maybe stockpiling a shopping cart full of them. Let's not forget the machete.

Yes, my angel, I suppose pain was a lifeline. In order to insulate, you must first build a formidable wall. You must allow the flame, or electricity, to numb you good. Over. And over. And over again. The pain is easier to endure when you inflict it on yourself, than when someone else hurts you. The only person who knows your pain tolerance is you.

Point in case, when Dr. C gave me another shot the other day, I snatched it from his hand and said, "It won't hurt so bad if I do it." But then again, sometimes we hurt ourselves more than others.

I never saw my sister's pain. My pain sat first and blinded me. Time travel doesn't exist yet. If I'm still alive when it does, I plan to go back. Tell my sister sorry. Then hug her. And never let go. Lizzie

I heard someone knocking at my psych-room door.

"Knock, knock," Nodin said, opening my door. "How's life going, Lizzie?" He shined that million-dollar smile. I was pretty sure he could make millions on that smile. It was all firework energy. Oh, dear Jesus, he was handsome.

Ruh-roh, Emma teased. *Here comes your dreamboat.*

"Shh."

I smiled and said nothing to Nodin. Every time he was around, I fixed my hair.

Because he's your dreamboat. Emma whispered

Nodin has long, dark hair and brown skin. He told me once he was indigenous. From the Little Basket Tribe, somewhere in New Mexico near the Colorado border. On the Plains, he'd said. I wanted to walk the Great Plains with Nodin beside me.

He also said his name meant "wind." I'd agree. He was the wind that stole my breath.

"Are you ready for group today?"

I was in love with Nodin. And I was goanna marry him one day. He was nineteen. We were two years apart. It could work.

How would that happen? Emma interrupts. *Chances are, you'll never see Nodin on the outside.*

"Never say never, Emma," I muttered.

"What was that?" Nodin said, eyes narrow.

"Oh." I smiled shyly. "Nothing."

He smiled back. "Are you ready?"

"Yep." My voice sounded too bubbly.

I apologize for my sister's rudeness. I can see Emma twirling her finger around her temple right now. *She can be a little weirdo sometimes.* Making that well-mannered voice she does when mocking me.

As we walked down the corridor, most every door was closed on this wing. As though the darkness was collapsing over me. Though Nodin was the light that I followed within the dark. Even his gait was pleasing.

He strode like a seasoned dancer. If someone asked me to describe Nodin in one word, I'd say *beautiful*. Nodin was beautiful.

"Here we are." Nodin showcased the door like a magician's sleight of hand. And his chiseled veins ran through his hands and up his muscular arms like lightning bolts. I took it back. Nodin was a God.

I peeked inside the therapy suite and could see the girls sitting on chairs. Forming a circle in the middle of the room. Those ugly, little chairs hurt my butt. The girls looked bored as they waited for Dr. C to arrive. Blondie, whose real name was Becky, was hunched over with her chin in her hand. Destiny kept calling Becky Blondie because she always upstaged her. Dr. C had to stop the group session every time to remind Destiny that Blondie wasn't Becky's real name. Destiny and Becky argued a lot. Destiny kept saying, "I'd stop if she quit upstaging." Every time Destiny called Becky Blondie, Becky's face turned sad with a side of tomatoes. And I recognized that look. I felt the same way when they called me Killer Girl in juvie. Her Blondie was my Killer Girl.

I smiled my best smile at Nodin and twisted my hair around my first digit. "See you in an hour," I said, as though we had plans for the evening. Oh, dear Jesus, I wish.

We weren't allowed to walk around the halls unattended. They only allowed us floppy pens to write with. Well, correction, they allowed floppy pens until Janet disassembled the pen and fished it up her veins. After that, we were only allowed golf pencils. No eraser. We might erase ourselves in the middle of the night. Or hurt someone else. So they had people like Nodin escort us to group. To sessions. To lunch. Watch over us. Make sure we weren't offing ourselves.

"Oh." Paranoia was rightfully installed on his face. "Didn't anyone tell you?"

"Tell me?" My heart was thumping a hundred miles an hour.

"Uh, yeah." Nodin averted his eyes. His beautiful mahoganies landed on the floor. "This is my last day." He peeked at his watch. "I leave at eleven thirty."

"Why?" My voice quivered.

"Fall semester starts tomorrow."

My eyes searched his mahoganies, trying to read his emotions. "It's fall?"

He gave me a sympathetic look. "Yeah, but I'll be back next summer."

Next summer. *Oh, dear Jesus, Nodin. I hope I won't be here next summer.* The sad part, the worst part, I never got to go outside. I didn't even realize it was nearing autumn. I missed the sharp weather. Golden leaves sifting to the earth. The smell of snow. The bite of winter.

Nodin was about to leave, but I said, "What's the name of your school?"

"Oh," Nodin said, adverting his eyes again, "we're not supposed to say. It's against the rules."

Fuck the rules Nodin, we have a thing.

He noticed my teary eyes. He drew closer and whispered, "DU." Then he walked away.

You totally lucked out, bitch. What are the chances!? Emma blared. *You know that place inside and out.*

The only vacant chair left in the group was next to JC—Joanna Camden. I didn't mind sitting next to JC, it just seemed JC didn't enjoy sitting next to me. Or anyone, for that matter. She always sneered every time I sat beside her.

JC was usually quiet, though she complained the plastic chairs were filthy. Well, sticky. To JC, *everything* was sticky. She smashed her hands in her lap most of the time to protect them from getting sticky. She was afraid to touch anything.

JC shared in the last session about witnessing her grandmother die. Her grandmother bleached every horizontal and veridical surface in the house. Even the dish water had concentrated amounts of bleach in it. Because everything was too sticky. Most of the time, they sat in their undies, on the carpet, to eat meals on paper plates and specialized composite utensils. Ones that didn't stick to skin. They even sat on the carpet to watch TV. JC's grandmother claimed the sofa was too sticky. JC proclaimed it velvety. But now she questioned whether it was sticky after all. And ever since JC's grandmother had died, she couldn't sleep anymore. Or go to school. She couldn't even leave her bedroom. She passed out a lot whenever she was around sizable crowds. Small ones too. She said it was the noise people made that freaked her out.

She was an ECT girl too. Enrolled in the program longer than me.

She still passed out in group sometimes, so I figured ECT applications weren't working for her.

Dr. C said everyone's brain chemistry works differently. What works for one person might not work for another. So I guess I had a chance, however slight it might be.

I didn't think you could erase all the bad. All the pain. Not ever. No matter how much electricity they pumped through your brain. I thought the only way to rid the madness from the deep within was the electric chair.

"Lizzie," Dr. C rifled through the papers on his clipboard, "you haven't taken part in group the last two sessions." He was strategic when setting the clipboard on his lap. Then tucked a pen inside his shirt pocket. "As a group, we discussed unhealthy ways we all cope," he flapped his hand and motioned to a few girls to lower their voices, "and process trauma. Especially when things are being done to you, and you have no control over it. I've shared," he glanced at a few more girls, "we've all shared. Except you. We'd like to know what challenges you face when you encounter trauma and how you coped."

Something negative settled on my face, I think, because Becky answered Dr. C's question instead. "I don't think Lizzie's ready to share, Dr. C."

"God!" Destiny yelled. "You're always thinking, Blondie. Always running your mouth."

"Destiny, we've discussed name-calling in group before. We must respect everyone's feelings. You know Becky doesn't like being called Blondie. This circle is a judgment-free zone." Dr. C scribbles something on the clipboard. "I'm giving you one demerit."

"That's bullshit!" Destiny rose. "Blondie isn't even a curse word. It's a descriptor."

"Destiny," Dr. C motioned for Destiny to sit, "we've discussed this before. You know, as well as I do, Becky doesn't like being called Blondie. Most of the group has agreed that Blondie, in this context, is hurtful. It's doesn't have to be a curse word to hurt someone's feelings."

Oh, dear Jesus. I can see Emma's eyes rolling. *Why's Destiny so hot for Becky?*

Destiny plopped down on her chair with a loud thud.

"Lizzie...," Dr. C continued.

All eyes were on me.

"Let's start small. Name one unhealthy way you cope with trauma." Dr. C peeled his arms open wide. "It can be anything. Remember, there are no right answers. No wrong answers. There are no dumb questions either. Everyone in this room is a bright star. I'm a firm believer that simple answers are the pathway toward genius."

Laura cracked up and covered her mouth.

Lizzie, Emma's angry voice boiled, *Don't you dare share. Don't you dare.*

"I... I..." I took a breath. I was digging at my thumb cuticle, feeling my skin rip apart. I looked at Destiny, and she glued angry eyes to the checkered tile. "I hurt myself sometimes."

Becky raised her hand. Dr. C looked at me with scrunched brows but got distracted by Becky. He waved his hand to acknowledge her. "I'm pleased you want to add something to the discussion, Becky. Let's allow Lizzie to explore this a little more. Then you can have the floor." Dr. C locked eyes on me. "Lizzie, thank you for sharing with the group. I know this is a difficult subject for you. When you say you hurt yourself sometimes, can you share what triggers those emotions?"

You've said plenty. Emma is pissed. *You know the rules.*

I followed Destiny's lead, looking down at the checkered floor, shaking my head.

"Oh, Dr. C," Becky said. She thrashed her hand in the air. "Dr. C."

"Becky," Dr. C gave her a side-eye, "I'll call on you as soon as Lizzie has had her turn. I'd like to explore this a little further."

"Dr. C said put your hand down, damn," Destiny said.

Becky lowered her hand. Her face melted to sadness. She crossed her arms. "Lizzie," Dr. C peered at me, "this is a safe space. You're safe."

If you tell, Emma warned, *you know what will happen next.*

"Shut up!"

"Lizzie, who are you telling to shut up?" Dr. C adjusted his sitting position.

The girls were staring at me with melted clown faces.

I can't carry the secret anymore, Emma. Forgive me. You couldn't either. Look what happened to you.

I say with a gentle, ephemeral tone, "I hurt myself when Andrew touched me."

I warned you, Emma whispered. *Now look what you've done to yourself.*

◦

Polaroid World

—MY MIND in the jaws of ECT

He threatened to knock me out. And he did knock my lights out, right before Emma died. I got smart with Andrew. I talked back and gave a dirty look. Abby distracted me, and while I gave Andrew his medicine, he hit me, and I lost consciousness. I recalled a little after that.

I woke on Andrews's floor. Muffy was licking me. I was naked. I tried to stand, but a sharp pain paralyzed my lower back. I found my jeans and underwear strewn beside Andrew's bed. I collected what I could and dressed. Andrew was snoring. I stared at him for a good while, while he slept. Was he sleeping? Or was he a faker? Yeah, he was a faker. I saw his left eye snap open, then close.

I hobbled to the bathroom and took a shower. I bathed under the water until it poured icicles all over. That's when I began to feel something. Ravenous tingles electrified me. Before the cold water weighed me down, I was numb inside and out. Hypnotic. Invisible. An automated spirit roaming the house, tending to the needs of the living.

Like a flesh-eating plague that had invaded my senses. I heard nothing. I smelled nothing. The wetness felt dulled. I only saw tunnels. No light. No birds tapping at the window, as they did every morning. The birds like to cause a raucous in the trees outside Andrew's window. Perching here and there. Darting at full speed. Swooping crazily in the air. Bickering. They loved to bicker. You never could tell if they were friends or enemies. But not today. Never again. The silence clouded over once Andrew struck me down.

When I sit in the courtroom, I shrink in my chair. Sometimes I want to shrink so small I transport myself into the quantum.

Way up here I'm a girl governed. And therefore, must play by those rules or get burned alive.

But even if I'm able to transform myself smaller than microscopic. A million times smaller than microscopic. And free fall into the quantum. I would have escaped the laws of men. But even if I could escape, I would have eluded nothing. Because way down below, I'm still governed by the laws of physics.

Quantum mechanics dictates a completely different set of rules. And these rules may be worse than the upper realm.

God made me a girl in this realm, ruled by men. I imagine God would not change his mind in the quantum. God would create me to be dominated by some other thing. And so, it matters little if I live in the quantum or upper. Escape is impossible. No perfect utopia to tread upon. In any world. I will remain a slave to whatever forces press upon me.

So, I have created my realm. Inside Polaroid World. Emma is there. I see her. I think she sees me too. At least I'd like to think she sees me.

Polaroid world is not a matter of control or rules. It's a matter of luck. My world welcomes anything, big or small. Whatever strikes the lens is welcome. No gods. No men. But only when my eye decides, when Emma gives me the signal, the click of a button captures utopia. A frame. A still-life of perfection. Surgery. The taste of bombolone on my lips.

There's just one problem. My success withers at the speed of light. Every time I think I've found the magical portal–Emma vanishes from the picture. Then I realize, what if the secret door does not live in America? What if it's in Norway? Or China. Emma wanted to visit those places. I think I must travel to these places. And see what it's like. I'm not getting any younger. And time is running paper-thin.

I never wanted to live in this life. I desire to reach the stars. I desire to live in another world free of this, whatever this is. Because there is another door. A secret door that eludes us all. It's the entrance to utopia. And we must spend our lives hunting it down. Because that's where our true family resides. And they are waiting for us to come home.

Still, another complication enters my mind. What if something inside the heart hides at the door? How does one travel inside the heart? That's maybe the craziest idea yet.

I will find a home. I will travel to Norway first. Emma mentioned Norway way more than China. And when I do, Emma will be waiting there for me. I just know it.

EIGHTEEN
LOST TOGETHER

Yesterday, Nurse Molly and Dr. C sat me down to chitchat about my test results. The look on their faces made think I'd done something terrible.

"Test results like these," Nurse Molly, all psychoanalytical, "would be easier to absorb if you had support from family or friends."

Dr. C gave me a look that seemed to befall some deep turmoil. As though he wasn't sure how to navigate delivering bad news from two feet away. He was wincing hard. The news must have been the devil's work.

"Lizzie," Dr. C casually crossed his leg, left to right. His voice robotic and crisp. Nurse Molly hovered nearby, as though Dr. C needed a spotter to help with all the heavy lifting. Plus the two chaperones standing by. More like wardens than anything else. Crowding the doorway like Goliath wallflowers. "We received some concerning news about your test results. Dr. Peterson, the OB-GYN you saw yesterday on the seventh floor, well, the news isn't positive, Lizzie. I know this may be very difficult to hear."

"He said it was probably nothing." My voice was now frightened. "He said not hearing the baby's heartbeat isn't always a bad sign. I might not be that far along."

"Yes, we discussed that as well." Dr. C's face grew more serious. "He also had another concern, but he didn't want to alarm you before he made a final determination about the results."

"He said everything would be okay..." My heart fluttered.

"Lizzie," Dr. C said. "Dr. Peterson confirmed the pregnancy is ectopic."

Ectopic, WTF, Emma said. *Lizzie, that doesn't sound good.*

"Hush your dirty, little mouth!"

Dr. C ignored my outburst. "Dr. Peterson is highly recommending induced abortion because of the fetus's location. It's ectopic, no question. He wants to prep you for the procedure this afternoon. We can't afford to waste any time."

"He said the baby would be okay." My eyes were floating, and I looked at Nurse Molly. "He said the baby would be okay. Right? You were there."

Nurse Molly wore a mask of shame and adverted her eyes.

I shook my head. "No, I won't let you take my baby. I'm sure the baby will be fine."

"No," Dr. C said. "I'm afraid the fetus isn't fine, Lizzie. Dr. Peterson went over the test results carefully and determined the fetus is about ten weeks in development. It doesn't have a heartbeat. There's no question about it, the fetus is implanted outside the womb. Ectopic pregnancies can lead to death if not treated. This is very serious."

Dr. C gave me a stern face, as though he was angry. I'd never seen Dr. C get angry before. I was quiet for a second. Trying to think about what to say next. *Emma, I'm sorry for yelling at you. Come back, please. I don't know what to do. We can't let them take the baby.*

"Lizzie." Dr. C resituates his butt. "Nurse Molly tells me you asked for menstrual pads today. We need to know how many pads you've used so far. This is very significant."

Dr. C kept using the word *very* for everything. Tears rolled. I could feel my lips quivering. Baby Fay came back to curse me. Then something else came. "I want to speak to Dr. Peterson's manager." I almost screamed.

That idea just popped into my head. I had no idea if Dr. Peterson had a manager. I was just hoping he did. I saw it on television once. It couldn't hurt, right?

Do you see Nurse Molly over there, smirking? Emma said. Rolling her eyes and folding her arms. *What does she care? It's not her baby.*

"That's very reasonable, Lizzie," Dr. C said with encouragement. "I'd request a second opinion as well if I were in your shoes. Dr. Peterson was ahead of you on this one. He forwarded the test results to another OB-GYN for review. And she recommended an induced abortion as well. Your safety is paramount here. The hospital has stringent guidelines for preventing patient deaths. You don't have a choice here, kiddo, you really don't."

Lizzie, Emma whispered. *Don't do anything stupid. I know how you get.*

I wondered how many times a heart could break before it crumbled completely. If my heart stopped now, maybe the world would celebrate. I glared at Dr. C. "I can't, Dr. C. I can't do it. You don't understand."

Dr. C shook his head. "I'm really sorry."

I rose. Dr. C looked a little nervous. Nurse Molly backed away from the chitchat circle, as if I would smack her. Which, I'd never gotten violent during my stint in the hospital. I had one little outburst in juvie, and now the universe thought I was a psychotic beast. That minor episode permanently stained my record. And soon to join the list, Killer Girl. Maybe that's why everyone was so scared of me?

The chaperones edged closer, ready to snatch me up, if need be. My eyes were a slushy mess. "Please..." I mopped my eyes with my palms. My digits jittery. I clung to my belly, as though I'd felt the baby kick. "Don't you see? If I let the baby die, then all of this," I wave my hands in the air, "was for nothing."

Dr. C nodded, giving the chaperones the go-ahead. One chaperone wrenched my arm, subduing me. I tried to wiggle free, but his hands were like Hercules's. And he kept squeezing tighter until my arms stung.

"No!" I screamed. "Let me go!" I whipped my head over my shoulders and peered at him with hateful eyes. "Ooow, you're hurting me."

"Stop fighting, then." His breath smelled of tuna.

"Ooow." I glared at Dr. C as he loaded a syringe. I couldn't break free. I tried to kick his shins with my heel, but it did nothing. The chaperone overpowered me the way Andrew used to.

Lizzie, Emma said. *Dr. C's right, you could die. Don't end up like me.*

"Lizzie." Dr. C handed Nurse Molly the vial and walked toward me with the syringe in his left hand. "I'm going to give you a sedative. It will make you feel sleepy."

I repelled my body away from the needle and tried backing away. But I hit a muscular wall called a chaperone. The chaperone was bulldozing me closer to Dr. C, still gripping my arms. His muscular body rammed hard against me. I could feel his everything smashed against my back. His breath grazing the top of my head. "Stop! I don't like being touched...ow!"

I finally went limp and stopped fighting, as I did when Andrew violated me. It was best not to fight. It would all be over soon. Hopefully. Maybe. *They will do whatever. Just smile, Lizzie.*

My bare feet screeched against the checkered vinyl. I watched as the needle invaded my space. I peered at Dr. C with puppy eyes. Face full of tears. "Please, Dr. C, don't."

He said nothing. His face was blank and calculating. I wondered if I'd worn the same face when I'd killed Andrew and Abby. I wondered if I looked that empty. I wondered if Andrew knew I was ready to kill him.

Dr. C grabbed hold of my arm, aimed, and stabbed the needle deep within my flesh.

All I could do was scream.

NINETEEN
HAPPY TREE FRIENDS

IT HAD BEEN two days since my procedure. The cramps were still razor sharp. Wrenching my hollow womb. I hadn't slept because the pain had gnawed at me. Aggravating me. Toying with me. And laying on my side didn't help, as it often did when my period came. Normally, I'd ball my body tight, and somehow that would work. It would cool the flame in my tummy. Even though it didn't ease the cramps.

I filled one pad today, and it wasn't even noon. Dr. Peterson warned me the bleeding would be heavy at first. But then it would get lighter as days went on. So he'd said, before he knocked me out. Given another famous cocktail through IV. Isn't karma a little beast?

I sat on the sofa, staring at the television. They let me watch TV now. My consolation prize for letting them give me an abortion. Dr. Peterson said the court was asking for a DNA sample from my baby. Correction, from the fetus.

Dr. Peterson and Dr. C cornered me. They wanted to know the baby's father. I told them I was still a virgin. You should have seen the look on Dr. Peterson's face. He almost laughed. At least I made someone laugh. Although Dr. C didn't even bat an eye.

I was convinced they already knew the answer. They wanted to hear me admit the truth. But, as we know, just lies serve a purpose. Of course,

I refused to tell. How else was it going to go? DNA doesn't lie. Soon the entire world would know what had happened in that house. As far as Andrew went, well, he was fucked twice over.

How did I know the baby didn't belong to Mario or Lincoln? Simple. I'd peed on a stick before sleeping with them. That was a cloudy day with a side of whatever. When my eyes locked onto the pink stoplight, I wailed for the entire day.

I thought long and hard about drinking a gallon of bleach too. But I couldn't kill my baby. Emma didn't drink bleach until after we'd buried Baby Fay in the cellar. Now I knew what Emma had felt that day. If there was a gallon of bleach within reach, I'd drink the whole goddamn bottle too.

I had no idea what was playing on the screen. It could have been blank for all I cared.

For some reason, JC decided to plop down next to me on the sofa. "Do you wanna see something cool?" JC's mischievous smile lit up the room.

I stared at JC, vacant, sedated, and then looked back at the screen. I saw JC playing with the remote out of the corner of my eye. I had no idea they didn't let patients touch the remote. JC aimed the remote at the television, and *Happy Tree Friends* flashed on the screen. The volume was low. I couldn't hear what the characters were saying.

"Turn it off," I said in a faraway tone.

Look! Emma celebrated. *Oh, how I miss this show. Come on, you remember, don't you?* Happy Tree Friends *always makes people laugh.*

I peered at JC, my eyelids droopy. My voice was lethargic. "Turn it off."

"It'll make you feel better."

I was sick of everyone forcing me to do things, convincing me it was for my own good. It was obvious none of these things were making me feel better. Couldn't anyone see what was happening? I wasn't better. I'd never be better. Didn't they get that?

I'd gone into a severe depression after getting an abortion. Where Dr. C had pumped my system full of drugs, so I'd forget. For two days, I'd felt numb inside. Everything inside, bone dry, including my soul. I kept checking my pulse just to make sure I was still alive. I thought maybe I'd died and was serving time in hell. Or purgatory. Here's the thing: a mountain of drugs can't erase memories. If they could, everyone would do them nonstop.

Yet, seeing *Happy Tree Friends* stirred powerful emotions. Buried emotion I'd almost forgotten. The only time Emma would belly laugh was when we watched *Happy Tree Friends*.

Oh, Lizzie, here comes my favorite part. I could hear Emma belly laugh inside my head. My parched skin drank my warm tears. They barely made it to my cheeks before they fizzled out. And, for whatever reason, I joined my angel and started laughing when the blood and guts began.

I despised *Happy Tree Friends*. It was gory as hell. Not suited for children. Not suited for anyone. Emma had an exotic sense of humor, but somehow, I kept laughing with tears rolling down my face.

See, I told you this is funny.

I was laughing hysterically. I couldn't stop. My tummy was racked with paralyzing pain because I was convulsing so hard from laughing. My face was on fire. My mouth was sore. My eyes swelled to where the *Happy Tree Friends* melted into a bloody slushy from the tears.

Out of nowhere, Becky joined this sick party and sat next to me, opposite JC, sandwiching me on the couch. Becky whispered something in my ear. I couldn't hear what she said. Becky nudged me hard and raised her tone. "What are you going to name your baby?"

I heard one girl behind us gasp. Little did I know, Destiny was watching Becky like a stalker. I immediately shut my mouth. No more laughter. No more anything. *Happy Tree Friends* melted into the background. The room went eerily still.

My face, once filled with joy, turned horror-struck with a hint of betrayal.

"Yo!" Destiny's voice rumbled from behind. "Shut your fucking mouth, Blondie."

Becky turned to meet Destiny's gaze. "I just wanted to know the baby's name."

"Becky," JC said, stunned. "Not cool at all."

"What did I say?"

"Dude," Destiny charged over to the front of the sofa, "she lost the baby."

Becky looked at me. "I didn't know. I swear."

I squeezed Becky's hands hard, like I wanted to smash something. My heart hurt. I was blinded by tears again. I peered at her, my voice crying. I said, "Stardust Angel." Because I never wanted to forget Emma. I wanted to remember good things for a change. I wanted Becky to know her name. I wanted everyone to know her name.

Lizzie... I could see Emma placing a hand over heart, touched. *Are you serious? You'd really name your baby after me?*

"That's total rizz." Becky returned the favor and squeezed my hand.

Destiny sat on the coffee table. Her soft eyes bore down on me. "Are you good?"

JC draped an arm over me. "Lizzie."

I quickly mopped my eyes dry, frustrated. "I'm okay." But I was far from okay.

"Lizzie..." Destiny peered at me, concerned.

I fabricated a smile. Fresh tears spurted. "I'm okay." I looked at Becky, then JC. "Really."

Lizzie. Chill.

"I'm sorry." Becky squeezed my hand again.

"I'm okay!" I screamed a thundering cry. My fists clenched. My arms trembling. My face all tomatoes. All the hurt spewing from my soul. All the torment finally allowed to escape the confines of my heart. "I'm okay!"

I kept screaming. And everywhere I looked, all I saw were melted clown faces.

Oh no. They're coming to put you down again.

TWENTY
CATCH RELEASE

I DIDN'T KNOW Emma kept a secret diary. Not until Detective Rose told me during the interview. I thought I knew my sister inside and out. I suspect everyone hides a little piece of themselves. Away from the people they love. Keeping something for yourself is purely survival. The truth hurts bad sometimes. The truth really, really hurts sometimes.

Even the people you love most don't deserve your truth. Keep something for yourself. You can't give it all away. It's impossible. It will break you. And whatever's left for yourself keeps you going one more day. Otherwise, you'll have nothing left to hang on to. I knew Emma had her reasons to lock herself away. To protect herself.

I woke this morning when the light filtered through the greasy windows. The glass looked as though hordes of children had gone crazy and rubbed their dirty paws all over. If I smashed my face against the glass just right, I got a glimpse of the street below.

Sometimes I see people going about their day. Billows of frost exiting their mouths and waltzing upward. Children skipping against a cold snap. Heading somewhere grand, perhaps. A park. Walking the dog. School. Anywhere besides the fifth floor of a psych unit.

Sometimes I wondered where all these people were heading. What home did they arrive to once they got to wherever they were going? Was it like mine? It made my heart race just thinking about how many Emmas were out there.

Every time I glimpsed someone walking below, I'd think, *Is that a duplicate angel? Should I smash the window and holler, "Don't go home? Run while you still have a chance! Leave everything behind and start anew while you have the strength!"*

Then I'd think, maybe that's what happened to Emma. Maybe some girl from a fifth-story window got her attention. And begged her to run away. To never go home. To start anew. And maybe when she did what she did, that was her way of starting fresh. Not running away but starting over, from scratch.

Andrew played a game I dubbed Catch and Release. Among many things, he was an artist at playing feeble. But when he caught me, he brutalized me. He used psychosocial warfare on his prey first, and then got on top of me. Pinned me down and sunk his knees into my chest so I couldn't breathe. He didn't look strong, but he harnessed the devil's will. And just when I thought I'd pass out, he'd spring off and hover over me as I crawled toward my bedroom. Coughing. Trying to scream when nothing would come out. And there he was above me, mocking every inch I took. Inch by inch. I was a little dummy because I thought he'd let me escape. And he waited for me to get as far as the door. Then he'd pounce again. Drive a knee into my stomach.

This went on until I stopped fighting and gave up. As if it were my decision. When in reality, I'd surrendered the moment he knocked me to the ground.

That was the twist. I never could escape. He made me think all these devastating outcomes were because of my bad choices. And if I were smarter, then I'd free myself from the torment. His elation stemmed from proving I was nothing more than a dummy.

In the end, I laid, letting him do whatever he wanted. Sometimes I'd just close my eyes and pretend I was elsewhere. Out of mind. Slip away, as though I had the power to transport to another dimension. Where he couldn't hurt me.

I could see Nurse Molly out of the corner of my eye. Standing in the doorway. Inspecting me as though I was a bug. Ever since the abortion day, Nurse Molly had escorted me to group. Escorted me to ECT. Escorted me everywhere around the ward.

I walked over to Nurse Molly and followed behind her, her stone bracelets rattling around her wrists. Her gait wasn't glorious like Nodin. Her essential-oil perfume saturated my nose and mouth. As though I was being suffocated by a toxic muffler. I could nearly taste the waxy oil.

When we reached group, I said, "Have you heard from Nodin?"

"Lizzie," Nurse Molly snapped, annoyed as hell, "I already explained this to you. I can't give out personal information about employees. Instead of worrying about boys, you need to concentrate on yourself." She placed her hands out, guiding me as though I wasn't capable of walking through a doorway.

Destiny and JC had saved a seat for me. After my outburst, we now had a friendship group happening. Destiny, JC, Becky, and me. We all sat together in a group and hung out together in the game room and TV room too.

Destiny didn't call Becky "Blondie" anymore. They still bickered, though. I think they were on the mend. JC didn't repel my presence either. I'd learned my lesson from juvie. It was best to be honest when relationships started to bud. The other day, while in group, I shared why I went to the slammer in the first place, though I didn't tell them I'd killed Andrew and Abby. I said, "I was charged with manslaughter."

The room got super quiet. No one even rustled in their seat. Not even Dr. C. Although his reaction was a mystery. He sat there, bug-eyed, as though a car would run him down. I thought he already knew. Maybe he was surprised I'd share something so traumatizing.

Yes, Dr. C, it was traumatizing. I was forced to kill Andrew and Abby. And I did it all for nothing. The baby didn't survive. Emma didn't survive. Baby Fay didn't survive. I was the only one who survived. Now what?

Once the room digested the weight of my confession, the girls bombarded me with questions, but Dr. C intervened and shut down the whole conversation. He reached toward the ceiling and raised his voice. Which he never did. Yell, I meant. I figured I was probably breaking him. I broke everyone, eventually.

"Lizzie, I'm uncomfortable with the direction of this conversation. I see a lot of curious faces here. I know this subject must be incredibly difficult to discuss. And thank you for sharing with the group. That requires a lot of courage on your part. That being said, I'm required by law to report crimes involving harm to yourself and others. As a group," he waved his hands around, "we don't need to know specifics. I'm concerned about your well-being. Legal ramifications are my primary concern here. And it's best we move on to another subject. Are we all in agreement here? For Lizzie's sake?"

Every girl in the room nodded. Some kept staring at me. Trying to read my mind. Was I a murderer? Did I kill my parents? I imagine they were toying with those ideas. Analyzing how I did it, perhaps. Was it a bloodbath, like a slasher film? Did I stab Abby forty times, then give Andrew forty-one? I could see it in their eyes. They were tallying the carnage.

TWENTY-ONE
MUSIC HEAD

DR. C RUSHED into the group and sat. Hair ruffled. He kept his nose glued to the clipboard in his hand. He smoothed wrinkles from his khaki slacks and set the clipboard on his lap. He folded his hands and laid them on the clipboard.

"Okay." Dr. C sighed. "Who would like to share a happy memory? Remember, a happy memory can be any event in your life. Eating a snow cone in the park or riding a bike on a beautiful day. Listening to your favorite music while driving in the car, windows rolled down."

Nobody rushed to raise a hand. Someone sniffled. Chairs squeaked against the checkered floor. I saw Stacey picking at her digits. Holding them up to the light, bored.

"Okay, then." Dr. C's voice perked up. "I'll call on someone." He peered at each of us with hawk eyes. Then homed in on me, then Stacey, then back again. "Lizzie, you haven't shared a happy memory with the group. Why don't you try it?"

My heart tingled from excitement. Not happy excitement. More driven by anxiety. Although Dr. C brought up a subject I know well. Music.

"Okay," I said in a baby voice. Then I cleared my throat and looked around the room. "Umm, well, Emma and I loved listening to music together. So, that was happy, I guess."

"Lizzie," Dr. C adjusted his bottom in the seat, "let's explore a little more. Emma and you enjoyed listening to music together. That sounds like a bonding moment. We can all relate." He eyed various girls in the group. "We connect through music. Tell us more about that moment. Did Emma and you have a favorite place to listen to music? Was there something special about this bonding experience that left an impression on you?"

"Yes." I felt too shy to speak. "They didn't allow us to listen to music."

One girl cracked up. Destiny squeezed my hand as though she knew my pain.

"What about a cell phone?" Lydia said. "Did they let you have one?"

I shook my head.

"Did you have a computer?"

"I think we're diverting a little," Dr. C said. "Let's stick to the happy memory. You didn't have permission to listen to music. So, somewhere along the way, Emma and you listened to music. Let's explore that." Dr. C nodded at me to speak.

"Umm..." My eyes sprinted around the room. "A boy. Well, not a boy." I touched my chin. "I think he was Emma's age, or close to it."

"What was his name?"

"Derrick, I think. Emma talked to him most."

"I'm confused, Dr. C," Bethany said. "Lizzie said Emma enjoyed listening to music. Now she's talking about a boy named Derrick."

Dr. C nodded and placed his finger to his lips. "Let Lizzie explore. Everybody explores in their own way."

"Okay," I said, frustrated. "Emma always threw out the trash. And Derrick was our next-door neighbor. Our driveway connected with his. So, every time Emma threw out the trash, she'd talk to him."

"Were they boyfriend and girlfriend?"

"No. But I think they liked each other."

"Then what happened?"

"Andrew's window faced the driveway." I huffed. "He saw them talking and got *really* mad. He shouted out the window at Derrick to leave Emma alone. He even talked to Derrick's dad once."

"So," Lydia twirled her hands with impatience, "what happened?"

"Nothing. They moved away. But before they moved, Derrick left a big box on our doorstep. It had a CD player and headphones and tons of CDs."

Someone cracked up.

"Why leave a box of CDs? That's weird."

"Because." I was near tears. "Emma told Derrick she liked music. And we didn't have music in the house. So, he gave us music. I don't know."

"What kind of music did he give you?"

"Everything." I rubbed my eyes. "He gave us everything."

"Like Taylor Swift?"

"Come on," Bethany said. "No boy's going to listen to Taylor Swift. And if he does, it's on the down."

"R.E.M., Rage Against the Machine, Trisha Yearwood." I spewed Emma's CD collection while counting my digits. I glared at everyone while frustration built. "You know, just stuff."

"Damn," Destiny said, "Derrick's all over the place."

"All right," Dr. C interjected. "Now that we have more context, let's discuss the happy memories associated with the music."

I felt Destiny's warm hand squeeze mine. I was doing my best not to cry. Though my eyes welled.

"Lizzie," Dr. C said, "is this more of a sad memory than a happy one?"

"It's both." My voice quivered. "It makes me sad and happy."

"I love those kinds of memories," Becky murmured.

"Well," Dr. C crossed his legs and peered at me, "often happy memories are associated with sad moments. This is our brain's way of processing trauma. What you're experiencing," Dr. C finger quoted, "is textbook normal. And it's okay to feel all these feelings at one time."

"Dr. C," Bethany pointed out, "you're not supposed to say *normal*."

"Yes, Bethany," Dr. C's eyes swirled, "you're right. I don't enjoy using the word *normal*. Especially for mental health. We all process differently. There's no such thing as normal. Everybody's normal is different. Which cancels out the definition of normal. But in this context, I'm just making a point. Please continue."

"Emma and I, we'd sneak downstairs and listen to music at night while everyone was asleep. Emma would get silly. And I would too. They didn't allow us to get silly. We had to be..." I peered at everyone, hoping for positive confirmation. But everyone had sad eyes.

"Please continue, Lizzie," Dr. C gave me that stern glance of his.

"Perfect," I said, almost relieved. "We had to be perfect. We had to be super quiet."

"And what did the music provide you?"

"We could finally be ourselves," I said in a faraway voice, a voice tumbling down a well. "Music kind of set us free, I guess."

Dr. C motioned me to continue, even though I didn't want to. I could feel the tears bubbling to the surface

"When we danced and listened to music and laughed, it was like we were living someplace else. Someplace magical. Our house just faded away. Everything did. I don't know where we ended up. But it was just far away from Andrew." I began crying.

"Thank you for sharing, Lizzie." Dr. C passed a box of Kleenex down the line so it would reach me. "That was a powerful observation."

Some girls in the group were teary-eyed. I could hear the sniffles ripple around the circle. Destiny held my hand even tighter. And JC was holding my hand too.

"Now," I whimpered, "when I hear certain songs, I cry. I can't help it. Because I think of Emma. Music isn't the same for me anymore. It haunts me."

TWENTY-TWO
FIRST ADVISEMENT

"Your Honor," the prosecutor rose, "the state is requesting a million-dollar bond for Ms. Mondragon."

"Your Honor," Maxine rose too, "my client has a clean record. She doesn't pose a flight risk. She doesn't even have a driver's license. May I remind the court my client is only seventeen."

"A seventeen-year-old who killed her parents and murdered her unborn baby." The prosecutor glared at Maxine. "From what I understand, your client can afford such luxuries."

"Your Honor," Maxine softened her tone, "the prosecution wants to paint my client as a monster any way he can. Ms. Mondragon had undergone an abortion because of a medical emergency that may have cost her life. She has undergone intensive therapy while admitted into psychiatric care. If I may, Your Honor," Maxine gestured Etten to the stand, "Doctor Lee would like to address the court. Ms. Mondragon was under her care before being placed in custody."

"Objection, Your Honor," the prosecutor said. "This is a bond hearing, not a trial."

"Overruled." The judge gave Etten the go-ahead. "The court will allow Doctor Lee to provide more context."

"Good morning, Your Honor." Etten gave Maxine a scared look, though Maxine motioned her to carry on. "Ms. Mondragon has been under my care since January. Patient confidentiality prevents me from discussing our sessions in depth; however, from a clinical standpoint, Ms. Mondragon experienced horrific abuse for most of her life while living in the Mondragon household. I've never treated a patient so severely traumatized. Ms. Mondragon's incarceration is more damaging to her mental and emotional health than the court may realize."

"Your Honor," the prosecutor flips his hands around, "what does this have to do with—"

"Take your seat, Counselor," the judge said. "You'll get your chance."

Etten looked at the prosecutor, then the judge. "Ms. Mondragon is in a fragile state. She went from incarceration to being transferred to psychiatric care at CU. It's crucial for Ms. Mondragon to be placed in a safe and trusting environment."

"Doctor Lee," the judge's tone grew curious, "correct me if I'm wrong, but if Ms. Mondragon is in a fragile state, as you suggest, isn't psychiatric care the safest place for her?"

"No, Your Honor."

The judge rifled through papers. "Correct me if I'm mistaken again," he peered at Maxine, "Counselor, the court agreed to transfer Ms. Mondragon to the psychiatric center, as you requested. Doctor Lee's assessment heavily influenced my decision." The judge looked at Etten, then Maxine. He threw up his hands. "If I may be so frank, what has changed?"

"Your Honor," Etten said, "while under psychiatric care, Ms. Mondragon has undergone several ECT treatments, an abortion procedure, and prescribed countless antipsychotic medications. None of which has been successful. She's not improving."

"Is there a reason she's not improving?"

"Your Honor," Etten gulped hard and folded her hands. "She feels betrayed. She doesn't trust the staff. And trust is an enormous factor for someone who's experienced unthinkable abuse most of their life."

"Is there a reason she doesn't trust the folks down at CU?"

"Your Honor," Etten said, "she believes that someone could have saved her baby. Ms. Mondragon also believes they forced her to have an abortion."

The judge beamed bug eyes. "Did they force Ms. Mondragon to have an abortion, Doctor Lee?"

"No." Etten waved her hands. "The staff acted appropriately under the circumstance and performed a lifesaving procedure. Ms. Mondragon cannot process major life events, including the abortion, while under their care." Etten glared at the prosecutor. "She grew up in an extremely abusive household where she couldn't trust anyone, except for her sister. Her sister committed suicide. Then her parents passed away. I understand that someone murdered an acquaintance at the detention center. Then, they whisked her away to a psychiatric center and performed an emergency abortion. All these situations occurred within a month of each other. Ms. Mondragon needs a safe space to process all these catastrophic events. She will not improve in a hospital setting or jail. These are not suitable environments for her care. The psychiatric center was a temporary solution." She peered at Maxine. "She'll benefit most from intense, one-on-one therapy where she can build trust. Trust is the key here. She requires a stable, controlled environment where she can rebuild her life."

The judge seemed overwhelmed. He sighed.

"Your Honor—"

The judge aimed a finger at the prosecutor. "Counselor, I'm not ready for you. You'll know when I'm ready for you because my eyes will look in your direction. Do I make myself clear?"

"Yes, Your Honor."

"Now have a seat."

"Doctor Lee, Counselor," the judge sat taller, "I suspect you've devised a game plan for Ms. Mondragon."

Maxine stood and looked at Etten. "Yes, Your Honor, we have."

The judge placed his finger on his lip. "Paint me a picture of Ms. Mondragon's financials, Counselor."

"Your Honor," Maxine made eye contact with the prosecutor, "her inheritance is going through formal probate."

"She can't access the funds," the judge said.

"Yes, Your Honor." Maxine peered at Etten. "We're prepared to fund Ms. Mondragon's bond ourselves. But we petition the court to lower the bond."

"Who's *we*, Counselor?"

"Doctor Lee, Hana Yu, and myself."

"I think I've heard enough for today. Ms. Mondragon has no criminal record. Is not a flight risk. From what counsel testified here today, she doesn't pose a danger to society." He sat there for a minute, thinking.

The prosecutor rose, seething.

"I'm releasing Ms. Mondragon on her own recognizance. She will remain in the care of Hana Yu."

"Your Honor!"

"That's my ruling, Counselor."

TWENTY-THREE
R LALIQUE

IT HAD BEEN a week since they let me leave the hospital. I missed Destiny and JC and Becky. I wondered if they mentioned me at group. It's hard to leave your friends behind in a place like that. If I had a choice, I'd free them all. The right way this time.

The winter air was thick and icy as I sat on a stool in the backyard. The smell of tree sap and pine tickled my nose. Emma's camera rested in my frozen, jittery hands. Her camera was all that mattered now.

I sat outside every morning. If I could help it. I wouldn't limit myself to four walls ever again. Vicious dictators were gone for good. Fingers crossed. I felt like I hadn't seen the sun in years. The sky. I felt like juvie and the hospital had buried me deep in the cellar alongside Baby Fay. Because they were good at banishing the light and all those cotton clouds. How would anyone know they existed without the sun?

My lungs burned as though circulating fresh air was toxic to my system. More laborious than huffing artificial. That endless supply of mold and dust and microbial mixed better. The ventilation system at CU must have weakened me.

Hana wanted to celebrate my release by taking me to an Italian restaurant. Instead, the only place I wanted to go was Andrew's home.

The authorities had finally given us the green light after months of fighting.

I paced the house for a little while, alone. Hana stood on the porch until I gave permission to tag along. First upstairs, then down. I stayed in Emma's room for a while, sobbing. The house lay lifeless. Apparitions hiding behind every door. Sort of like a house rescued from a fire. Everything remained untouched and sound, as though salvation were still possible. Except the flame sucked the soul out of everything.

How can you breathe life into soulless things? To be fair, I didn't know how I'd survived in this place as long as I had. But somehow, I did.

Muffy's bowl, where I sometimes poured half-and-half instead of water, was sitting near the kitchen table. And a squeaking-clean tuna can, which Muffy had licked clean, sat beside it. I could still smell tuna residue fuming from the tin. Muffy's bad breath clinging to that bowl. Her essence. Emma's essence. Andrew. Abby.

But I couldn't smell my own, as though I never was. Though, I was here. Even though the house had shunned me. Spit me out onto the street like rain from roof gutters.

Nurse Maggie had said that Muffy had snuck outside when someone left the door wide open. While the paramedics loaded my body into the ambulance. She claimed she'd tried to lure Muffy back in. But Muffy took off instead. Who could blame her? She saw her chance and took it. I'd tried many times. So did Emma. The only ones snug as a bug inside that house were Andrew and Abby.

Although, I suspected Nurse Maggie had lied about doing her best to lure Muffy back inside. Nurse Maggie, as we all know, lied on the fly. She was a beautiful liar. Like me. Maybe she had fallen asleep again. Resting her little face on the kitchen table, power-napping, when the paramedics hauled me away.

I stood in Abby's doorway for a while. I never once laid eyes on her last resting place. Hana noticed Abby's collection of glass figurines. Said they were expensive. R Lalique or something.

Hana asked if I wanted to keep the figurines. I said no without hesitation. My tone raised, as though how dare she ask.

"I want to smash them to smithereens."

Hana put her hand on my shoulder. "Do you have a baseball bat?"

I giggled. "I wish."

"I'll go downstairs and find something."

I gave her my blessing with an encouraging look. Once I heard the steps creaking all the way down, I imagined Hana making her way to the kitchen.

I eased the door shut behind me. Now I was alone in Abby's room. Truth is sobering. I didn't need a bat or mop handle or whatever else to smash these figurines. I had my paws. I had my pain. My anger. And that was enough.

I snatched the first figurine, and I was going to smash it against the wall, but I hesitated. I inspected it. Admired it. I wondered how Abby could love this piece of glass more than she loved me. More than she loved Emma. Why was this naked thing so special? Why wasn't I more precious than a thing?

It just happened. It flew from my hand, sailed through the air, and shattered against the wall. Then I picked up another. And another. Soon, I started screaming. I smashed everything my hands could grab. I went wild. I unleashed everything inside myself. Bloody Jesus hanging on the wall, broken to bits. Glass flying everywhere. Everything shattered. My heart too.

"Lizzie." Hana interrupted my outrage.

When I turned to face her, huffing and puffing, reeling from my hell, Hana flinched. The look on my face repulsed her. My angry, killer-girl eyes. My outburst repulsed her. I repulsed her. And all I could do was crumble to the floor and wail. Worse than Mario. Worse than Lincoln. Worse than the girl on the second story. I did it better.

Once Hana got me to calm down, I collected a few things from Emma's room. The Cure T-shirt, some jeans. It was all just random shit. Shit that was important to my sister. I went downstairs and loaded Emma's CDs into plastic bags and left.

I had to leave. I wasn't strong enough to bear the weight of the house. Of Andrew's sins. Of mine. I wished to remove myself from all this sorrow and death.

Yet, I soon realized a hard reality: I would never be free of this place.

Never. I would never leave it behind in the rearview mirror, like some distant mountain skyline because, somehow, I was stuck on repeat.

TWENTY-FOUR
A MILLION FOLLOWS

"I can't tell you how thrilled I was that you agreed to an interview, Lizzie." Bridgett Pressman's voice was poppy. The *New York Times* columnist had contacted Hana several times for an interview. She scooped both my hands in hers and warmly shook, her eyes drowning in champagne bubbles as though a bad day had never crossed her path.

I didn't know how to respond. I was too nervous.

Bridgett sat on Hana's sofa in the living room and settled in. Hana and Maxine sat on the other side of the room. Etten couldn't make the interview because she had patients to see.

Bridgett set a digital recorder on the coffee table. "I'd like to record our interview. We agreed not to videotape. But a digital recorder helps my process. It's a way for me to go back and retrieve some moments during the interview. That's my process." She laughed. Almost seemed more nervous than me. Maybe she knew I was a killer girl.

I peered at Maxine for guidance. Maxine stood. "Mrs. Pressman, we have no objections to using a recording device; however, we agreed there is to be no discussion of the trial. Or any reference to the death of Ms. Mondragon's parents. No reference. We agreed to grant this interview solely to discuss Ms. Mondragon's photography and art career."

This didn't faze Bridgett. "I'm aware how rare this interview is." She looked at me. "Thank you for allowing us to interview you. I know this is a rare privilege. And I want you to feel comfortable. I want you to just be yourself. If I ask an uncomfortable question, don't feel pressure to answer it. It won't be authentic if it's forced. So, if that happens, let me know, and we'll move on to the next question." She smiled at me. Her teeth glistened like pearls.

I started picking at my thumb cuticle. I fidgeted in my seat.

Bridgett pulled a pad and pen from her bag. "I really enjoy interviewing young people. The youngest person I interviewed was eight years old. I know you'll do great. Trust me, I'm fascinated by young minds. What can I say? I gravitate toward our future leaders."

"Were they an artist too?"

"No," she waved her hand, "he was a math prodigy. But in a way, you could describe math as an art form. He certainly made a convincing argument."

I was trying to relax, but I couldn't. My mind was racing, and the jitters inflamed my knees. I wanted to bounce them. I must have been spilling my nerves, because Hana and Maxine looked worried.

But you wouldn't know it because Bridgett was going about things as though nothing bothered her. If a tornado blew through I'm sure she'd keep on smiling.

"Here we go," Bridgett said, pressing a red button on the digital recorder. "Lizzie, interviewing someone isn't a natural process. Most people aren't comfortable talking about themselves or providing intimate details about their life. I know artists deeply immerse themselves in their private world. Which is how they create masterpieces. What I aspire to do when I interview someone for the first time is capture that moment. I want to help you capture this moment. *Your* moment. The moment you're in right now. What inspires you right now? What drives you right now? What does your world look like right now? That's what I want to capture. So, what I'd like for you to do is stay in this moment, okay?"

"Yes," I said, unsure of myself. Unsure of what Bridgett was talking about.

"I'm going to start off with something easy. What inspired you to pick up the camera and start taking photographs?"

"Well..." I glanced at Hana and Maxine, as though they might help me answer the question, then I turned my attention to Bridgett. "After my sister died..." My eyes welled. I closed them for a second. I knew I could do this. I cleared my throat and looked at Bridgett. I took a deep breath. "I found the camera when I was going through my sister's stuff."

"Is that the same camera around your neck?" Bridgett pointed at Emma's camera.

"Yes." I lifted the camera. "This is Emma's."

"I can't think of one photographer who still uses Polaroid." Emma's camera mesmerized Bridgett. Her eyes told a tale. "Is that why you chose Polaroid as your medium, because it was Emma's camera?"

"Well," I squirmed, "it chose me."

"Lizzie," Bridgett peered at me, "I want to talk about how you found the camera by accident and why you used Emma's camera for your medium."

"I didn't know Emma had the camera. She kept it a secret," I said, my voice stronger than before. "I never saw her use it. Then, after she died, I found it in a shoebox. She kept these photographs in the shoebox too. They were beautiful. I mean, *are* beautiful." I started to tear up again. "I just sort of realized that my sister was a genius. I mean, she was my genius, but I didn't know she was *a* genius. And I couldn't share that moment with her. Does that make sense?"

"Absolutely." Bridgett perched at the edge of her seat. I could see her mind change gears. Her eyes glistened with excitement. "May I see one of your sister's photographs?"

"I can't." I calmed myself, fighting the tears. "They don't belong to me, and I'm not sure Emma would want people to see them. She never let me see them. I feel like I stole something from her by snooping."

"Are your sister's photographs reminiscent of your work?" Bridgett's eyes narrowed.

I shook my head. "Emma was better than me. I tried to snap a good one, but mine looked nothing like hers."

Bridgett dead-eyed me and shook her head. "There was obviously a genetic link between you two girls. It's not uncommon for more than one sibling in the family to be gifted."

"Emma was gifted." I shied away. My eyes landed on the area rug. "I just wanted to see my sister again. I think the camera was important to her. And I thought I might see her again if..."

"Let's travel back in time for a minute to when you discovered the camera inside the shoebox and thumbed through Emma's photographs. From what you describe, this was an emotionally difficult time for you. I would go as far as to call it a pivotal moment. What inspired you to take pictures with Emma's camera?"

"I think I heard Emma say, 'Take a picture of yourself.'"

Bridgett didn't seem stunned by this. She didn't even bat an eye.

"And I did what she told me to do. I took a photo of myself. It felt good. Exciting. Like something great was about to happen. I don't know what, but something." I ripped my thumb cuticle apart. Blood oozed. "I didn't expect Emma's camera to make me feel that way. And I didn't feel alone anymore. I felt like Emma was looking over my shoulder. She was right there. And while I was waiting for the image to develop, I saw..."

"What did you see?" Bridgett hung on my every word.

"My reflection in the mirror."

"What did the reflection tell you?" Bridgett said, as though she was inside my head, rummaging around for the truth. "Did the mirror speak to you?"

"I felt pretty. Maybe beautiful," I said, tears welling again. "I don't know. I just felt beautiful for the first time in my life."

"What did you do next? Did you scrutinize the self-portrait you just took with Emma's camera, or did you scrutinize your reflection?"

"My selfie," I said, annoyed. "I don't even really know the difference between selfie and self-portrait."

Bridgett covered her mouth. I saw a large smile rise out of her hands. She fought not to laugh. To keep her composure. Her professionalism. "You're wise to point that out, Lizzie. I was just as confused as you. So, I had to speak with the curator to find the answer."

"What is it?"

"It can be both. But, in the art world, a selfie is generally considered a replaceable image, disposable even. Easily replaced if one isn't satisfied. Whereas a self-portrait is permanent. Meant to stand the test of time. Not replaceable. I do want to discuss your self-portrait; that is what MoMA has officially named your photograph. But we were onto something just a second ago about your reflection and self-portrait."

"What do you think I should call it?"

"I think, without question, it's a self-portrait. I don't think you meant it any other way. The image is timeless. It will stand the test of time. And I do believe our talents choose us. And even though you may not have meant it consciously, to snap a self-portrait, the artistic side of you, your powerful gift, somewhere in your subconscious, took over. Which is common. Brilliant artists are often tormented by their subconscious mind. The image is truly exceptional. And it's obvious why MoMA chose to acquire the image as part of their permanent collection."

She stared at me. I knew what she wanted from me. I could see it in her eyes. It was my turn now.

"When I saw my self-portrait, I was sad. It didn't match my reflection in the mirror."

"How so?" Bridgett's intrigued eyes narrowed.

"It scared me, and the mirror lied." My eyes rose out of the sadness. "I started thinking maybe Emma's camera was the truth. The real world. And everything else was just...not real. A lie. And Emma's camera was the only way I'd know the truth. The only way to find it."

"Lizzie," Bridgett was now boiling over with intrigue, "you said your self-portrait scared you. Can you elaborate?"

Maxine rose as worry cradled her face. Then Hana rose too.

"I didn't see beauty in my self-portrait. I saw pain. I saw a lost girl. A girl who wore hell, and then some. My picture wasn't as beautiful as Emma's. Emma was taking pictures in heaven. And I was taking pictures in hell. That's what I saw...I saw...I saw."

Bridgett searched my eyes, eager for the words to race from my mouth. But they never did. The moment passed. Tears were forming in her eyes. She collected herself and sat taller.

"I must tell you, I saw your solo exhibition in New York, and your work is," Bridgett squinted, searching for the right words, "ethereal. Dreamlike. I'd even describe some pieces as hauntingly raw. Your pieces invoke haunting emotions. And that's what puzzles the art world. You're only seventeen and using antique equipment to capture images that photographers spend a lifetime to capture. Which, I think it's safe to say, most photographers will never reach the levels you effortlessly do." Bridgett gazed into my eyes with a serious look. "Your photographs are extraordinary, Lizzie. You may see hell in those images, but I see something very different. Yes, I agree some of these images are hard to face. I think there's no other way to capture these moments. That's your artistic subconscious kicking in. And it challenges us to see the world as it is, unfiltered. Yet, you capture people's essence so clearly, so raw, it's deeply poetic. It's painful and beautiful all at once. I'd say if Emma captured heaven, then you're capturing the soul."

I didn't know what to say. What could I say to that?

"When I interview artists, I always ask this question, and I think it's an important one to ask: Do you think your art has the power to influence positive change in the world?"

"No. I can't even change my own world."

"Well, I'm sure millions of followers would disagree. Have you read the latest posts on your fan page? I know I have. And they're inspiring. You've started a movement. Particularly with the unhoused population and survivors of abuse. Those are the images you seem to gravitate to. I mean to say, those are the subject matters you capture in your work."

"I used to get excited to read the latest posts on social media. But now, I don't read them anymore or go on social media."

"Is there a reason you don't go on social media anymore?" Bridgett asked, not allowing me to answer the first question. "People see you as a champion. I suppose you're a social movement of your own. You're a hero to millions of teenage girls. Let's just say that."

"I enjoyed talking to people online at first. Some posts really touched me. Some made me cry, in a good way. The amount of people who believe in me amazed me. Strangers believe in me. It was weird because I don't think I'm special." I looked at Hana and Maxine, then back at Bridgett. "But then some people started posting hate."

"Will you share some comments they posted?"

"Someone, I think it was a girl, said I deserve to die because I was a baby killer."

"How do you know it was a girl?"

"Because another fan hunted her down and found out who she was. He exposed her identity. I guess you can find anyone on the internet."

"Do you mind sharing more?"

"Bridgette," Maxine stood again. "I think we should move on to other topics. This is deeply painful for Lizzie."

I peered at Maxine, then Bridgett. "Are you going to write about this in your article?"

Bridgett looked at me, then Maxine. "I wouldn't write something of this matter in my article. I won't give bullies a platform to celebrate hate. I was more curious on a personal level." She looked at me with sad eyes. "I don't get personal in interviews. I want you to know I'm a fan of yours. So, I'm breaking my rule here. My daughter has experienced similar bullying on social media. I was more curious about how you got rid of these bullies."

"I don't think you can." I try to hold back the concern on my face. "They wished me dead. Someone claimed they'd find me and mutilate my body. A lot of comments about raping me and wanting me dead." I laughed. Not like what I said was funny. It wasn't. That laugh betrayed madness. "How can you do both?"

Bridgett appeared horrified by what I'd said.

"Anyway, fans tried to hunt these trollers down, but it just got worse. It was like a gigantic war had broken out on my fan page. The threats were so scary, I didn't want anyone to get hurt. So I just removed myself from social media. It's calmer now."

"Why do you think so many people wish you harm?"

"Media coverage about the trial. My abortion. The media found out about the abortion and posted it online." I stared in Bridgett's eyes. "That's the thing people don't get. I never wanted an abortion. It wasn't my choice. It was get an abortion or die."

"You made a wise decision, Lizzie. Sounds like it to me. I would have made the same choice without hesitation."

"The doctors made it for me." I laughed again, my eyes swirling around. "I was ready to die for my baby. Thankfully, they intervened. Or I would have died."

"Lizzie," Maxine said, her eyes sharp. "It's best to stick to our talking points. You're skirting a fine line."

"People are just mean." I bobbed my head. "Really mean. People are cruel." I changed my stance because cruel was more fitting. "If your daughter ever needs someone to talk to, I'm here. I know what it feels like when people destroy you on social media. It's soul crushing."

"Lizzie." Maxine raised her tone.

Bridgett appeared spellbound. More like shook. She smoothed her shoulder-length hair and cleared her throat. "Yes. Well. Thank you for that insight." She paused to collect her thoughts. "Oh, yes, are you passionate about topics like abuse and the unhoused? Or do these topics call to you? You know, fuel your artistic expression?"

My heart beat in my throat. Tingles raced beneath my skin like tiny pinballs going in every direction. "As far as that goes, it's always been Emma's choice. She tells me what to do and I do it. I think she wants to tell her story, and the only way she can do that is by telling other people's stories. I think Emma celebrates survivors. Maybe because she didn't survive. I'm just the person looking through the lens and pressing the button. Emma does the rest, mostly."

"Well," Bridgett said, "Emma sounds like a remarkable young woman. And even though Emma is the driving force behind your photographs, you, Lizzie, are remarkable too. Don't let anyone say otherwise. The art world considers you blue chip status."

My face didn't hide the fact that I was clueless. This was the first time I'd heard someone call me "blue chip."

"Blue chip means you're a sound investment. Someone mentioned *bulletproof* to me the other day. So, there you have it, you're bulletproof."

"Bulletproof," I giggled, "I wish."

"Oh, I think it's safe to say this is another record. You're the youngest blue chip artist in history. This is unprecedented because you haven't established a well-known body of work. You're sitting alongside the likes of Adams. In fact, they're calling you the Adams of the twenty-first century. Not in the technical sense. Adams cast a light on the west.

Rather, you cast a light on social topics of the twenty-first century. People who are invisible in the public eye. Sexual abuse survivors, for example. You're a big deal. Your art is now considered a bulletproof investment that will only grow more valuable as the years march ahead. Meaning, your children, and many more, will see your art hanging in the finest museums all over the world. What do you think about that?"

I liked when Bridgett said *big deal*. It just sounded dreamy.

"I hope I remain bulletproof," I said playfully.

Bridgett reached in her bag and fished out a business card. She scribbled a phone number on the back of the card alongside a name: *Phoebe*.

"My daughter's a big fan." Bridgett handed me the card. "Your encouragement would mean a lot to her, I'm sure."

"Is this her cell phone number?"

"Yes."

"Hana just bought me a cell phone. I can text her." I placed my digit on my chin. "But I enjoy talking to people over the phone better. I like hearing people's voices."

"Yes." Bridgett smiled. "We're of the same mind. Listen, you're the real deal, Lizzie. I know you may not agree to another interview, and I can't fault you for that, but I'm fascinated by your story. You're one of the most interesting people I've covered. You were unfiltered with me, just as your photographs are. Would you consider allowing me another interview?"

I thought for a moment. My lips squeezed together. "Yes, but I have a request."

"Okay." Bridgett's curiosity was on high alert.

"I'd like to take a picture of you."

"Of me?" Bridgett's eyes widened. She began to fidget with her neckline.

"Yes."

"What would you do with it?"

"Give it to you."

"Me?"

"You gave me something special today, and it's my turn to give you something."

"I'd love for you to take my picture, but I'm unclear what I gave you?"

"You're going to tell the world about Emma," I said as though it should be painfully obvious. "Your words will allow her to live on. Her story will live on too. That's a gift. That's all I want. That's all I ever wanted."

TWENTY-FIVE
CHASING BOMBOLONE

"Is everything okay?" Hana asked. "You've been quiet today." A nervous laugh escaped. Then she pointed at my plate. "You haven't touched your food."

The waiter bombarded our booth with two glasses of cucumber water before I could answer, then planted more silky napkins on the table.

Hana had ordered truffle tagliatelle. The creamy sauce kept spraying all over the white linen tablecloth whenever she twirled her fork a little too fast to scoop the pasta.

"Can I get you anything else?" the server said. She looked Emma beautiful. A real toughie, though. Emma was a real toughie. I thought I was a real toughie too, though having to be courageous isn't the same as being courageous.

I imagined a stylist had shaved the side of her hair. And left the outside long and flowy. Exact in every way. She folded and hiked her pressed sleeves to her elbows. Reveling geometric tattoos printed on both arms. Moon. Sun. Stars. Brail. Her arms bore a roadmap to the universe. She didn't wear hell and then some. Instead, she wore a treasure map to the cosmos. Wherever she was going, I wanted to join her.

172

Hana peered at me with those eyes, desperate to read my mind. "What's going on inside there?" she often asked. I thought I scared her a little. And I thought she believed, if she could read my mind, the world would right itself. Or, even better, I would right myself. I wished that were true. I wished you could read someone's mind and right all the wrongs the world could ever hurl. But that only happens in fairy tales.

"No," Hana said to the waitress. "I think we're all set. Thank you so much." Hana added "so" to everything. It was sweet.

You know someone's kind when they're nice to servers. Because, usually, if someone is kind to a server, they're kind to everyone else. And that was true in Hana's case.

Hana had kind eyes. Kindness radiated from her like a bright star. It was clear to see. Just as clear as evil. It was the ones where you couldn't read past the facade that scared me the most.

Italian food was my favorite, and I was still searching for those bombolone I ate in New York. No restaurant in Denver served them. Anyway, today, right before we walked into this fancy Italian restaurant, an older gentleman was standing on the corner with a cardboard sign. It read: *Lost my wife. Lost my dog. Let's be real. I need a beer.*

Hana handed the gentleman a twenty. The gentleman gave her a hug with tears in his eyes. I asked him what his name was. He said, "Roger." His voice was hoarse. The sun must have dried up whatever liquid remained in him. I could tell he hadn't moved from that spot in days. Light snow had collected around him and then froze to a sheen. Neither drink nor food sat near him. His hands wouldn't stop shaking as he held the sign. I imagined he hadn't eaten today. I imagined Roger was siphoning fumes.

I carried my Polaroid camera around my neck everywhere I went. I couldn't hear Emma anymore. ECT had wiped her voice from my mind. But sometimes I saw her when I snapped a picture, clear as a cloudless day.

"It's great to meet you, Roger." I shook his hand with confidence and brought attention to the camera around my neck. "You caught my eye. May I take your picture?"

At first, he looked a little embarrassed and shy. I thought he figured I was poking fun at him. Funny thing is people often get fidgety when a stranger asks to take their picture. I guided his hand and said, "If you allow me to take your picture, I promise I'll be kind and respectful. I want to capture you as you are right now."

Hana had helped me come up with that last part. It worked most of the time. It was all in how you said it. If you said the wrong thing, using the wrong tone, well, then good luck. You might get your lights knocked out. And you should. Because names hurt.

Roger fixed his hair. Tucked his shirt deep in his pants. Then tightened his belt. His bangs covered his right eye, so I tucked the strands behind his ear to help. Getting into Roger's personal space made me realize how handsome Roger was. I bet he was a real dreamboat at my age. "Where should I stand?" he asked, shuffling this way and that. "Right here or over there."

"Stand where you're most comfortable," I said, squinting through the lens. "You don't have to smile or pose. Just find a comfortable spot and be yourself. Like I wasn't even here."

I saw Hana out of the corner of my eye, standing at a distance. She patiently waited for me to take his picture and allowing Roger and me more room to work. Roger stood on the corner and leaned against the metal pole of a street sign, assuming a stoic stance. I saw his thoughtful eyes, which lead to the heart. He smiled a humble smile, then said, "Is this good?"

I pursed my lips tight because I was peering through the lens. "Are you comfortable?"

"Yeah." He looked uncomfortable, but he wouldn't admit it. I never did either.

"Give me a sec."

I thought Roger figured something was wrong. His face grew concerned. "I'm okay. It just takes me a bit. I only have one shot at this. And I want to get it right."

Part of that statement was true, but some was a lie. I waited to see if Emma would grace the lens today. I spent most of my picture-taking time waiting for her. If Emma didn't grace the lens in thirty seconds, I took the picture. If she graced the lens, then I waited thirty seconds more before I snapped the picture. I held on to Emma as long as I could.

You want to know something crazy? If Emma graced the lens, her

Polaroids went for six times the amount. Just recently, one of Emma's Polaroids sold for eighty-eight grand. Thanks to an anonymous buyer from Houston. People all over the world bought Emma's Polaroids. Places I'd never heard of. Even famous people bought Emma's Polaroids. Emma was a stardust angel behind the Polaroid. Let's not forget, this was Emma's camera. I was just keeping it warm for her until we met again.

Lucky for both of us, Emma graced the lens today. And it was a glittering day. I waited thirty seconds, enough time for Emma to fade away. I closed my eyes and whispered, "I love you," because she was inside the lens. Then I snapped the picture. And also, you should always tell people you love—I love you—because you never know.

I fanned the Polaroid between my thumb and forefinger away from the light to develop the image. I yanked my Sharpie from my back pocket and signed my name on the white border. I handed Roger the picture. "Thank you for trusting me."

"What's this for?" He was puzzled by the Polaroid in his hand.

"It's yours."

Roger inspected the photo. He played with his hair some more, as though looking at his reflection. He stroked his cheek. He was mesmerized as he showed me the photo, disbelief in what his eyes were telling him. "Is this what I look like?"

I nodded.

He tried to hand back the photograph.

"No, that's yours."

He stared at it a little longer. "This is art. I can't believe this is me."

I handed him a business card from the gallery. Jamie Hart was my handler.

"What's this for?"

"You can keep it. Or sell it."

He held the photo to his chest. "Why would I do something like that?"

"Just in case."

"I'm never goanna sell it, ma'am."

That was the first time someone has called me ma'am. "Well, if you change your mind, call them first. They'll sell it at a good price."

Roger inspected the picture again, as though it were a precious heirloom instead of a photograph. "Thanks, but I'm keeping this. You don't sell something like this."

What I'd learned along the way was, sometimes you had to let go of your angels. Not forever. For a little while. Until you met again. Because you would meet again.

Before Emma passed, she'd told me she couldn't wait to become a Stardust Angel. But just like everything in our lives, the key ingredient was to endure before we could claim the prize. "Essentially," Emma had said, "the universe has to feast on your dead body first. Tissue and bones. Basically, your entire existence until there's nothing left. That's the price. But after that, you come back as a guardian of the universe. As a Stardust Angel." She'd told me we came from stardust, and we returned to stardust once we died. And, within a blink, I'd become a Stardust Angel too. Join her somewhere in the universe so we could be together.

"Where did you go just now?" Hana asked, returning my mind to the Italian restaurant.

I glanced at the pasta sitting in my bone-colored, geometric bowl. "I guess."

"Lizzie," Hana scrunched her brow and reached her hand over the table to squeeze my wrist. "Is there something on your mind?"

Hana's eyes were so gentle. She'd make a perfect mother. I wish I'd had a mom like her.

I pulled my hand free. "I want to tell you something, but I'm afraid of what you'll think of me."

"Afraid?" Hana perked her posture and placed her hands on the table, one on top of the other, as though she were anxious. "Tell me, you don't have to be scared."

I held my breath and said in a quick swoop, "I want to go to Norway. I need to go there."

"Oh, okay." Hana smiled with relief, hand clutching heart. "I can take some time off this summer, maybe two or three weeks."

My face turned grimmer. "No, what I meant to say is, I need to go to Norway alone." Why? Because Emma had loved Norway. She always talked about going there.

Hana's eyes inspected mine. Trying to read my mind. "Oh, I don't think that's possible."

"I have my passport now."

"Yes." Hana sat even taller. "That's true, but—"

"I have money too."

"Yes."

"I need to go to Norway."

"Lizzie, the court appointed me as your guardian. And I'm your conservator as well. I have legal obligations set by the court."

"Hana..." I could feel the tears activating. My voice cracked. "I can't stay here."

"Why not?" Hana's pulse appeared to be racing. "Is this because of Graham?"

"I'm not a good person," I said, a few tears drooling from my eyes. "You deserve a good person in your life."

Hana grabbed my wrists. "Lizzie. You *are* a good person. You're so kind. And you have a big heart."

"I murdered them, Hana. I murdered Andrew and Abby," I whimpered. "I researched it on the internet. I knew what I was doing. Don't you understand? I murdered them on purpose. I wanted them dead."

Hana's grip weakened. Her thoughts were transparent. Her eyes told the tale, sparkling with heartbreak and betrayal. I knew that look because it had belonged to me first. Or perhaps Emma. Hana's hands retreated.

Now, the tears were flowing fast. My body was trembling. "I don't regret what I did. That's why I can't stay here anymore. It hurts too much."

Hana sat speechless. Her hand hovering over her mouth. Branded by the look of betrayal. After a few seconds, Hana opened her mouth to say something, when a little girl walked up to our table. She had dark hair like Baby Fay. She bore a strong resemblance.

I quickly mopped my face with my sleeve.

"Excuse me, miss, are you Lizzie Mondragon?" Her voice was precious. The little girl was maybe eleven.

I cleared my weak voice. I tried to smile, but it crumbled on the way up. "I'm Lizzie."

The little girl's mother was hovering close. She had dark hair too. She was a mirror image of the little girl. "My name's Rebecca." The girl pointed at her chest.

I saw something hiding in Rebecca's hand. "I like your name, Rebecca." I glanced at Hana. She'd composed herself. A fake smile on her lips. I'd never seen Hana fake anything. And she was good at it. Girls may be inherently better at hiding whatever horror comes their way.

Rebecca handed me a pen that had a fuzzy gremlin for an eraser and a glittery pad of paper. "Can I have your autograph?"

"Sure." I smiled big, tears swimming. I took the pen and pad.

"I want to be a photographer just like you. I'm saving my allowance so I can buy a camera like yours."

Her mother was smiling behind Rebecca, wearing proud eyes.

"These are scarce." I stopped signing the pad midstroke. I looked up, and out of the corner of my eye, I saw Emma standing beside Rebecca, almost protective. My sister was no longer an apparition of the lens. No longer tethered to the house. Or any other. That included me. She was finally tangible. Real. But mostly, she was free to do as she pleased. Everyone wanted my sister's camera. Or one like it. It was at this moment I saw my sister's purpose. My purpose. This is how stardust angels are formed. I unlatched the strap around my neck and handed Emma's camera to Rebecca.

Hana rose. "Lizzie." She raised her voice, as though trying to prevent an accident.

I didn't know what I was doing. My mind, my hands no longer belonged to me. Rebecca tilted the camera this way and that. Inspecting certain details. Amazed by the buttons. Just like I was when I'd first held Emma's camera shortly after she'd died. "This was my sister's." My voice was ready to wail. Heartbreak energy. "I want you to take care of it. It's very special."

"Is it a magic camera?"

"Yeah," I cried. "Magic."

"Ma'am." Hana's eyes were flashing caution. "Your daughter can't have the camera."

"This is my heart." My vision blurred.

Rebecca's mother peered at Hana, then me. "Rebecca, give it back."

I locked eyes on Rebecca's mother. "My sister wants Rebecca to have it."

"No." Rebecca's mother shook her head. "We can't accept this."

Rebecca tried to return the camera, but I forced it back into her hands. I peered at Hana. "Emma's finally free. I'm sorry. I don't deserve your forgiveness."

Then I turned around and headed for the entrance of the restaurant. Fast as I could, before my heart exploded into smithereens in front of all those strangers.

TWENTY-SIX
SPRING TO FALL

I MADE it halfway down the block. My vison slurry. I felt aimless and lost in an alien world. When I heard Hana screaming my name in the distance, I could smell Emma's shampoo sifting through the air. I could feel Emma. She was collapsing all around me.

I continued to walk fast until everything inside disintegrated. I collapsed onto the sidewalk and wailed. Pedestrians stared at me as they made their way to wherever they were going. Watching a girl fall to pieces in the middle of lunch hour traffic seemed to them—a typical Monday on the Sixteenth Street Mall.

Hana caught up and helped me to my feet. I couldn't stop this thunderous crying. Hana kept saying, "We can go back and get the camera."

"I can't breathe," I managed to say through the tears. My body was trembling.

Once we got to the car, Hana called Etten over Bluetooth. I was inconsolable. The pain was too great. I couldn't catch my breath. "Etten, it's Hana," her voice riddled with panic. I figured Etten could hear me crying in the background. "Lizzie gave Emma's camera to some girl. What do I do?"

"Hana, listen to me carefully." Etten paused, her voice high alert.

"Lizzie, remember the coping strategies. Remember to take deep breaths. In through the nose, exhale through the mouth. Remember the strategies."

"I can't breathe!"

"What the hell do I do? I've never seen her like this."

"Shit," Etten's voice was terrified. "Drive her home quickly. I'll meet you there."

"I can't breathe!"

"Should I take her to the emergency room?"

"No. She's at a critical point. Taking her to the emergency room poses more risk. She's traumatized by hospital settings now. Drive to the house. I'm heading there now. Lizzie, remember the breathing exercises. Remember how to use touch therapy?"

"She's nodding."

"Good. If one doesn't work, move on to the next until you find the one that works. Breathe in through the nose, out through the mouth. Remember, tap, tap, tap, tap. Hana, does Lizzie have her fidget spinner?"

"Lizzie, did you bring it with you?" Hana whispered. I saw the tears in her eyes. I'd broken her heart.

I screamed.

TWENTY-SEVEN
COVET

I DON'T KNOW how far we drove, but I reached a wall I couldn't climb. "Stop the car!"

Hana looked at me with those eyes. I was still wailing. Hyperventilating. She pulled to the side of the road. The car screeched to a halt, and I flung open my door. I tried to get out, but I collapsed into myself again. The world turned to starlight around me.

Hana ran over to the passenger's side and kneeled to meet my eye. "Lizzie, I'm right here. I won't leave you. I would never leave you."

I peered at her, and my face melted into a sad clown face. My voice shattered into a thousand pieces on the side of the road like those R. Lalique's did. "My heart hurts so bad. I can't carry this anymore. Why does it hurt so bad?" I bawled my fist. "I didn't think letting Emma go would hurt this bad. Why did Emma have to die? Why did Baby Fay have to die? What kind of world is this?"

"Listen to me," Hana cradled my shoulders. "I love you. We'll get through this."

I squeezed Hana so tight. Not for love. Not for what she'd just said a second ago but because I'd reached the precipice of hurt. "Tell me how to stop the pain. How do I get rid of it?"

"I don't know..." Hana's voice was only pieces.

WHEN PAIN SPILLS in every direction, you try to outrun it using the power of your mind. The pain comes in waves. In one moment, you convince yourself you can run a little faster, longer. Then you cry even more. But when the pain reaches your soul, there's nowhere left to run.

I cried. Then I calmed down. Then I cried more. Each perceived victory spurred a renewed descent. No matter where my eyes landed, I saw Emma. Every detail in my mind brought her back.

The moment the car reached the driveway, Etten was waiting for us. Maxine was there too. Etten was carrying her medical bag. They both wore funeral faces.

Maxine kept fidgeting with her hands. Hana helped me to my room, while Etten and Maxine followed close behind. I laid in bed, turned to my side, and kept sobbing.

"Lizzie," Etten walked over to my side of the bed and drew a syringe and vial from her medical bag, "I'm going to give you a sedative. It's going to make you sleepy."

I shook my head. Etten had given me a sedative before. Sedatives helped me when I got like this. Although Hana was probably right—I had reached a new milestone.

The smell of rubbing alcohol filled my nose. The needle looked jumbo gauge and a mile long. She injected the icy liquid into my vein. I heard a train sounding its horn in the distance. I didn't even feel the needle prick my skin. And within minutes, I was erased from this place.

I ENVISIONED this happened after Etten injected me with a bottle of eraser:

"What the hell happened?" Etten said, while standing in the hallway. "She was making actual progress."

"Shhh," Hana whispered and gestured. "Let's talk in the kitchen."

They slipped into the kitchen and sat at the table. Hana stared off into space. "What happened?"

"I don't know." Hana flailed her hands. "Today she was very quiet.

She didn't eat much. She didn't say much. I thought she was having a down day. I thought going to an Italian restaurant would cheer her up."

"Did you ask her how she was feeling before you took her there?" Etten asked.

"Yes, Etten." Hana sharpened an eye. "Of course I asked her. I talked to her. She kept saying everything was fine. What was I supposed to do? You told me not to force her to talk about things. You told me just to observe when she retreated into herself. You told—"

"Okay." Etten held out a hand. "I'm sorry, I'm just," she tilted her hand, "I'm too emotionally involved. I never get involved with my patients' personal lives. It's unethical. How can I treat her when I'm too emotionally involved?"

Maxine snickered. "We're all emotionally attached to Lizzie. We've crossed many lines, professionally speaking." Maxine peered at Hana. "Why did she give her camera away?"

Hana gave them a grave look. "That's not the worst part. It's what she said before she gave Emma's camera to the little girl." Hana's eyes rose high.

"Okay," Etten said, "let's take a breather."

"Lizzie took a man's picture on the street. She seemed fine. She started talking a little more, so I thought everything was fine. Then we ordered food at the restaurant. But she got quiet again. And she didn't touch her food. I asked if she was hungry..."

"What, Hana?" Maxine revealed her palms. "You're making me nervous."

"Spit it out," Etten said.

"She then told me...well...that she killed her parents...on purpose." Hana was on the verge of tears.

"That's not uncommon," Etten said. "Patients who've faced extreme trauma can feel responsible. They can even fantasize about killing their parents. Some patients hallucinate and think they've murdered someone."

"No, Etten." Hana glanced at both of them with serious eyes. "She searched the internet on how do to it. She did it on purpose. You weren't there. She looked me square in the eye and said, *I killed them on purpose*. And she meant it. She confessed. She asked me to forgive her."

"My God." Etten covered her face. "I'm legally obligated to report premeditated murder. I could lose my license if I don't."

"Did you know?" Hana glared at Maxine.

"Lizzie never confessed."

"Then you suspected?"

"I didn't ask Lizzie if she committed murder."

"But you knew."

"I suspected she might have toyed with the idea. Flesh-eating chemicals. Oil drums. Tarps in the cellar. It was suspicious."

Hana's eyes narrowed. "Why didn't you tell us that?"

"Listen," Maxine raised her tone and pointed at Etten, then Hana, "I was protecting you and you and Lizzie. What does it matter anyway?"

"Do you realize how traumatizing that can be for a young girl to carry that bullshit around for the rest of her life?" Hana said.

"Do *you*?" Maxine shifted her fingers. "Do you think Lizzie should go to jail?"

Hana got quiet.

"Nobody wants to answer now, huh? Lizzie doesn't deserve to spend the rest of her life in jail. You told me yourself, Etten. It's nearly impossible to win an insanity plea. Lizzie killed her parents under the greatest trauma most of us will never comprehend. The world is better off without Andrew Mondragon. I don't care how he died. She killed them to save the baby. To save herself." Maxine looked at both of them. "A good attorney knows when to keep their mouth shut. I knew better than to ask the question."

"That's not the point." Hana stared at Maxine in disbelief. "We went to the same law school."

Maxine sharpened her glare. "I'm a criminal-defense attorney. There's a difference. You know what I meant." Maxine then glared at Etten. "You're not required by law to report what you've heard here today. You came here as a friend, not as a psychiatrist. This is a moral dilemma, not a legal one. I think we," Maxine shifted her fingers in each direction, "should agree right now to carry this secret to the grave. We owe her that much."

"Tell me you didn't know, Etten!"

"Well." Etten gave a guilty look.

"You knew?"

"Yes."

"Aren't you supposed to report that?" Hana said. "I mean, you could lose your license and everything, remember?"

"Listen," Etten flailed her hands, "before you get all self-rightness, let me explain."

"Oh," Maxine glared, "I should step out."

"Sit down," Hana shouted.

Maxine raised her hands in surrender.

"That took a lot of trust and courage for her to confess to you." Etten said.

"Courage?"

"You know what, Hana, get a grip. She was only a danger to Andrew and Abby. And guess what? They're dead."

"Amen to that." Maxine smiled.

"What do we do now?" Hana said.

"We do nothing," Maxine said. "Nobody needs to know. We stay the course and help Lizzie as best we can."

"I gave her a sedative." Etten's eyes landed on the granite countertop.

"She wants to travel to Norway."

"Norway?" Etten and Maxine said at the same time.

"She doesn't have a passport." Maxine looked at Hana. "Right?"

Hana shrugged. "Well, she does now. She wants to go alone. She says it hurts too much living here. That's where Emma wanted to go"

"What else did she say?" Etten said.

"That she's a bad person and doesn't deserve good people in her life." Hana started crying.

"Hana, honey." Maxine scrunched her face and squeezed Hana's arm.

"First Graham, now Lizzie." Hana said. "What should I do? Should I let her go?"

Maxine looked at Etten. "Lizzie isn't in a healthy space right now. Allowing her to travel to Norway by herself would be reckless. She could hurt herself. Her sister committed suicide, let's not forget that. Her family history isn't great with mental health. From what Lizzie shared during our sessions, I believe her father suffered from severe mental illness."

"You think?" Maxine said.

"She could get kidnapped," Etten said, ignoring Maxine's comment.

"You weren't there." Hana peered at Etten. "She had broken down. She said her heart hurt so bad. If you could have heard her voice. There was nothing I could do to make things better. I couldn't help her."

"I think you should let her go," Maxine said.

"Maxine!" Etten chimed in. "Why are we entertaining this? Lizzie is a severally traumatized child with years of psychological, emotional, and physical abuse. And now we're just going to let her travel to Norway, on the other side of the planet?"

"Do we know anyone in Norway?" Maxine said.

Etten gave Maxine a side-eye.

"Yeah," Hana sniffled.

"Who?" Etten and Maxine said.

"You know who," Hana said, annoyed. "Alexa Whitmore."

"Alexa Whitmore moved to Norway?"

"Yeah," Hana said. "Don't you remember from the reunion? Alexa told me she was moving her clothing business to Norway because the country was innovative and had a stable economy." Hana wiped her tears.

"I don't think Alexa would be a good mentor," Maxine said.

Hana glared at Maxine. "I know. You asked if we knew anyone in Norway. We do."

"Okay."

"That still doesn't explain why Lizzie gave Emma's camera away," Etten said. "We all know how important that camera is to Lizzie. That's her lifeline."

Hana gave a frightful glare and said, "It's Emma's birthday today."

"Shit," Maxine spewed. "That explains it."

"That's the problem," Hana said. "Emma was Lizzie's world. We didn't take that into account. We're too damn concerned about the camera when we should have focused on Emma."

"We should have focused on Emma *and* the camera." Maxine gave a sympathetic smile.

"But the fucking camera," Etten whined, raising a fist.

"I know, Etten, I tried to get it back from that little girl, but Lizzie wouldn't let me."

"You should have stood your ground and taken it back."

"Just listen for one second." Hana wiped more tears. "After she told me she'd killed her parents, a little girl walked up to our table and requested an autograph. That happens a lot now when we go places. People just walk up to her, requesting autographs. She has a following."

"Five million, I heard," Maxine muttered.

Hana's eyes sparkled with disbelief. "Her last photograph sold for eighty-eight grand. You should see her bank account."

"Well," Maxine said, "that explains a lot. She has the funds. She has a passport."

"She's still seventeen," Etten pointed out. "You're the legal guardian. Besides, I doubt the airlines would allow a seventeen-year-old to buy a ticket to Norway and travel there by herself."

"Don't be so sure," Maxine said, "my nephew traveled to Europe on his own, and he's only thirteen."

"If you could have heard how devastated Lizzie sounded. It's heartbreaking. That's the important part you guys are missing. The things that happened to her in that house are so evil, so painful. I don't think we can help her. I don't know if anyone can. I think we might do Lizzie more harm."

"I completely disagree," Etten said. "You're right, though, that Lizzie went through hell in that house. Nobody's arguing that. Lizzie didn't have a safe space to process trauma she experienced, before us. Much less express those deeply painful feelings. It takes time. Trust. It doesn't happen overnight." Etten grabbed a bottled water and took a swig. "Everything you just said, aside from that last part, is the biggest reason not to let her go."

TWENTY-EIGHT

WHAT A BOTTLE OF
ERASER CANNOT REMOVE

I woke up at 5:03 a.m. The sun still slumbered in the east while the light scattered everywhere else. I thought I'd woken inside Andrew's world again—the day after I did what I did. Andrew's house had never been so empty and soundless before that day. Hana's house had a similar aura when nothing stirred in the twilight.

I didn't dream of Emma. Sedatives had a funny way of stealing things from me. Stealing things I cherished most. ECT stole things from me too. Now I knew what I had to do to stop the world from stealing whatever I had left.

Emma had taught me so many things. The one that stood out the most was that when there was no one left to protect you from harm, you had to first protect yourself.

Dr. C had told the group that you must stabilize yourself before helping others. Even if both of you are lying on the floor, bleeding to death. First, save yourself.

At first, I thought that was cruel. Though Dr. C was good at explaining his analogies. If you don't stop yourself from bleeding out, you'll die before you can save the person next to you.

And then it hit me. That's what had happened to Emma. She'd tried stopping me from bleeding out. And ignored her own injuries and bled out first. I guess her blood flowed faster than mine. Emma was faster at everything. Even dying.

My path was foggy before I gave away Emma's camera. I wandered through the jungle in darkness, searching for my place. Trying to figure out where I belonged. Who I belonged to. What I belonged to. And then when I gave away Emma's camera, unbelievable pain struck me down. This was no ordinary pain. This pain also provided a gentle light. This light gave me the ability to see far as I could. I saw everything I ever needed to in one glance.

Soon, gentle snow would fall on Denver and pack the corners of windows and doorways and sidewalks and streets and park benches. You could smell the wet pavement in the air. You could smell it sweating from evergreens when they rocked in the wind gushing from the summit. The grass still sharp enough to poke through the ice. The sidewalks glistening. The smell of winter infecting everything it touched. Inhaling and exhaling all that lived among.

All those things I'd miss. Funny thing is the things I'd miss the most were the simple things I saw every day. The things that grow on you. Absorb you. Become you.

These were the things I would miss the most. The smell of snow in the air. Pine sap drooling outside my window. The mountain skyline that hugs the city. Those mountains growing more invisible by the day. Not because you were weary of looking at them but because your eyes had grown comfortable with the image living inside your head. And now these things that were once a wonder were invisible to you. They saw you, but you didn't see them. Not anymore.

And if you thought I would drink a gallon of bleach like Emma or run in the bathroom and end my life, you were mistaken. Emma did what she did so I could live. So I could have a real life. And I wouldn't dishonor my sister in that way. I chose to live so that Emma would live too.

❖

Jonathan Jackson sent a package along with a letter, gifting me a rare Polaroid camera. Only a handful remain. One sits in a museum somewhere.

The camera had belonged to his father and had been sitting, get this, in a shoebox for twenty years. Small world, right? He'd inherited the camera after his father had died. It had been collecting dust in a safe somewhere in Vermont.

Jonathan Jackson described his late father as a wildlife enthusiast. He loved birds. He loved snapping photos of birds and animals and nature. His father aspired to be a photographer but relied on his day job as a school janitor to make ends meet for their small family. It took his father over two years to scrape together enough money to buy the camera. Money was very tight.

So, when Jonathan Jackson read my story in the *New York Times*, the rare Polaroid camera came to mind. He had forgotten about the camera and put it in a safe.

My story inspired him, and he shipped the camera. In his letter, written from a typewriter, he wrote:

Ms. Lizzie Mondragon,

> *I'm a little embarrassed and humbled to admit I have never heard of you before reading your news article in the New York Times. Your story touched me deeply. After reading your article, I searched the internet for examples of your work. I say this with most sincerity, your photographs meet the level of some of the greatest photographers of our time. I send my father's Polaroid camera to you in hopes my father's dream to become a photographer lives within you. I know you will continue to create masterworks with your ability, and I humbly ask for you to accept my father's camera. Not as charity but as encouragement to continue the work you do. Frankly, the world is a better place because of people like you. I know my father, were he still alive, would have gladly helped a fellow photographer.*

Jonathan Jackson must have shed a few tears when he mailed his father's camera. Think about it. He'd kept his father's camera in a safe all those years. It must have caused him mixed emotions. I know it broke my heart to give Emma's camera to Rebecca. But it was time for me to listen. Instead of doing. Maybe when Rebecca's ready, she'll pass it along to someone in need, like herself. And so maybe Jonathan Jackson was hoping his father's camera would live longer in my hands than hiding in a safe. Which it would. And I intended to honor Jonathan Jackson's wishes.

I sent Jonathan Jackson a heartfelt letter in response, along with a signed Polaroid. I took a couple weeks to mail the letter because Emma had refused to grace the lens. I waited a while to capture her. I almost gave up. I thought Emma had ditched me for good. But then a little yellow bird perched on the windowsill one morning when a drizzle had swept through. And a gray blanket swallowed the sky. I ran to my bedroom and snatched Emma's camera, hoping I had enough time to snap a photograph before that bright bird fluttered away and evaporated in all that cold and dismal. And I made it. And Emma graced the lens.

Jonathan Jackson gave me the essence of his father. And I gave him Emma. Fair is fair. From one heart to the next.

Hana would never let me leave. They would do anything in their power to keep me here. Not out of spite but out of fear. And I wouldn't live in fear anymore. I couldn't stay anymore. Home was where Emma was. Emma was always home. If I stayed here, I would end up like Emma, and I needed to stop the bleeding.

Etten had explained during one of our sessions, about not rushing into reliving past traumas. She told me it could be dangerous if I tried to confront everything all at once and that I should only face things head-on when ready.

The truth was, I relived these traumas every day. Denver was where Emma and I had taken care of each other. Denver was where my story began. And every day it destroyed a piece of me. I didn't want Denver to be the place where my story ended.

No matter how much I googled. Prepared for the unexpected. The people I loved the most always fell away from me. For the first time, I googled nothing. For the first time, I learned to live. I was bound by nothing. Our freedom belonged to us.

I quickly packed essentials into a small carry-on Hana bought me before we flew to New York. Much of my carry-on consisted of film, along with clothes and toiletries. I looped Mr. Jackson's Polaroid strap around my neck. It hung lower than Emma's, the weight heavier. But I liked it. His camera had more buttons. I didn't know what they did yet, but I'd find out.

While I waited for my Lyft driver, I wrote Hana a letter. I didn't know where I'd end up. I only knew where my first destination was— Norway. And sometimes, that's plenty. And I wanted Hana to know where I was going and that I'd be okay.

Without Hana, Maxine, and Etten, I wouldn't be going anywhere. I'd probably be living in the hospital still. Or worse, serving time in prison.

I wondered if they realized they'd already saved my life. And that I was so grateful to have found them. Well, they found me. Maybe they looked at my departure as a failure, but it was really a win.

I was scared too. But what isn't scary in life?

TWENTY-NINE
SMALL WORLD

The Lyft driver parked near the curb at the departure area of DIA. "Do you know what airline flies to Norway?"

"Norway..." I could see him staring at me in the rearview mirror, thinking. "That's a million miles from here."

"Yeah," I smiled.

"Try Virgin Airlines."

"Okay, thanks."

"No, no." He placed a finger on his lip. "Better yet, try American. They fly anywhere in the world. You can't go wrong with American. My sister says they're the best."

"Okay. Thank you, sir." I got out of the car.

"Hold on." He peered at me with vetting eyes. "You look familiar. I've seen you somewhere." He squinted his eye at me. "Do you live in the Capitol Hill area?"

I shook my head. "I better get going. It's cold."

"Okay, sorry, you just look very familiar."

"I can take your picture if you want." I presented Jonathan Jackson's camera. My hands were trembling. I blew a cloud of frost when I spoke.

"Nah." He waved me off. "Leave me a good tip, if you want."

"Okay." My teeth chattered.

AFTER WAITING in line for thirty minutes at the American Airlines ticket counter, my turn finally came. I walked up to the laminated counter, where a woman in her twenties, slender, with dazzling red hair, gave me meanie eyes.

"Hello," I said with Little Bo-Peep energy. "I'd like a flight to Oslo."

She tapped at the keyboard. Her eyes jetting left to right, right to left. "The next flight leaves at 8:22 a.m. Gate A-66."

My heart sank. By that time, Hana would be up and about. She'd read my letter and call the authorities. "Okay, I'll take it."

"You're lucky, there's only one seat left. But it's a flagship first seat."

I nodded like money was no object. "Flagship first."

"Do you have twelve thousand dollars?" She snickered. "Because that's what a flagship first ticket costs to travel to Oslo this morning."

Oh, dear Jesus. I opened my wallet and forked over my debit card. She snapped it from my hand. "I need to see your passport too."

She studied my documentation for a hot minute. Peering at my debit card, my passport, then at me. "There's spending limits on debit cards, love."

I opened the bank app on my cell phone and set my debit card limit for travel. Hana taught me that little trick in New York. "It should go through now." My smile, not so convincing.

"You're only seventeen. Are you traveling with your parents?"

"No," I said, my lips twisted.

"Hang on, love." She smiled. "I need to run this by my supervisor. I'll be right back."

She walked over to another attendant dressed in a bright-colored coat. After some talking, they peered at me, embroiled in a debate. Like that time when the officers had detained me at the gamer café.

Emma, if you're watching over me, please help. I started picking at my thumb cuticle.

After she was done chatting with her supervisor, she walked back over. "Okay, love. You're good to go."

My heart leapt. I wanted to scale the counter and hug her.

"Do you have luggage to check?"

I quickly showed her my carry-on with excitement in my eyes. "I have this."

"We can check it in here, or you can carry it with you on the aircraft."

"I'll carry it with me." I tried containing the excitement ravaging my body. "How long is the flight?"

She looked at the computer screen again. "Twelve and a half hours. What's your email address, love?"

"mystardustangel@gmail.com."

She stared at me for a second, smirking. Every time I told someone my email address, they gave me that look. "Cell phone?"

"Yes."

"What's your number? I'll text you the boarding pass and confirmation number. Once you receive the text, you'll walk over to Jeppesen Terminal, Concourse A." She pointed behind her. "The bridge is the fastest way."

FLAGSHIP FIRST CAME with complimentary slippers, blankets, and a night mask. Not a Ferrari. When I got settled into my seat, the flight attendant asked if I wanted champagne or a cocktail. I said, with a faint smirk, "Champagne?"

I'm thinking maybe the rules don't apply to flagship first. Maybe sailing in the clouds has the same set of rules as sailing the seas. Rules are just guidelines anyway. Sometimes things that first appear bad, are good. And things that seem good, are bad in disguise.

I took it all in stride. The last time I got tossed, I ended up in the hospital with a concussion and landing myself in a murder trial.

I shared a divided cubicle with another person, and she kept staring at me. I waved and gave her a friendly smile as I sipped my champagne.

The woman rubbed her wrist, as though in pain. "Enjoy the champagne, dear. Enjoy it while you can. What I wouldn't do to have a sip."

"It's free," I said. "I can get you one, if you want."

"You're sweet." The woman smiled. She was pristine as a marble floor. "I can't drink that stuff anymore," she held up her hand, still massaging her wrist, "that stuff will flare the gout."

I winced, imagining gout was awful. "I'm sorry."

"Why are you sorry?" She frowned. "It's not your fault. Blame it on genetics. That's the real culprit." She smiled. "No, I'll do fine, dear."

"I can take your picture if you like." I held up Jonathan Jackson's camera.

"Oh." The woman flailed her hand as if embarrassed or shy. She straightened her silk blouse and fiddled with her flawless hair. "I'm a complete mess."

"I think you're beautiful."

Her eyes sparkled with disbelief. She stares at me, thinking, blushing. The woman smiled and straightened her posture, folding her hands in her lap, posing playfully, "How's this?"

I peered through the lens. "That's perfect."

Say cheese, Emma whispered.

"Emma…"

"What's that, dear?"

I snapped the picture, and the photograph paper slowly ejected from the slot. I waved the paper between my digits to expose the image. I wanted to see Emma. And I saw her. I signed the white border and handed the photograph to the woman.

She carefully inspected the photograph for a minute, then searched my eyes. I could see tears forming. "You're a true artist, dear. A real gift."

"Have you ever been to Norway?" I asked.

She dried her eyes with her wrist. "No. It's my first time."

"Me too."

"You're young to be traveling alone," the woman said. "I was adventurous too when I was about your age. I wanted to see the world."

"And did you?"

"Not at first." She giggled. "I fell in love with a boy. Then we traveled all over the world together. He despised flying. But he did it for me. He'd walk through fire for me."

"What happened?"

"I'm sorry, dear," the woman said, sharpening her face as if recovering from a daydream. "I married the boy, of course."

"Where is he now?"

A somber expression extinguished her light. She averted her eyes. "He passed away a year ago. He went peacefully, and I'm thankful for that."

My inner light dimmed too. "My sister died," I said, as though it had happened yesterday.

"I imagine that was an incredibly tough time in your life."

"It still hurts."

"Yes, I imagine it does." The woman placed her hand on the divider. "Time doesn't have the power to heal everything. But it hurts less the more time moves on, I can promise you that."

I started to fade into myself. I felt my body melting into the seat.

"I don't want to make you feel uncomfortable, but I know who you are. I recognized you the moment you stepped onto the plane."

My heart palpitated beneath tissue and bone. My eyes sprung. Tingles electrified me.

"You're a courageous young woman. We're rooting for you."

Emma, what should I say in return? I don't know what to say. A few seconds tolled, and Emma didn't respond. The woman was waiting for me to say something.

"I don't feel courageous." My voice tumbled out.

"Most courageous women don't even know they're courageous. That's what makes them so powerful." She raised her finger. "Courageous women push the world forward. You will do exactly that."

THIRTY
THE LETTER

HANA YU WOKE AT NINE. Her head hurt, as though she were hungover. The sun was sizzling through satin drapes. Normally, the gentle dawn would have forced her eyes open. She rarely slept past eight. But not after yesterday.

She had tossed and turned all night, obsessing over Lizzie. She had even gotten out of bed a few times to check on the girl, and sometime around four, she finally drifted to sleep.

Hana forwent her usual morning rituals of dressing and brushing her teeth. Instead, the first thing on her mind was Lizzie. Hana wasted no time going to Lizzie's room.

The bedroom was spotless. Organized. The bed made.

"Lizzie," Hana said, thinking she might be in the bathroom getting ready for the day.

But Hana didn't see the bathroom light on. So she walked over to the other side of the bed. When Hana realized Lizzie wasn't there, she headed down the stairs to the kitchen.

"Lizzie!" she shouted.

A strange emptiness consumed the house. The only noise was from her bare feet smacking the polished wood floor.

"Lizzie?"

Panic charged her heart when Lizzie didn't respond. Hana looked at the sink. The stove. Those granite countertops for crumbs. For water rings. A dirty dish. Any sign that Lizzie had eaten breakfast. To her dismay, the kitchen mirrored its state from last night. Three dirty wine glasses still sitting in the copper sink. The empty bottle of wine near the microwave. Lizzie, if she were here, would have cleaned up. She always did, even when the mess didn't belong to her. Lizzie was clean to a fault. Hana had repeatedly assured Lizzie that the occasional messiness was acceptable. It was okay not to pick up after herself every time. She didn't have to be perfect. Things didn't have to look perfect all the time. But all the coaching in the world wouldn't change Lizzie. Lizzie would always be Lizzie.

Hana rushed to the garage and saw Lizzie's car parked there. A dated Camry. Emma's old car. The only items kept from the Mondragon house were Emma's things.

A hard realization began to build inside Hana, and she sprinted toward the patio door, where Lizzie would sometimes sit on a garden stool in the backyard, snapping photos on a sunny morning. The sun glaring through the windows like a magnifying glass.

But when Hana peered out the sliding glass door, Lizzie wasn't sitting in her usual spot. Hana slid open the door and called for Lizzie with a touch of heartbreak. But nothing.

Hana bolted upstairs to retrieve her cell phone. Her fingers twitched. She had to cover her heart, hoping to slow it down. In a matter of seconds, she located Lizzie's whereabouts using the My Phone app: Lizzie was at the Denver International Airport.

Hana headed for Lizzie's room again, not bothering to tear her eyes away from the phone. An alert pulsed. A text from Lizzie's bank flashed: $12,430.15.

Once in Lizzie's room, Hana started flinging open drawers and yanking open the closet doors, taking a quick inventory of what was missing. Strangely, very few items. Most of her clothes still hung in the closet. Drawers full of tank tops and socks.

Hana sat on Lizzie's side of the bed, still peering at the little pin illuminating on the map with Lizzie's exact location. She called Etten and put her on speaker.

"Etten," Hana's voice was pain stricken, "Lizzie's gone. She's at the airport. What should I do?"

"Don't call the police, whatever you do," Etten said. "It was a traumatic experience for her being arrested the first time. This will only make things worse."

"What should I do?" Hana's voice cracked, tears reaching the cusp.

"Are her clothes missing?"

"Some of them." Hana sniffled.

"What about her camera?"

Hana flung the phone on the bed and started riffling through Lizzie's room.

"Hana, I'm dialing Maxine." Etten's voice echoed from the speaker.

"It's not here. It's gone." Hana's voice was full of terror.

"This is Maxine, you know what to do." Then a piercing beep followed the message.

"Shit!" Etten said. "She might be in court today."

Hana spotted a white envelope on the nightstand.

"Drive to the airport," Etten said. "There's still time. She told you yesterday where she was going."

"I'll call you back," Hana said.

Hana read from the letter.

Dear Hana,

Please forgive me for leaving. I lived most of my life pretending to be something I wasn't. They taught us to pretend. So we pretended all these horrible things weren't happening. I no longer want to live in the dark. I want to live an honest life.

The people I love go. I'm tired of everyone leaving me behind. It's better to leave first.

You gave me a good home. I thought Emma was the only good thing in the world. Now I know there are many good things.

I could stay here with you forever. We could eat Italian every day. Because that's who you are. You would eat Italian every day for me. Even if you didn't want to. You'd do just about anything for me, except let me go.

But I'm scared I'll grow comfortable with you in this place. In this life. It's funny how we can grow comfortable with things. Get used to things, even bad things, so much so they become invisible. Bad things are easy to absorb and live with, once the tears stop. Once the heart settles. Once the mind rationalizes the horror.

I know what's good and what's bad in my head. But my heart can't tell the difference. I know what I did was wrong. That's what my brain tells me. But my heart leads me elsewhere. It corrupts my mind. I cannot trust myself with good and bad.

And it terrifies me to realize I can live here with you forever, not knowing if this is a good or bad life. I can't trust that I'm living a good life. Emma sacrificed her life for me. I know Emma did what she did so I could have a good life. The only way I'll know this life is pure is to search for it. Wherever that is.

It's not here. I see that now. I don't know where a good life is, but I'll spend the rest of my life hunting it down.

You told me once, when we were eating popcorn on the sofa and watching a movie, if I had one wish, what would it be? I wish to find the goodness in the world.

Please don't be sad for me. Be happy about all the good things we shared. You gave me the strength to do this. You showed me I deserve good things when I never thought I did.

Be happy knowing I'll find the good. I will.

Love, Lizzie

THIRTY-ONE
VILLAGES WE ESCAPE

HANA YU and Maxine Williams sat before the judge. Etten Lee positioned herself behind them; the judge's chamber was short on chairs. He forwent the traditional rayon robe and wore a tropical shirt and funny pants as though he were playing on some golf course in the Bahamas.

Judge Caprio gave them a concerning gaze before he sat. His blue eyes reflected a hint of worry. He plopped down and dragged the seat closer to the desk. "Counselors," he stares at Hana and Maxine, then Etten, "Doctor Lee. Shall we begin?"

"Your Honor, we requested to speak with you about hypothetical scenarios regarding Lizzie." Maxine curled her fingers.

Judge Caprio nodded. "Okay, everyone, just take a breather. It's clear we've hit a snag somewhere along the way. It's never a good sign when the prevailing party requests an emergency meeting."

Etten edged closer to his desk. Hands clenched. "Your Honor, I'm legally required—"

Judge Caprio put his hand out as though she was harming him. "Doctor Lee, would you consider yourself a person of faith?"

Etten looked at Hana, then Maxine, then peered at the judge, perplexed. "My parents, I suppose."

"That wasn't the question."

Etten's eyes traveled the room, thinking of what to say. "I have faith in science and medicine. Does that count?"

Judge Caprio straightened his posture, "It does. Science and medicine are indeed a religion. I imagine it requires a lot of faith to heal the sick. I hate to imagine a society without science and medicine."

Etten relaxed a little and scooted further from the desk. "Your Honor."

"Is science a perfect system?"

"No."

"Is medicine a perfect system?"

"No." Etten looked at Hana and Maxine.

"Why do you suppose that is, Doctor Lee?" Judge Caprio held his finger high. "I can see your scientific mind working. A textbook answer isn't required."

Etten thought for a moment. Her eyes darting elsewhere. "Humans, Your Honor."

Judge Caprio clapped. "We're not perfect." He raised his hands toward the ceiling. "God made certain of that."

Hana and Maxine kept staring at each other. "I don't understand, Your Honor."

Judge Caprio sipped coffee from a pottery mug sitting on his desk, "The law isn't perfect. Some things don't deserve the attention we feed it."

Judge Caprio looked at each of them. He folded his hands and leaned way back. "Let me guess, she ran away."

Hana said. "How did you know?"

He looked at each of them again. "I would. I'd run so far, you'd never catch me. I suppose that's what Ms. Mondragon's doing. I suspect she's searching for her freedom. I can't blame her."

"She's only seventeen, Your Honor," Etten said.

Judge Caprio wagged his finger, wearing a serious face "I've been a judge forty years and seen a lot of defendants enter my courtroom. I've seen a lot of survivors take the stand. I watched the prosecution rip Ms. Mondragon apart. Dragged her name through the mud for all to see. She sat attentively in the defense's corner. She behaved better than most adults. Make no mistake, Ms. Mondragon is a force. You do her a disservice by feeling sorry for her and treating her like a helpless victim. She's none of those things." Judge Caprio pointed at the ceiling again. "Believe me, I know the good when I see it. She doesn't pose a danger to herself or anyone else. It's time to close the book. It's time for Ms. Mondragon to find a life of her own. Maybe living under a different sky will do her some good. She deserves all the good she can get. You want my advice, let her find happiness, wherever that may be."

Hana started to cry. Maxine squeezed her hand. Etten placed her hand on Hana's shoulder. Judge Caprio produced a sympathetic smile. "She won't forget any of you. She'll remember all the things you've done for her. I know she'll include you in her life when the time is right."

"We have a hearing in two months."

"Here's what I propose." Judge Caprio thumbed through his calendar. "Emancipation. No more checkups. I'm not up to speed on how the court distributes an inheritance. Although I read somewhere the age of collecting such wealth is twenty-one."

"Yes." Hana sniffled.

"Then we must safeguard Ms. Mondragon's financial future. Ensure that her needs are met wherever she goes. Does everyone agree?" Judge Caprio peered at each of them.

Maxine looked at Hana. Hana looked at Etten. They all peered at each other. Hana lowered her head and nodded. Maxine said, "Yes, Your Honor."

"Doctor Lee," Judge Caprio held out his hand, "you're the last one."

"I'm sorry, Hana, Maxine, but I don't agree."

"Etten," Maxine said.

Hana just looked up and stared.

"Which part don't you agree with, Doctor Lee?"

"Letting a severely mentally ill kid fend for herself." Etten's voice was far away. "Lizzie requires intense psychotherapeutic treatment, among other things. She's not well, Your Honor."

"Oh." Judge Caprio rubbed his chin. "I've never heard a case quite like Ms. Mondragon's, Doctor Lee." He scooted his chair closer to the desk. "Have you ever treated a patient like Ms. Mondragon?"

"No."

"There are no perfect systems that I'm aware of. I know you hold a lot of power for Ms. Mondragon's future. Your recommendations heavily influenced the court system." Judge Caprio leaned back. "Let me ask you this, Doctor Lee, in your professional opinion, do you think Lizzie has improved while under your care? My aim isn't to insult your abilities. I'm asking you an honest question. Cast profession aside. Cast pride aside. I'm asking you as a person. Slide your feet in her shoes for a moment. Think about all the things she has endured."

Etten's eyes beamed. Her face turned angry. Prideful. She glared at Hana, who still had tears in her eyes. Then she cast her eyes on Maxine, who sort of shrugged, her expression willful. When she looked at Judge Caprio, something came to her.

Her life, for a second, flashed in technicolor. She saw her teenage self in the village where she grew up. After passing the bar, she had made one trip back home. And while she was there visiting her grandmother and mother, her father passed. She was no stranger to loss. Her brother died when she was twelve. She couldn't wait to go back to the States the moment she set foot in the village. She aspired to be someplace else, anywhere, except the village where she was born. Because, in her mind's eye, if she stayed any longer, she feared she might never escape.

She homed in on Lizzie's desperation to escape this life. Escape whatever compresses a human down to nothing. Like Lizzie, Etten had aspired to be something other than whatever everyone expected her to be. To be acknowledged. She wanted people to see her as an individual who had hopes and dreams of her own.

"Thank you for seeing us on such short notice, Your Honor," Etten said. Her expression was blank. She stood tall. "We'll file a continuance, as advised. Lizzie will continue her current—" Etten paused.

Hana and Maxine nervously inspected Etten. Judge Caprio was captivated and seemed to levitate from his seat, eagerly awaiting her next words.

"I'll recommend the court to emancipate."

THIRTY-TWO
EMMA, IN NORWAY

Years Later

"Lizzie, Lizzie," Kiley shouted, alarmed. Running up to me with her ten-year frame. When she reached me, she panted and barreled over with her tiny hands clutching her knees. "It's Jessica. She's doing that thing again." She flailed her hand in the air. "You gotta come quick." Kiley jetted away, motioning me to follow.

"I'm right behind you." I said, concern chiseled on my face.

Kiley and I closed in on Jessica. I saw her sitting on the ground with her knees to her chin, arms wrapped around herself, near the climbing wall, her auburn hair draping her face.

Within seconds of arriving, Kiley stood guard, as though she was Jessica's protector. And she was. "Jessica," I said, "would it be okay if I sat next to you?"

I asked permission because I was requesting to invade her personal space. And you should always ask permission when doing that. Especially with children.

The strands of her hair shook vigorously, mop-like. Access denied.

Kiley knelt and whispered, "Is it okay if I sit next to you, Jessica?"

Jessica didn't respond right away, but eventually she nodded.

Kiley sat beside Jessica. I could now hear Jessica softly crying.

I knew this cry because I, too, had cried like this many times. I pulled a fidget spinner from my pocket—I carried more than one now—and spun the fidget between my fingers so Jessica could hear. *Zzzzz. Zzzzzzz. Zzzzz.* "Would you like a fidget, Jessica?"

Jessica extended her curled palm. I placed the fidget there, and she began spinning it.

Meanwhile, Kiley murmured something to Jessica, and whatever she'd said worked. Jessica lifted her head and swept the hair from her face. I searched Jessica's eyes. I didn't know her pain, and I wouldn't pretend to. Because I didn't know her pain. Still, I could empathize. From one trauma warrior to the next. We were stargazing. I saw her star, and she saw mine.

The lunch bell pierced the sky with a harsh racket. Other students on the playground stopped what they were doing, looked up, and rushed toward the door. Screams, jibber jabber, and laughter was all around. The sound of tiny feet beat the composite ground, like a well-trained army, ready to infiltrate enemy lines.

"Oh no," Kiley said with excitement. She wrapped her arm around Jessica. "Jessica, it's lunch." Then Kiley peered up at me with her sparkling blues. "Lizzie, what do we do? I don't think Jessica wants to go."

"Then we wait," I said. "Until Jessica's ready to go back inside."

Kiley wore angst on her face. She locked eyes with her best friend, then looked at the door, likely hungry. But her love for her friend outweighed her needs, and she settled in her spot, clinging tighter to Jessica. "It's gonna be okay," Kiley told her.

"Jessica..." Now I was trying to save two children. One needed emotional support, and one needed food. "May I please sit next to you? I think Kiley might be hungry."

Jessica glanced at Kiley. And Kiley and Jessica searched each other's eyes. Kiley remained stoic and brave. Though Jessica picked up on something else, maybe Kiley's growling stomach. The tables turned abruptly. Now, Jessica was more concerned about Kiley than herself.

"I'm ready to go inside, Kiley." Jessica wiped her nose.

I'd learned valuable lessons in the last few years. Trauma survivors thrive when they're the masters of their own destiny. And at Emma Academy, all survivors were the masters of their own destinies. The students set the pace. And this, right here, about Jessica and Kiley, was a typical day at the Academy.

When you give trauma survivors a safe space to be the master of their bodies, their minds, their emotions, their dignity, that's when the healing begins. I knew this from personal experience. Bodily-autonomy theft is the ultimate violation. And at Emma Academy, we were courageous. We were warriors. Not victims.

Out of the corner of my eye, I saw a familiar face standing off to my right. I took my eyes away from the girls and peered at Nodin. Yes, that same Nodin.

He gave me a look of concern, curious to know what was going on with the girls. I shrugged and lifted my hands.

Nodin headed toward us, but I shook my head and flicked my hand for him to go to lunch without us. And he did just that.

Kiley still had her arm draped over Jessica as they walked toward the door.

Emma Academy spun to life one day while eating bombolone outside an Italian restaurant in Oslo, and they were just as good as New York City.

The truth is it would take many lifetimes to spend my Polaroid fortune. Emma always taught me to do for others, even when you can't do for yourself. Besides, Emma would have killed me spending all that money doing otherwise. I'm joking. Kind of.

Emma Academy focused on trauma-responsive schooling. It turned out, Norwegians loved the idea, and I got support from the Norwegian government to make this dream come true. They also fast-tracked my citizenship. While this wasn't the normal procedure for seeking citizenship in Norway, my ten million followers made it possible.

I considered it fair that Andrew's eight million dollars should cover trauma treatment for whomever needed it. Emma Academy accepted everyone, and our teachers had strong backgrounds in trauma—informed-trauma specialists, to be exact. We also had six psychiatrists on board. Three psychologists. Every staff member specialized in trauma outreach.

Don't worry, I kept some of the money for myself. I bought a cottage. And a car. And a fancy stereo with lots of CDS. I needed little else.

Oh, and I set up a trust for Kit's brother, who was in foster care. I gifted him a million dollars.

THIRTY-THREE
ANGEL NUMBER

I no longer needed to buy Polaroid film. I guess Polaroid was making a screaming comeback because of me and my work as a brand ambassador for the company. My fan page, apparently, after this, grew fifteen million strong, which was flattering and humbling, though I had Emma to thank for my success. None of this would have been possible without her.

Concerning Nodin, I told you I would marry him. The moment I saw him, it was carved in stone. He was kind and beautiful. How do people grow more beautiful the longer you know them? It's simply a mystery.

I didn't marry Nodin right away. I had things to do first. The details of how our paths crossed and how we fell in love is a different tale for a different time.

Also, I did something I thought I'd never do; I graduated. Not high school, *college*. Well, GED first, then everything else. I had a feeling I wouldn't graduate from high school. The cards didn't land in my favor on that one.

A year after dating Nodin, he got down on a knee and lifted a ring to my eyesight and proposed. He said, "I want to spend the rest of my life with you. Will you marry me?" His eyes sparkled, all goo-goo.

My eyes watered. My lips quivered. "No, I'm not ready." I felt so bad, but I wasn't ready.

His face turned to dust. "When will you be ready?"

"I still have too many things to do," I told him. "We love each other, isn't that enough?"

He closed the ring box and stood there for a minute with a determined expression. "I'll show you how much I love you. Then you'll have to marry me."

I smirked. He was adorable. What he meant to say was, "I'll be so good to you, your heart will have no other choice but to surrender." And he was right. I did.

He was so beautiful and pure, he thought there was something wrong with him. Truth is, I was afraid to love him. That I would eventually break him. I'd lay awake thinking it's only a matter of time. The ghosts of Andrew and Abby would avenge their deaths. Running was not sustainable. The sins of the past are timeless. I was not.

After a year, he cooked a special dinner by candlelight and proposed again. I said, "No."

He cried, "Do you not love me?"

"Of course I love you, but why do I have to marry you to prove my love?"

"Do you want to spend the rest of your life with me?"

"Yes."

"Then what's the problem?"

I kissed him on the lips and searched his eyes. "When I'm ready, you'll know."

Two weeks later, after cutting the ribbon on the front steps of Emma Academy, a little girl tripped and fell, scraping her knee. She screamed. Nodin consoled her. Consoling a child requires skill; some approaches succeed, others fail. Nodin comforted the little girl flawlessly. I was sensitive to these matters. So, I knew the signs. And that's all it took. That was a big sign.

I didn't wait for the cutting ceremony to finish. When the heart calls, you must answer. I walked up to Nodin and peered into his eyes and said, "Do you still want to marry me?"

"You know I do."

"Then let's get married."

"Are you serious?"

I nodded and smiled.

"Okay," he said with excitement.

"Let's get married now."

"Right now?"

"Yes, right now. Time's running paper-thin."

Well, sadly, life doesn't imitate the movies in Norway, and we didn't get married that day. We didn't marry the next day either. If we lived in America, most likely. In Norway, getting married is tough. Especially when a brand-new citizen of Norway is trying to marry a noncitizen. They had granted Nodin a residential visa; however, substantial obstacles stood between us and legal matrimony. Luckily, it all worked out. My sizable contribution to Emma's Academy moved the immovable.

Two years later, I gave birth to a little girl. I named her Stardust Angel. She had dark, shiny hair and Emma's eyes—forest. Stardust Angel carried my sister's beauty. I was thankful for that. It turned out, Emma wasn't living in Norway. She had never left my side. She had been hiding inside my fallopian tube the entire time, just waiting for the right moment. Her timing was flawless.

Interesting fact: Norwegians pickle herring. They have similar things to American pickles, but the brine is sweeter. Far from American dill pickles. And when I was pregnant with Baby Stardust Angel, all I craved were dill pickles and peanut butter on rye—not a Norwegian staple. Norway has boatloads of rye. Good luck finding the other stuff. Nodin found peanut butter and dill pickles, thankfully, and that was all I ate for nine months.

When Baby Stardust Angel was two, she developed an obsession with dill pickles and peanut butter on rye too. If you create the monster, you must feed the monster, remember? And Baby Stardust Angel was a little weirdo, just like her mother. I imagined this was what my sister would have said if she were still alive.

Once Baby Stardust Angel was born, I no longer saw Emma

through the lens. To be fair, I cried a lot when Emma no longer graced my lens. Not as bad as before. No comparison to the time I gave Emma's camera away. Where I fell to pieces on the sidewalk and needed to be sedated. But I cried good and hard.

Then I realized, after a few days, Emma was sitting right next to me. She was right in front of me. Her tiny, delicate hands touched me every day. Emma could finally fly from the cage of the lens.

Emma always wanted a Ferrari. She was obsessed with them. I didn't know why. She told me once, at the kitchen table, that a Ferrari is the fastest car on the planet. And I believed her. So, I thought it was only appropriate to buy Baby Stardust Angel a Ferrari. It was lollipop colored and sitting in our garage. Kidding. Did you think I'd buy a baby a real Ferrari? Well, only kind of kidding. It was a toy Ferrari, battery powered.

Get this, one day, after Stardust Angel turned six, I said, "Do you want to go on a walk with me, Baby Stardust Angel?"

I flinched at her reaction. If you could have seen the fury coming from her eyes, you'd have flinched too. She glared at me and raised her voice. "I'm not a baby!"

I held up my hands, surrendering. "I'm sorry." Tears formed in my eyes. I was a little hurt by her reaction, being so used to calling her Baby Stardust Angel that I hadn't realized she was too old to be called a baby. My mistake. I'd never seen Emma get so mad like that.

"My name is Stardust Angel!"

"I'm sorry," I said, my voice shaky. "You're right."

I'd missed something precious during her outburst. I was so busy feeling hurt I didn't absorb the situation. Two weeks later, when I called her Stardust Angel, she corrected me. "My name isn't Stardust Angel."

"Oh," I said, concern written all over my face. "You don't like being called Stardust Angel?"

"I'm Ferrari."

"You mean, you like Ferraris?"

"No," she said with conviction, "call me Ferrari."

Oh, dear Jesus. Everyone is obsessed with the goddamn Ferrari. I might add, Ferrari, a.k.a. Stardust Angel, loved driving the battery-powered Ferrari around the block; however she was getting too big to ride in the toy Ferrari anymore. So, we put it up.

When we meet new people and introduce our daughter as Ferrari, they often ask us why we named her that. Usually with a confused expression. Although, one person visiting from America laughed when I told them we'd named our kid Stardust Angel. He said, "Are you guys from a hippie commune or something?"

I said the only thing I could say, "Of course," and snickered.

"We didn't," I said, half joking, half serious about her name being Ferrari.

"Well," they said, meanie eyed, while glaring at Nodin and me, "who did?"

Nodin and I looked at each other and said, "She did."

I could only imagine what strangers discussed about us in private. "Lizzie and Nodin allow their daughter to run the show." Or "The kid calls the shots in the house. Who's the parent? Them or the child?"

Well, that was true. We let Ferrari call the shots. She was the master of her own destiny. And she knew it. I wasn't raising a daughter with social norms of what a girl should be and shouldn't. I was neither raising a princess nor a queen. There's nothing wrong with either thing. To be fair, I was raising a Stardust Angel.

If you're wondering if I still took Polaroids, the answer is yes. At our last fundraiser, one of my photographs sold for seven figures. Just know that every penny—correction, kroner—was going toward the construction of a second school. I figured we'd name it the Ferrari Academy.

The downside of the Emma Academy was not having enough space. Norwegians are gifted builders and architects. State-of-the-art quality. They advised us to build bigger than our original plan, leave plenty of room for growth. We overbuilt, like they advised. But Emma Academy filled up fast. And then we had to create a waiting list and couldn't accept any more students.

Countless Emmas urgently needed the Academy. I wouldn't forsake them. I'd snap a million photos. Sell my blood. Do whatever it took to build another academy.

I no longer searched for Emma through the lens. I trusted my own instincts now. And when I snapped a photograph, it was purely me. My eyes. My heart. My soul. When you held one of my photos in your hand, you were getting my everything.

Two years ago, I received a package in the mail from Rebecca Montoya, the little girl I had given Emma's camera to; she regifted the old camera, and I'd since passed it along to another little girl named Liv. Rebecca included a beautiful photograph she'd taken with Emma's camera. I couldn't quite assemble the right words to explain her process—a forward-thinking art. Art of the future. And I was in love with her work. It took my breath away. She labeled the photograph:

RM 1/1.

And every so often she'd send me photographs marked:

RM 1/1.

She became a big deal. The first photograph she sent me, I forwarded the image to the gallery. And they loved it. They were eager to represent her. Now, I suspected she traveled the world, just as I did.

Breathtaking mountains encircled our cottage and loomed like mighty rock gods. And when I closed my eyes, I saw Denver. And even though I was peering up at a different sky, I knew Emma was with me. Ferrari had her own room. We had a room for ourselves. We had a kitchen, dining room, living room, and a decent-sized backyard with majestic views. And it was good. It was plenty. What more could I dream?

And when I lie in Nodin's arms at night, staring at the ceiling, and the house was still, no Ferrari zooming down the hallway, I was confident I'd found home.

Am I a good person? I didn't know. I thought about that a great deal. I murdered my parents and got away with it. In a sense. But do you ever really escape something like that? I'd suspect most people would want to know if I regretted killing my parents. If I was sorry. Heartfelt sorry. Had I repented? If given a second chance, would I do it again?

Well, some things, I'd always keep to myself.

How about this: you decide. You decide if I'm evil. You decide if I should burn in hell for all eternity. That's what Abby had told me. That I'd burn in hell for all eternity if I ever told a soul what Andrew had done to us. I was supposed to honor my father and mother, no matter what. That's what the Bible says.

If you think I should burn, then let me burn. But I've got news for you: I burn every day. Remember what I said initially about not playing the angel? I may have lied. But I never lied to you. I never pretended with you. You know my unfiltered story.

You do with it whatever you want. I didn't tell my story to prey on your sympathy. To change your mind. To manipulate you. I told my story. I was the master of my story. You got a glimpse of what it was like to walk in my shoes.

I wasn't in a good headspace back then. I knew I was pregnant with Andrews's baby. And I was afraid something bad would happen to my baby, like what happened to Baby Fay. I thought I was saving an innocent life.

I tried and failed. I failed Emma. Baby Fay. My baby. You don't have to lug that guilt around with you everywhere you go for the rest of your life. I do. There's not a day that's goes by that I don't think about all the things I should have done.

Dr. C told the group most catastrophic events that happen in our lives are out of our hands. "So, take comfort knowing you couldn't do anything about it."

And maybe that's true. Maybe everything that happened in my life was out of my hands.

The woman on the plane was correct in saying time doesn't heal all wounds. And after nine years, the pain in my heart didn't hurt nearly as bad as it used to. Or maybe I absorbed the pain. Until I became the pain. The pain was now invisible.

My heart didn't scream at the speed of light anymore when I said his name. I knew a monster once, and his name was Andrew. You mustn't fear something so much you cannot call it by its name.

When you don't call its name, then the monster continues to thrive in the darkness, doing its work, extinguishing the souls and replenishing it with soot.

I wouldn't celebrate Andrew. Or muster sympathy. The world had one fewer Andrew, and that was a good thing.

Though, with a deranged and twisted heart, I had to admit, as with all things I'd confessed to you during my story, I hated Andrew for all the wrong reasons and not nearly enough for the right ones.

I supposed, in a twisted sense, a very disturbed sense, if he were alive today, I'd thank him—shortly after slipping him a deadly cocktail.

It appeared the monster had forced purpose on me. My purpose wasn't of my own choosing—it's not everyone's goal to seek fulfillment in life's meaning. Andrew gave my work meaning.

So, yes, initially, I despised him for cursing me with this devastating burden. Torment consumed me nightly. Seeing the many survivors in the world. How many Emmas existed. It took me a long time to call this reality by its name. To allow myself to love someone. To trust someone. To have a child.

And now I thanked him for this purpose. But I'd come to realize a disturbing thing—there's no short supply of monsters. Monsters seemed to flood the world. And not enough people cared to rid the world of monsters. And often the warrior who tried to defeat the monster was silenced.

Recently, a sixteen-year-old was denied a protection order by a Kansas City judge due to only one instance of molestation. The judge told her he'd grant her a protection order if she'd been molested multiple times.

People must always battle monsters because monsters govern our lands. And I'd never stop fighting until the Andrews of the world were extinguished. That was my promise—the monsters of the world would perish, and I'd lead the charge till my dying breath.

I heard Ferrari screaming for my attention from down the hall. She wanted me to braid her hair. And she could get a little pushy sometimes. I wondered where she got it from...

Here it goes. This was my wish. I had come to terms with harsh realities. I couldn't save all the Emmas in the world, but maybe, just maybe, we could together. Because what I realized now was that Emma was right all along. Stardust forms the human soul. And we will return to our former place among the stars together after the universe feasts upon our dead bodies.

Just kidding. I have no idea... Well, semikidding.

Lizzie.

P.S. Hana, Maxine and Etten will arrive at noon for the ribbon ceremony at Ferrari Academy. Without them, I would not be here, confessing my story, in Norway. They are the best mothers anyone could hope for.

AFTERWORD

Lizzie came to me on a flight to Ohio. My daughter sat to my right, gazing out the window, her eyes lost in the lush clouds below. At the time, my mother was gravely ill. We'd argued before I left Colorado, and my heart ached throughout the flight. She consumed my every thought. Then, Lizzie appeared. I didn't stop writing her story until three weeks had passed.

Eight months later, my mother died. It took me two years to find the courage to return to Lizzie's story and polish it.

I may have written Lizzie, but her story is not mine alone. Lizzie belonged to my mother. She belongs to every girl and woman.

If you or a loved one or anyone you know has become a victim of sexual assault, please contact RAINN.

Rape, Abuse, and Incest National Network (RAINN)'s mission is to create and operate the National Sexual Assault Hotline (800.656.HOPE, online.rainn.org, rainn.org/es) in partnership with more than one thousand local sexual assault service providers across the country and operate the DoD Safe Helpline for the Department of

Defense. RAINN also carries out programs to prevent sexual violence, help survivors, and make sure perpetrators are brought to justice. Financial and other information about our charity's purpose, programs, and activities can be obtained by contacting Development Department, RAINN, 1220 L ST NW Suite 500 WASHINGTON, DC, 20005, United States, 202.544.1034.